ALAN MORRIS & GILBERT MORRIS

ADVENTURES
Katy Steele

IMPERIAL INTRIGUE

Tyndale House Publishers, Inc.
Wheaton, Illinois

Library of Congress Cataloging-in-Publication Data

Morris, Alan B., date
   Imperial intrigue / Alan Morris & Gilbert Morris.
      p.   cm. — (The Katy Steele adventures ; 2)
    ISBN 0-8423-2040-7 (pbk. : alk. paper)
    1. Frontier and pioneer life—West (U.S.)—Fiction.   2. Private investigators—West
(U.S.)—Fiction.   3. Women detectives—West (U.S.)—Fiction.   I. Morris, Gilbert.
  II. Title.   III. Series: Morris, Alan B., date   Katy Steele adventures ; 2.
  PS3563.O87395I47   1996
  813′.54—dc20
                                                   96-8251

Printed in the United States of America

01   00   99   98   97   96
7   6   5   4   3   2   1

To Zachary Alan Morris . . .

I thank God that He gave you to me.

A son's love is a brilliant light to the father's path.

CONTENTS

1 A Royal Party 1

2 Carnicero 17

3 Dos Culebras 33

4 Dance of Anger 47

5 Bait 59

6 A Short Count 71

7 A Father's Confession 87

8 Unwelcome Intuitions 101

9 Accusations 115

10 Fritz 131

11 A Fierce Thunder 145

12 A Stranger and a Brother 159

13 Fury's Challenge 175

14 Ominous Messages 189

15 Murderous Ventures 203

16 Roses and Verbena 219

CHAPTER ONE

A Royal Party

S am Bronte stepped aside to let a lady pass on Toulouse Street in New Orleans. Quite unconsciously, he laid his hand on a wrought-iron fence sporting a particularly ornate design of flowers as he tipped his hat. The hot August sun of 1868 had cast its blazing glare on the fence for almost eight hours, and Sam swore he could hear his hand sizzle like bacon on a griddle just before he jerked it away with a cry of "Owww!"

"Guardez vous! C'est très chaud!" the woman warned belatedly with the smallest of smiles. She wore a white sundress that reflected light so brightly that Sam would have squinted had he not been doing so already—from pain.

"Merci, mad'moiselle." Sam's attempt to smile only reached grimace level. He watched her stroll down the street, as he gently massaged his stinging hand. *New Orleans ladies,* he thought, shaking his head with a wry grin. *They're so . . . saucy!* It wasn't the first encounter he'd had with their brassiness. He'd been staring intently at the French Opera House on Toulouse earlier and hadn't noticed a woman walk by with a small child until he'd heard an "Ahem!" from behind him.

"Don't you tip your hat to ladies, sir?" she'd demanded with raised eyebrows. Sam had mumbled an apology, tipped his hat, then stared at her receding back disbelievingly. Since that moment he'd kept a careful eye out for approaching females.

Sam considered the imprint of the fence on his palm, a red stripe from little finger to thumb. He shook his head yet again—this time with self-reproach—and pulled his already-soaked handkerchief from the back pocket of his plaid trousers to wipe his sweating face. The New Orleans heat was like nothing he'd ever experienced. Besides the obvious high temperature, there was a humidity in the air that seemed to actually press down on a man with liquid weight. A few times during the day, Sam had had to stop and catch his breath, feeling as if his lungs were sponging more water from the air than oxygen.

He continued walking back toward the St. Louis Hotel, turning left on St. Louis Street. He'd ventured out in the mid-morning to see the French Opera House, taking his time along the way to appreciate the fine Spanish architecture of the buildings and houses. The Opera House was everything he'd imagined and more. Sam was a thespian and had been in many playhouses across the land, but compared to this theater, which could seat two thousand people, all the others were mere children's playrooms. The natives loved their opera, he'd learned from the manager, who'd claimed it wasn't unusual for the poorer residents to plan their food budget around the cost of opera tickets.

Crossing Bourbon Street, Sam glanced at Antoine's Restaurant, where he and Katy Steele would take their visitors for dinner that evening. Thinking of Katy, his detective partner, Sam wondered again why she'd wanted to stay in the hotel instead of accompanying him while he explored. *Those rooms must be like ovens!*

Sam waited until a carriage passed by on Royal Street before he crossed and bounded lightly up the steps of the St. Louis Hotel. His energetic stride halted abruptly as he entered, much the same as it had when he and Katy had arrived the night before. The Grand Stairway of the hotel was so awe inspiring that one couldn't help but stare open-mouthed for a few seconds. Fully ten feet wide, it spiraled sharply to the second and third floors in majestic beauty. Local citizens claimed that it was the most striking sight in the city, and Sam had no reason to argue with the assertion.

"Sam!" he heard someone call. He turned toward the registration desk and saw Katy wave and start toward him. He noted with an appreciative eye the way her cotton dress, which was a robin's-egg blue, complemented both her figure and her green eyes. As usual, she wore her long, ash-blonde hair pinned up, but this time it was topped with a Dolly Varden hat that perfectly matched her dress. Her cheeks were flushed slightly, whether from heat or exertion Sam didn't know.

"Someone's been shopping," Sam commented as they met.

"Oh, just this and that," she said, her hands going to the hat for an unneeded adjustment. "Do you like it?" She put her arms out and turned once for his inspection.

"It fits you perfectly. Where did you buy it?"

"Right here in the ladies' shop," she answered proudly. Taking his arm, she steered him toward the restaurant. "Come on. Let's go have some coffee."

"Only if it's iced. I don't think my body can stand another temperature hike."

They found a table beside an open window and ordered. Sam told her of the impressive Opera House and his encounters with the ladies of the city.

Laughing, Katy said, "It sounds like your good looks won't pardon a *faux pas* with the ladies of this town!" She watched his white teeth flash in a grin as he swept his black hair from his still-sweating forehead. Sam was easygoing, with a quick laugh, and Katy could see why women were attracted to him. His boyish expression, combined with astonishingly blue eyes against tanned skin, had magnetized many women.

Their coffee arrived, and after taking a huge gulp, Sam emitted a satisfied "Aaahhhh!" Putting the cup down, he asked, "Are you ready for your next great adventure?"

"Yes—as long as there are no explosives around, thank you very much." Katy made the comment lightly, but her face reflected the dread that she still felt when thinking about a near-fatal incident.

After the murder of Katy's father, a railroad detective with the Central Pacific Railroad, they'd been hired to replace him with the task of finding the killer, who'd also been sabotaging the railroad. The criminal had revealed himself quite unexpectedly one night, and what followed was the most harrowing experience either of them had ever encountered. Katy had been tied up in a railroad tunnel that the killer was determined to blow up with dynamite, and Sam had defused the pile of explosives with only a fraction of a second to spare.

Katy had adored her father. The pain of losing him, especially in such a horrible way, was proving to be difficult to put behind her. "I still think about him every day," she murmured.

Sam didn't need to ask who she was talking about. He reached across the table and put his hand on hers. "I know," he said simply, but the sympathy in his voice touched her, and she smiled at him appreciatively.

To change the subject, Katy said, "I'm looking forward to meeting my first prince and princess."

"Ah, yes—the royalty arrives to brighten our day."

After they'd solved the railroad case, Katy had resigned herself to returning to her former career of teaching. But Leland Stanford, the president of the Central Pacific, had offered her and Sam the job of meeting and escorting Prince Johann and Princess Sophia Kessler and their party to a ranch in Texas. They were Austrians and would probably know little about the ways of the American West.

Sam leaned his elbows on the table and quoted: "'The hearts of princes kiss obedience, so much they love it; but to stubborn spirits they swell, and grow as terrible as storms.'"

Katy grimaced playfully. "Let me guess—Shakespeare, right?"

"Is there any other worth quoting?" Sam responded with an air of mock superiority.

"You apparently don't think so, since you quote him at any and every occasion. I'm not even going to guess on this one. What's it from, and what does it have to do with anything?"

"*Henry VIII.* And it means if you do everything he wants, when he wants it, without grumbling or complaining, he *might* let you kiss his hand."

"How do you know Prince Johann is like that?"

"I don't," he said, smiling, "I've just read about a lot of pompous fools in the European royalty. Maybe your prince is the exception."

"I certainly hope so."

Sam arched his back and stretched with a groan. The trip from California by stage had been hot, long, uncomfortable, and even dangerous at times. They'd spotted Indians on three occasions, but the stagecoach had fallen in with an escort of cavalry through the hostile territories and encountered no trouble. The food at the Way stations was another matter. To Sam it was nearly inedible; to Katy completely so. The first decent meal they'd consumed had been in Ft. Worth, and both of them had plunged into the meal of beef and beans with gusto. Sam had decided to try persuading the prince to take a coastal steamship to Corpus Christi, thereby shortening their trip in a coach to the ranch fifty miles below Abilene.

"Sore?"

Sam glanced at Katy with a wry smile. "Yes. I got lazy during the play, I'm afraid. Not much time for exercise."

When their assignment on the rail lines had ended several months ago, Sam had returned to the stage to perform in a brief run of *Sherlock Holmes.* Katy had gone to visit Mills College, her alma mater, determined to learn all she could in the library about Texas and Austria. She was going to be prepared for this new assignment.

5

"I've got to go change clothes," Sam said with a grimace. "Feels like I took a bath in these things."

"I'll just wait here for you," Katy said. She watched him walk out, noticing his white shirt clung to his back from perspiration. Reaching into her reticule, she took out a dark green fan painted with magnolia blossoms and unfolded it, grateful for the small breeze it offered. She felt sweat on her upper lip and, after glancing around to see if anyone was watching her, dabbed it away with a napkin.

Katy, too, was extremely tired from the trip. Her back and neck hurt from the bumpy stage ride and being in a sitting position for so long. Halfway through the miserable trip, she had begun to wonder if they should have refused the job, but the prince paid a generous salary, and she simply couldn't face going back to teaching. The experience on the railroad had convinced her that she had an adventurous spirit, and despite all the discomfort of the trip, she'd witnessed some breathtaking scenery of the West.

They were due at the steamship *Edelweiss* in an hour to meet the royal party and take them to dinner. Nervousness rose in Katy's stomach. Her mother had died while giving birth to her, and she had been raised in a lonely atmosphere by her father's sister, Agnes. Her aunt had discouraged any relationships Katy had sought, both with girls and boys, so she grew up a clinging wallflower, with no skill in interacting with people. Sam had instilled in her some much-needed confidence, but she still wasn't completely comfortable meeting strangers. People seemed to enjoy her company, however, and she was slowly losing her aloofness by the acceptance of others. It had been easy to blame Aunt Agnes for her social handicap, but after time she'd come to forgive her.

Katy was lost in reverie, thinking about the days to come, when Sam appeared at the table wearing a dark blue suit with a red cravat and vest and sporting a black derby hat. His shoulder-length hair was damp, as if he'd wet it and toweled it dry. Sam was somewhat prideful when it came to clothes; they draped his tall frame well, and he knew it.

"Trying to outdo me or just impress the princess?" she teased.

"Now, would I do that?"

"Of course."

Sam laughed. "Are you ready to go?"

"I suppose," Katy replied reluctantly.

"'Unto the breach,' then."

The *Edelweiss* was an oceangoing steamship with great paddle wheels on both sides. Austrian flags hung limply from both the bow and stern in the still, humid air. The sun was low enough on the horizon behind Sam and Katy to allow the warehouses on the waterfront to shield them from the heat. Nevertheless, the soggy atmosphere seemed to hold the burning rays of the setting sun.

Sam and Katy made their way up the gangplank, where they were met by a ship's officer who asked them their business in a strong German accent. "How may I help, plees?"

Sam said, "Permission to come aboard, *Kapitän*. I think we're expected by the prince—Samuel Bronte and Katherine Steele."

"Ist good. Dis vay plees." He turned to another officer and barked, *"Das Schiff ist Ihrer."* The junior officer saluted sharply, and the captain led them down a flight of narrow stairs and through a passageway. He stopped at one of the many doors and knocked sharply.

A muffled voice said, *"Kommen Sie herein!"* and the captain opened the door to allow Sam and Katy inside.

"Herr Samuel Brrronte und Fräulein Katherine Schteele, Excellency," announced the captain.

"Ah, yes. Thank you, *Kapitän* Hoffmann, that will be all." The man who spoke was over six feet tall, solidly built, with blonde hair and dark blue eyes. His smile was cordial, set in a long, square face

7

with a wide nose. "Mr. Bronte, Miss Steele, welcome to the *Edelweiss!* I am Prince Johann Kessler."

Sam gave a half bow, and Katy curtsied. "Thank you, Your Highness," Sam said.

Prince Johann turned to the other two people in the room. "This is my sister, the Princess Sophia, and my friend Wilhelm Kesselmeyer."

Sam and Katy bowed and curtsied to the princess. Sam saw what he thought was amusement in her blue eyes, as though the courtesies shown to royalty were amusing to her. Her hair was the exact blonde shade of Johann's, but long and thick, and her face had the same squarish quality of her brother's, but with softer features. Her mint-green dress and black, Basque-style jacket made of ribbon and braid bespoke elegance and wealth.

Kesselmeyer stepped forward and shook both their hands warmly. Short and pudgy with a round face, he had black, short-cropped hair and a noticeable gap between his front two teeth.

"How was the voyage, Your Highness?" Katy asked the princess.

"Tedious and long," she answered in the same clipped English as her brother. "After being confined to these tiny cabins for so long, I will be glad to see the wide-open space of America." Her voice was husky, as if sheathed in black velvet. She exuded disinterest.

"It took three weeks—the longest three weeks of *my* life," commented Wilhelm.

"Excuse me, please," Sam said to the prince, "but your English is almost perfect. I was wondering if you would have an interpreter, but you don't need one."

"My father, the emperor, is a great admirer of the British Empire. He insisted on the court taking lessons in case we ever paid a visit to that country. However, it never happened." He walked across the small, luxurious stateroom to a small bar and started pouring champagne into elegant, long-stemmed glasses.

"The arrangements you have made for us?" asked Sophia, in a tone that wasn't so much a question as an order to speak. The princess was studying both of them with an attentive eye—Sam with appreciation and Katy with a more critical appraisal.

"We have rooms at the St. Louis Hotel, if you'd like to stay there tonight," Sam said, "and we've arranged for dinner at a nearby restaurant called Antoine's."

"Wonderful!" exclaimed Wilhelm, rubbing his hands together. "I cannot wait to see my first southern belle!"

"Be careful," Sam advised, "they have teeth."

Wilhelm chuckled. "Just the way I like them."

Johann brought a tray of glasses filled with golden liquid. "A toast!" he declared, and everyone took a glass except Katy. Johann's eyebrows raised in surprise. "Miss Steele?"

"I'm—excuse me, but I don't drink."

The prince looked at Sophia and Wilhelm in confusion. Turning his gaze back to her, the surprised look had vanished to be replaced by a painted-on smile. "But, it is tradition before starting a new venture." He was obviously not accustomed to one of his suggestions being ignored, but he seemed more curious than offended.

She glanced at Sam, then the glass he held. She shook her head firmly. "I'm sorry. I really can't."

Johann studied her face. "Not even one drink, Miss Steele? For a prince?"

She shook her head again.

"*Gut!*" Johann exclaimed. "A woman of conviction. This is something I understand well. I salute you, Miss Steele." Without warning, he turned and bellowed, "Fritz!"

Katy glanced at Sophia and Wilhelm, but both seemed unaffected by the prince's abrupt behavior. Apparently it was nothing out of the norm.

An adjoining door opened on the other side of the room, and a short, squat man emerged. Though he was powerfully built, his smooth gait belied his bulk. Very short hair and heavy, bushy eyebrows gave him a menacing appearance. When his gaze fell on Katy and Sam, his hooded black eyes showed no greeting or emotion whatsoever.

"Bring Miss Steele a glass of water, Fritz. In our finest crystal!"

Embarrassed, Katy started to protest, but the prince held up a hand.

"Please indulge me in this, Miss Steele."

Katy smiled in response and nodded.

The servant returned within moments and handed her a beautifully crafted glass filled with water. Katy took it gratefully and raised her glass with the others.

"There, *that* is the spirit!" Johann exclaimed. *"Zum Woll!"* he toasted to Sophia and Wilhelm. To Sam and Katy he translated, "To life!" and then included everyone: "To Texas!"

Katy watched them down the bubbly liquid in one gulp and, after a brief moment, lifted her glass to her lips and sipped the cool beverage. She glanced at the prince and saw that he was smiling at her. She smiled in return, then set her glass down. As she did so, she realized Sophia watched her closely, but her eyes betrayed nothing.

Prince Johann set his glass down and turned to his servant, who stood beside him wordlessly. "Would you bring the carriage, Fritz?" he asked. Fritz bowed, turned on his heel, and disappeared through the door as quietly as he'd come. Johann turned to Katy and Sam and explained, "My bodyguard, though I do not know why I need one." He cleared his throat, as if embarrassed. "I know you were planning to take us by stage to the ranch, and I've taken the liberty to commission the building of my own carriage—large and comfortable enough to transport all of us and my servants tomorrow." He told Wilhelm, "We must send Fritz to find some horses, too."

"Sir, if I may," Sam suggested, "the trip would be very long and tedious by carriage. There's a coastal steamer shipping out tomorrow for Corpus Christi, Texas. Our journey would be shorter and less strenuous if you wanted to go that way."

Prince Johann put a finger on his lips in thought, mentally studying the map of Texas and Louisiana in his head. Finally he looked at Sam and said, "That is an excellent idea, Bronte! That *would* take some time off of the trip. But will we be able to take the carriage I have had built?"

"I believe so. I'll ask when I confirm our reservations."

Johann's eyebrows raised. "Hmmm. Already made them, eh? It looks as if we are in capable hands!" He gestured to the door. "Shall we go?"

Antoine Alciatore began his career in the kitchen of the *Hôtel de Noailles* at Marseille. When the chief chef was sick one evening, Antoine was ordered to prepare a beef order for a special party. The recipe proved to be a great success, and he was summoned to the party and asked the name of the dish. Considering the plate of mostly finished roast sitting in a pool of blood because of the rareness, Antoine couldn't help but think of his father's gory description of the beheading of Robespierre during the Revolution. So he christened it *Boeuf Robespierre.*

Antoine eventually came to New Orleans by way of New York and established his small restaurant in 1840. His specialty became *Dinde Talleyrand,* an exquisitely spiced turkey dish. He'd adjusted the kitchen shutters when cooking so the aroma would entice the bypassing public—and New Orleans came.

The dish was served by Antoine himself, delighted at the opportunity to cater to genuine royalty. Visions of the dining event in the next day's newspaper began to form in his head, and the prospect of future dollars from the free advertising planted a huge smile on his face.

Sam felt as if he'd tasted nothing better in his life. The turkey seemed to melt in his mouth without benefit of chewing. The pleasurable comments emitted around the table told him that he wasn't alone in his opinion.

"Johann, perhaps you can persuade this Antoine to follow us to Texas," Wilhelm said around a mouthful of meat.

"Do not talk with your mouth full," Johann admonished good-naturedly. "But it *is* a good idea."

"Your Highness, if I may ask, what brings you to America?" Katy asked.

The royal party stopped eating and looked at her sharply. Princess Sophia fixed her with a dark, clearly disapproving look. Apparently Katy had committed some kind of *faux pas,* and immediate regret that she'd opened her mouth swept over her.

Leave it to me to say the wrong thing, she thought, humiliated. Quickly she mumbled, "I'm sorry if—"

To everyone's surprise, Prince Johann burst out laughing. *"Ach!"* he said, "I will have to get used to the American way of directness!"

Wilhelm and Sophia each gave halfhearted chuckles. Fritz, sitting at the end of the long table by himself, wore his expressionless stare.

"Miss Steele, your straightforward nature is refreshing!" Johann commended. Katy nervously took a drink of her tea while he went on. "To answer your question, I am sure it is no secret that my country was quickly and soundly defeated in the war with the Prussians in only seven weeks. In fact, the war may very well go down in history as the Seven Weeks War instead of the Austro-Prussian War."

Katy nodded. She and Sam had followed the war through the *San Francisco Chronicle* during June and July. Napoleon III of France had calculated that the war would be long and tedious, since most of the southern and western states of the German Confederation sided with Austria. But the Prussians, with their superior arsenal of repeating rifles and advanced artillery, along with superbly trained troops led by the brilliant General Helmuth von Moltke, had annihilated the Austrians in only a month and a half.

Johann shook his head sadly. "The Prussians were lenient in their terms of surrender—in every area except punishment for my father. They confiscated our lands, raided our bank accounts, and took away everything but our titles."

"The brutes left nothing!" Princess Sophia said vehemently.

Johann nodded as he chewed his food, and after swallowing he said, "Fortunately, my father had stowed away some money in case of an emergency."

Katy had a feeling the amount that had been hidden was more than she would ever see in her life.

"My uncle Anton was a wanderer and found himself in America a few years ago with the opportunity to invest in some ranch property with a Mr. Carl Tyson. Tyson needed money fast and sold forty-nine percent of his ranch to my uncle. Being the kindly soul that he is, not to mention *rich* soul in his own right, Uncle Anton deeded the land to me. So, since I am no longer welcome in my own country, here I am, ready to make a new start." His face clouded. "But I do miss my homeland."

"Mr. Bronte, you have been awfully quiet," Sophia observed. "Do you have any questions?" She smiled and directed her full attention to his answer.

Sam wiped his mouth with his napkin and swallowed hurriedly before speaking. "As a matter of fact, I do, Your Highness. Prince Johann, have you ever owned or overseen a ranch before?"

Johann seemed surprised at the question and answered, "No."

"It's very hard work—and sometimes the, uh, money flow in the first few years is tight."

The prince had his eyebrows raised, listening but not understanding where Sam was going. "Yes? So?"

Sam cleared his throat. "What I'm trying to say is that it might be a good idea to look into the future of the ranch and your—resolve to see it through. Lots of experienced ranchers have gone bankrupt through events they couldn't control. Rustlers, Indians, bad weather—things like that are factors that need to be considered. Not to mention the hard work and dedication, along with careful money management." The three Austrians were staring at Sam with the same incredulous faces that Katy had been subjected to earlier. *Did I go too far?* he thought.

"Mr. Bronte," Wilhelm interjected, "if you think that my prince is not up to the task of simply running a farm for himself, you're sadly mistaken!"

Prince Johann put a hand on Wilhelm's arm. "No, no, Wilhelm, it is—how do you say?—OK."

Sophia fixed Sam with a glare. "Mr. Bronte, I have every confidence in my brother, even if you do not."

"Please don't misunderstand me, Your Highness. I only—"

"It is quite all right," Johann broke in. "Your opinion was asked by my sister—" he glanced at Sophia pointedly—"and you gave it as honestly as you could. There is no need to apologize."

The princess inclined her head to her brother but gave Sam a smoking glance before returning to her food.

Sam looked at Katy and gave her a minute "I tried" shrug. They'd discussed the subject on the way to New Orleans, and Sam decided he should at least try to broach the idea of the prince's selling his property and settling down in a more hospitable environment, one to which he was accustomed.

The rest of the dinner and dessert conversation was turned to more trivial interests, and Wilhelm eyed a few southern belles that entered Antoine's. The party ended on friendly terms, and to Sam there seemed to be no hard feelings about his openness. The prince and princess even elected to walk the short distance to the hotel instead of taking a carriage. Katy heard Johann instructing Fritz to fetch the prince's manservant, Sophia's maid, and their belongings first thing in the morning. Prince Johann was ready to see his ranch as soon as possible.

Sam walked Katy to her room and paused outside the door. "This may be tougher than we'd planned on."

"I know. I was thinking the same thing."

"I'm not going out there to be a cowboy, banker, and baby-sitter all rolled into one. Our orders are to get them settled in, show them the ropes—not run the whole ranch, and I think that's where we're headed." His face was grim and reluctant.

"Maybe they're more competent than they seem."

Sam shook his head doubtfully. "I certainly hope so."

Katy opened her door and leaned against the frame dreamily. "The prince is quite dashing, isn't he?"

"Yes—and he took a shine to you."

"Do you think so?"

"Sure. And I believe he got all the charm that was passed down the family line. The ice princess could turn a man to stone with her glares."

Katy patted his arm. "Just give her the ol' Bronte charm. She'll melt."

"I don't know. I think it would take molten lava for that."

CHAPTER TWO

Carnicero

Oberst Dietrich Friessner sat behind his huge rosewood desk and stared at the bucket in the middle of his office. The soft *ploink!* of raindrops falling into the pail from the tiny hole in the twelve-foot ceiling was rhythmic—at most times hypnotizing. But not to Friessner. Not this night.

The raucous sounds of a party drifted down the wide corridors of the *Hauptquartier,* and the *Oberst* thought again: *Narrheiten! Foolishness! Sometimes the stupidity of the Prussian Army is boundless! They celebrate a glorious victory over the Austrian dogs, yet there is nothing to celebrate!*

Although he continued to mentally berate his fellow officers, Friessner's expression didn't change from its usual stoic manner. In his mid forties, Friessner was considered handsome; with his dark hair, light blue eyes, and well-formed Roman nose, many women had succumbed to his charms. To add to his irresistability, the army uniform he constantly wore was perfectly cut to fit his lithe frame. The knee-length black coat hugged his broad shoulders down to his flat stomach and flared in a split-tail hem that was always crisply pressed. Ebony calf-length leather boots never failed to be spotless and glimmering. He'd wooed dozens of *mädchens* that had been considered by his friends to be unapproachable.

However, part of his foul mood had to be blamed on his indiscretions. His wife of twenty-two years had always suspected him, but now she'd caught him. He'd taken his newest conquest to a small, out-of-the-way café for a quick lunch. How was he to know that his wife regularly shopped at the dress store next door? Friessner had foolishly taken a table by the window, feeling particularly proud of his new girlfriend and wanting to show off his virility to the passersby on the street. One of the passersby happened to be his wife.

"Herr Regimentschef, your visitor is here," Friessner's adjutant called from the huge double doors at the entrance to his office.

"Send him in, *Oberleutnant." And now I have to deal with this creature,* Friessner thought darkly.

The man who came through the door was of average height, weight, and build. His face was average. His hair was average. His ears were average. Even his eyes were of a nondescript color: a slate gray with the irises outlined by dark circles. A gold-rimmed pair of glasses sat on his average nose, but Friessner had the distinct feeling that they were only a prop to give himself some semblance of identity.

Friessner spoke in halting Spanish: "Carnicero, I presume?"

The man gave a slight nod and smiled faintly.

"I have a . . . um . . ." Friessner despised trying to speak another language, and he felt at a severe disadvantage in front of this calmly smiling man. He seemed to be inwardly laughing at Friessner. *Or is it just my imagination?* The Spanish word for "translator" escaped him, so he snapped his fingers to his adjutant, who motioned for a private in Prussian uniform to enter. Friessner motioned to Carnicero and snapped to the round-eyed private, "Tell this man you are here to interpret our conversation."

The private began speaking rapid-fire Spanish to Carnicero, who kept his eyes on Friessner. Midway through the monologue, Carnicero interrupted in perfect German: "We'll have no language barrier, *Oberst.* As you can tell, my German is perfect."

18

The room was silent for a moment as Friessner felt his anger rising. The man had been playing games before he'd even spoken a word. With a curt gesture, Friessner dismissed the lieutenant and the private. After the door was closed, he asked tightly, "Why didn't you tell me of your talent . . . ?" *Before I made a fool of myself?* he finished in his mind. Instead, he let the sentence trail off and die somewhere between them.

Carnicero shrugged disinterestedly, looked down at the bucket at his feet for a moment, and sat down in a thickly padded chair without being asked. His movements were deliberate and smooth; he seemed the sort of man that was totally at ease, whatever his environment happened to be. Lazily glancing up at the ceiling, he ignored Friessner's question and commented needlessly, "Your ceiling leaks."

"And your language skills are excellent," Friessner grudgingly admired. He was gradually coming to hate Carnicero, and he'd only been in the man's presence for a few minutes.

"I also speak English, Italian, Greek, French, and Russian with equal proficiency."

"Very impressive."

"'Envy and wrath shorten the life,' *Herr Regimentschef.*"

Friessner stared, baffled. A raindrop hit the bucket of water. *Ploink!* "I beg your pardon?"

"At this moment, you are both envious of my language talent and angry about something. That combination of emotions—or sins, if you will—is hazardous to your well-being, according to the Apocrypha."

"The . . . Apocrypha?"

"Yes. Books of the Bible included in the Septuagint and Vulgate—Greek and Latin versions, respectively—but excluded from the Jewish and Protestant canons of the Old Testament. They were written anonymously, you see, and therefore couldn't be taken as gospel. At least not by the Jews or Protestants."

Ploink!

Dietrich Friessner considered himself a learned man. He was well read and had received the highest form of education that Prussia could give him. But he had no idea what Carnicero was talking about.

"Would you like to share your feelings of anger, *Herr Regimentschef?*" Carnicero asked, eyebrows raised in concern.

"No, I would not! Besides, I'm not angry!" Yet Friessner heard the defensiveness in his words and was sickened by it.

Carnicero clucked his tongue and gave Friessner a disapproving look. "That's too bad."

"Just a moment, *Señor* Carnicero, *I'll* ask the questions here!"

"As you wish. And it is just 'Carnicero'—not *señor.* 'Carnicero' in Spanish means—"

"I know what it means! You only wish to be known as 'butcher,' is that correct?" Friessner asked with heavy sarcasm. It was time to go on the offensive with this arrogant man.

"Yes. I believe in your country I would be called *Fleischer.*" Carnicero continued to regard Friessner with slight amusement— not at all fazed by his obvious dislike.

"Butcher," Friessner stated in a flat tone, unimpressed. "Is that your given name, or one you have chosen?"

Carnicero smiled.

Ploink!

Friessner waved a hand impatiently. "It doesn't matter."

"You are an important man, are you not?" Carnicero asked.

Friessner found himself confused again. "I have my own regiment, and I am chief of colonels."

"Then you really should request a better office from General von Moltke. One that has no hole in the roof."

"Enough!" Friessner's flat palm crashed down on the surface of his desk. He'd *never* had to deal with such insolence. With effort he attempted to calm down, but his eyes narrowed dangerously as he said, "We will discuss the matter on *my* agenda—not yours. Is that clear?"

"Yes."

"Thank you. Now, I have two people that I want out of the way as soon as possible, and another when you're done. You must travel to America—Texas, to be exact—and get rid of the prince and princess of Austria." Friessner leaned back in his chair to watch Carnicero's reaction. He was once again on the firm ground of authority and had sprung his own little surprise. But he was disappointed. Carnicero showed no surprise whatsoever.

"And the third person?"

"Their father, the emperor." Again, no reaction.

"Why?"

"That is not your concern."

Carnicero pursed his lips and nodded. Then he named his fee.

Friessner nearly fell out of his chair. "Out of the question."

"Then I wish you a very pleasant evening," Carnicero said lightly and started to stand.

"Wait!"

Carnicero looked at him, and Friessner felt a chill. The arrogant smile had vanished and been replaced by a stone nothingness. His eyeglasses reflected light from the lamp on the desk so that Friessner couldn't see his eyes—and he suddenly didn't want to.

"I'm waiting, *Herr Regimentschef.*"

"Is—uh—your price not negotiable?"

"No."

"But that's twice what I'd planned on paying!"

Carnicero's mouth turned down in a frown. "Then I must be losing my ability to gauge people. I was attempting to triple your asking price."

Friessner was beginning to sweat, and he decided to reason with him. Friessner would have to take enormous chances to gather

Carnicero's fee. He took a deep breath and explained, "Our victory over Austria was an empty one. Instead of taking over the country, Prince Bismarck ordered that lenient terms of surrender be given to them to avoid making the Russians nervous about our land gain. This is not acceptable."

"To whom?"

"To me! Austria is at our feet, and the longer we wait, the more time they have to rebuild their army and gather allies. So with the royal family out of the way, there is a natural opening for leadership in that country."

"And who is to be their leader? You?"

"I would serve if asked, of course."

Carnicero studied him for a moment, lost in thought. A rumble of thunder promised even more water for the bucket. "You are the only one behind this plot, are you not?"

Friessner shifted uncomfortably. "Yes."

"So if I carry out your plan, you would have access to the vaults of Austria—correct?"

"Well, I haven't been asked to *go* there yet—"

"But you will be. Otherwise, you wouldn't take such a chance." Carnicero stood, removed his glasses, and began to polish them on his shirt sleeve. "I believe you can afford my price, *Herr Regimentschef.* The only mistake that has been made here tonight is my misjudgment of your worth." He sighed heavily and replaced his glasses. "I will just have to live with that."

You're wrong, Friessner thought with despair. *I've made plenty of mistakes tonight.* He decided to go along with Carnicero's fee; after all, assassins could be hired to kill assassins, right? "Kill the prince and princess however you like. They are in the American West, where life is cheap. But the emperor's death must be an accident, do you understand?"

"Of course."

"Here is a map of Texas, with the prince's ranch circled."

Carnicero took the map and peered at it closely. "Dos Culebras. A ranch named after my own heart."

Friessner shook his head blankly. "What does it mean?"

Smiling wolfishly, Carnicero folded the map and put it inside his shirt to shield it from the rain outside. "It means 'Two Snakes.'"

———————

The royal party crossed the Gulf of Mexico to Corpus Christi without incident. Sam and Katy, still exhausted from their cross-country trip by stage, slept most of the way. When they arrived in port, Johann sent Fritz to buy a team of four horses for the special carriage he'd had built for them.

The carriage was shaped like a stagecoach, but larger, wider, and longer. Inside, three rows of benches faced forward, stretched across the width with red velvet padded seats. Three windows were on each side with matching velvet curtains. The rear had a built-in storage box, and Johann sent Otto, his manservant, to buy sandwiches, snacks, and pastries to store inside. Sam assured the prince that the pastries would be melted and sticky in the Texas heat before too long, but Johann had waved him off. Sam shook his head. For a man who was worried about how poor he was, Johann sure could spend money.

With Fritz and Otto's help, Sam managed to stow on top all the trunks the royal party had brought with them—nine in all. "What in the world do people need with so many clothes?" Sam asked neither man in particular. "I like clothes, too, but this is an overstatement."

Fritz ignored him.

"Dey loff deir closse," Otto confided. "Especially der princess. Many prrrretty drrresses." Otto's appearance was a little scary. His long face was acne scarred, with thick red lips and a large nose. One eyelid drooped noticeably, an unfortunate feature that had been the object of unmerciful teasing from other children as he was growing up. Now, at thirty-five years of age, he could lift his ugly head high since he was the sole manservant to the second-most important man in Austria. He did, however, avoid mirrors wherever possible.

Sam looked at the impassive Fritz. "How long have you been with the prince, Fritz?"

Fritz glanced at Sam, turned his huge body, and walked away without a word.

"Nice talking to you," Sam called to the broad back.

"Frrritz no shpeak English," Otto informed him.

"I haven't even heard him speak German."

"He no shpeak German, either. He haff no *zunge.*"

"No what?"

Otto thought for a moment, then stuck out his tongue and pointed at it.

"Ah, tongue!" Sam said. "He doesn't have a tongue? What happened to it?"

Otto made snipping motions with his fingers. "Verrry bahd mahn cut it out."

"Why? What did he do?"

Otto shrugged. "Only Prrrince Johann know dat."

Later that afternoon, the carriage was heading northwest with the sun shining directly into the windows on the left side of the carriage. Katy reached over and untied the red curtain on her window and let it fall into place to block out the glare. The custom-made coach was indeed more comfortable than a stagecoach, but there was no relief from the heat and dust that permeated the air rushing through the windows. Feeling as if she were coated with dirt, she glanced over at Wilhelm beside her. He had fallen asleep with his brown derby pulled down across his eyes, and a drop of sweat rolled down his cheek, leaving a white trail through his dusty face. *Oh, no! Am I that dirty, too?* Quickly she cast a glance at the prince and princess in front and to the right of her, removed a handkerchief from her reticule, and scrubbed at her face.

Just as she finished, Johann turned to look at her and smiled with white, perfect teeth. "I had no idea Texas was so *hot.*"

"And flat," Sophia added over her shoulder from beside her brother.

"This is my first time in Texas, too," Katy said. "I mean, except for the trip to New Orleans."

"That must have been a long, uncomfortable ride," Johann said, as he half turned and stretched his arm across the back of the bench. "You are from California, yes?"

Here I am, Katy thought with discomfort, *sweating like a field hand, and he wants to talk. His face doesn't even look dirty.* "Yes—I was born in Sacramento."

"You have gold there?"

"No, not me personally. But there was a gold rush back in the '40s."

"I would like to see California. You are not married?"

His directness took her by surprise, and her mouth worked before she answered, "Um—no, I'm not."

"And you and Mr. Bronte . . . ?"

"We're just friends. And coworkers."

"You have a very pretty face, Miss Steele. Very . . . innocent."

Sophia heard him and turned to look at Katy, who felt herself blushing like the sunset. Sophia stared at her for a moment, her eyes trailing down Katy's frame, before facing forward again. Her face revealed that she thought her brother was a bit daft.

"And you're very direct, Your Highness," Katy replied. "But thank you."

"Please, call me Johann."

Sophia was astounded at this and glanced at Katy again. Sam, sitting directly in front of them in the driver's seat, turned, smiled, and winked at Katy.

"Oh, I couldn't do that," Katy said, checking behind her to see if *everyone* was listening. Fritz was reading a book, its cover in

German, while Otto and Anna, Sophia's maid, gazed out the window in apparent ignorance. But servants were *always* listening to what was happening, weren't they?

"Why not?"

"It's—it just wouldn't be proper—would it?"

Johann smiled brilliantly again. "It is if I say it is."

Sophia called forward, "You look amused, Mr. Bronte. Do you find us so entertaining?"

Sam made no attempt to cover his devil-may-care grin. "I am often amused by life, Your Highness. Perpetually. I really can't help it; I just think amusing thoughts."

"How nice to be so easily entertained. Are we almost to the . . . what is it called?"

"Way station. I'm looking right at it."

They crowded forward to see three small buildings in the distance. Wilhelm woke up, looked around in confusion, then strained to see what everyone was looking at so intently. "Three buildings? I was expecting a small village."

Sam said, "No, Way stations are just stopovers for stagecoaches when the distance between cities is too long. Don't worry, they should have a well and plenty of supplies."

The station consisted of a main building, barn, and small storage shed. Tumbleweeds blew through the area like huge bouncing balls of dark cotton. The overall appearance was of hasty and fragile construction, and the whole site seemed in danger of being swallowed up into the ground by the flat Texas prairie that stretched for miles in every direction.

"We are staying *here?*" Sophia asked through numbed lips, her eyes huge.

"Beautiful, ain't it?" Sam drawled.

Katy attempted to keep her face neutral. Evidently, the princess had hoped to find a palace in the middle of nowhere.

Sam stopped the wagon, and from the front door of the main

building appeared an old man dressed only in stained denim pants and suspenders. His bare feet were filthy, and three days of gray stubble covered his heavily wrinkled face. He spat a stream of brown juice into the dust and said with a toothless grin, "Howdy, folks!"

"Howdy!" Sam said as he jumped down and opened the door of the carriage.

"Y'all come to stay overnight?"

Sam nodded. "If you've got the room."

"Oh, I got the room all right. Now last night I had a few sheepherders stay over and—lawsamighty!—they kept me up most o' the night with their stories! You people talkative? Gotta get my rest tonight."

Sam was helping Sophia down when he said, "This lady here will talk your ear off, if you don't watch it."

"Mr. Bronte!" Sophia said, aghast. To the man she began, "That is not true; I—" she stopped and shook her head in exasperation— "oh, why am I explaining myself to *you!*" She cast Sam a melting glare and walked away with a frown of distaste as she scanned the pitiful area.

The man watched her warily. "My name's Clem Reese. Y'all come on in and make yourselves at home."

The old man greeted everyone cheerily as they emerged, and they followed him inside. Sam mumbled to Katy about the horses, but Clem said, "Leave them hosses to me, son. You jest relax and get some vittles in ya. They's lamb stew in that big pot there"—he motioned to the stove—"and I baked some bread this mornin'." He leaned close to Johann, who shrank steadily away the closer he came, and said, "Throwed some halapeeners in it that'll put hair on your chest, young feller!" Clem cackled loudly and slapped Johann firmly on the back, then went outside leaving Johann staring after him in the same state of stunned silence.

"But—the floor is dirt!" Sophia exclaimed, still in shock over the condition of the place.

"That—that man touched you, Johann!" Wilhelm commented in awe. "He hit you!"

"He didn't mean anything by it," Sam told him.

Johann, still slightly in shock over Clem's show of camaraderie, stuttered, "What are hala—halapeen—?"

"Jalapeños," Katy finished. "They're a spicy—*very* spicy—Mexican pepper."

"Ah," he nodded, but gave no sign of how he felt about them.

A scream split the air, and everyone turned to see Sophia at the entrance to one of the bedrooms with her hands covering her mouth.

"What is it, Highness—a mouse?" Wilhelm asked.

"No—it is—it must be—" she closed the door to the room, swallowed, and with one side of her upper lip raised in distaste she said, "It must be *his* room. Do *not* go in there!" The sick look on her face assured them all that they didn't want to see Clem's room. They watched her step to another room and cautiously peer inside. Then she let out another screech and hurried back to the middle of the room. "This time it *was* a mouse!"

"That does it!" Wilhelm declared. "We cannot stay here!"

"OK," Sam said quickly, turning to the door, "I'll go stop Clem from unharnessing the horses. It's only about forty miles to Three Rivers—we could be there by tomorrow noon if we don't stop again." Sam was very tired of the royal party and their prissy ways, and part of him hoped they wouldn't stop him; then they could suffer the consequences of being cooped up in the carriage for eighteen more hours.

"No!" Johann barked. "This place may be bad, but think of the alternative, Wilhelm. We would travel all night and half of tomorrow. Besides, I *like* this place!"

"What!" Sophia cried. "Johann, it is filthy, the food is probably unpalatable, they have rats, and that man—Clem!" She shuddered. "He reminds me of that beggar that always came to the palace in Vienna. That man would *never* give up."

"Exactly. He reminds me of home."

Wilhelm walked to the bedroom Sophia had seen and his large nose wrinkled in distaste. He'd never slept in anything but kingly palaces and large, elegant hotel rooms, and the choice was a difficult one for him. But then he remembered the dust from the horse's hooves pouring through the windows of the carriage and the pain in his back from being jostled by huge bumps in the trail. "I suppose it is better than traveling all night."

Sophia looked at Katy. "I would have thought we could expect better accommodations from our chaperones."

Sam saw Katy's hazel eyes narrow and her mouth draw into a straight line. Before she could answer, he said, "Your Highness, there's no way to tell how the lodgings will be when you travel on the prairie. If you want to journey to out-of-the-way places, these stops are necessary."

The two women were staring at each other as Sam spoke, and he didn't even know if Sophia had heard him until she stated flatly, "Very well, Mr. Bronte."

Sam saw Katy withhold comment with effort and smiled inwardly. There was no doubt in his mind that she would have taken up for herself had he not intervened. He remembered when he first met her—how vulnerable and docile she'd been—and over time he'd watched her slowly climb from the protective shell she'd made for herself to blossom into a young woman that could take care of herself. A year ago, she would have been deeply hurt by Sophia's acid personality. Times had changed.

Sam suddenly noticed the heavy silence and suggested quickly, "Let's eat! I'm starved."

Clem's stew was less than savory. Too much salt and pepper made Wilhelm sneeze at once, and most of the potatoes had deep, dark bruises throughout. However, the cuts of lamb were tender and plentiful, and no one complained. The homemade bread was indeed fiery with the jalapeños added, and when Johann bit into the bread and chewed, his face turned red, and he gulped two cupfuls of water.

Struggling to keep from laughing, Katy cut a slice of bread for him. "Here, Your Highness. Let me cut some of the more ominous-looking peppers out for you."

"How can you tell the ones that are more . . . dangerous?"

"It's the seeds. Generally, the more seeds, the hotter the pepper."

"Ah."

"What is the purpose of eating something so unpleasant, Johann?" Sophia asked. Her own bread sat untouched on her plate.

"To experiment, Sophia! To sample the great American state of Texas!"

Sophia glanced around at their surroundings, and her face said that she'd sampled enough of the great state of Texas for one day.

Clem returned while they were pouring coffee from a large pot. "Helped yourselves, huh? That's fine—leave any for me?" He removed a particularly large wad of tobacco from his mouth and dropped it in a spitoon by the door.

"There is plenty left," Johann said.

"Hey, you people talk kinda funny. Whereabouts you from? Boston?"

"Austria."

"You don't say! Ain't that where them kangaroos are?"

"No. That is Aus*tral*ia."

Clem scratched his ear. "Always wanted to see one o' them kangaroos."

When Katy finished eating, she went out to the front porch and leaned on a post to gaze at the starry sky. She was accustomed to solitude, since much of her childhood had demanded it, and found herself feeling a bit claustrophobic from riding in the carriage all day. She was also tired of the princess's catty remarks and smoking glances. Johann's attention earlier had set something off in Sophia, but Katy was at a loss to know the reason.

The air had turned cooler since the sun's departure, and she hugged herself to stay warm.

"A bit cool, is it not?"

Katy turned and found Johann smiling at her. "Oh—Your Highness. I didn't hear you come out."

"Please Miss Steele—call me Johann. I would feel much better if you would."

"Maybe you would, but I'm not so sure about your sister."

He leaned on the other side of the post. "You must forgive Sophia. She is my big sister, and she has always watched out for me."

"I was wondering about your ages."

"I am twenty-six, and she is twenty-eight. She is slightly over-protective."

Slightly? Katy thought wryly, but she said nothing. Crickets had taken up their buzzing, and far away a coyote howled. She sighed deeply, content to breath in the cool, fresh air.

"Am I bothering you, Miss Steele? I can go back inside . . . ?"

"No, of course not. And if I'm to call you Johann, which I'm really uncomfortable about, you can call me Katy."

"Katy. A wonderful name. Why do you not go by Katherine?"

"It's my given name, but it's so formal, don't you think?"

"Yes, but it fits you. May I call you that?"

Katy smiled uncertainly. *Sam will have a good laugh over that.* "You can call me that, but it may take me a while to answer to it. My aunt is the only one that ever uses it."

"Ah! A woman I can understand."

Chuckling, Katy said, "Well, when you figure her out, tell *me* and we'll both know."

"Tell me about her."

Katy took her weight off the post and rubbed her arms vigorously. "I'd rather not. I should go inside—I'm pretty tired."

"I am sorry, Katherine. I did not mean—"

"No, it's all right. Maybe another time."

"I will look forward to it."

"Good night."

"*Gute Nacht,* Katherine." Johann watched her go inside, mentally chastising himself. *The first time I speak to her, I bring up a delicate subject and make her uncomfortable. What bad luck!* He'd been taken with her since their first meeting. Such sweet innocence, but mixed with a guarded wariness that bespoke self-consciousness. *She has beautiful cheeks and eyes. I must find a way to tell her that.*

He sat in a rocking chair on the porch and leaned his head on the high back. "Katherine," he whispered slowly, savoring each syllable. "Katherine."

CHAPTER THREE

Dos Culebras

On the seventh day of their journey, the party neared the ranch. They'd continued over the same plateau for sixty miles and stopped at a farmhouse for directions. The farmer told them to keep traveling to the end of the plateau and they would find Dos Culebras in a natural valley a few miles past the Concho River.

On the way they passed great herds of buffalo grazing on the vast prairie, eating every blade of grass in sight. Wildlife was plentiful; armadillos, prairie dogs, and coyotes all watched the lumbering carriage and then scurried away. They dined on quail and dove that Sam, Wilhelm, and Johann brought down from escaping coveys with fine, Austrian-made shotguns. Johann and Wilhelm proved to be excellent shots—almost as good as Sam.

Crossing the Concho River, they stopped beside a long, graceful bluff and splashed cool water on themselves. The reprieve from the stifling heat was refreshing, and the party was soon in a fine mood. Even Sophia laughed a few times when Johann splashed her. However, when they resumed their trip, everyone was more than ready to reach Dos Culebras.

Johann was riding beside Sam in the driver's seat when Sam asked, "Are you ready to brand a calf?" Sam genuinely liked Johann; during the trip he'd seen the prince display a boyish enthusiasm and charm. He showed signs of a pampered upbringing every once in a while, but not nearly as much as his sister.

"Oh, yes, I am anxious to try *everything* a real cowboy does!"

"You'd better not tell the foreman that. He's liable to put you to work mucking out the stables and mending fences. Not everything a cowboy does is roping cattle and driving herds."

Johann considered this information for a moment. "Then I am ready to do everything a cowboy does that is *fun.*"

They reached a barbed-wire fence and turned west to follow it to a road. Eventually they reached a sign identifying the land as Dos Culebras Ranch. On each side of the words were carvings of two rattlesnakes—one slithering toward the sky, the other toward the ground. Sam stopped the carriage on a small hill, and everyone crowded to the windows on the right to see the rich, green grasslands. No cattle were in sight, but the plateau was visible a few miles to the east stretching north.

"It is beautiful!" Sophia breathed, revealing a rare moment of pleasure. "And it is—ours?" she asked Sam with wide eyes.

"I don't know how it's sectioned off, but, yes, part of it is."

Johann was struck by the majesty of the wide-open plain, and his face glowed with pride at his piece of the world.

After finding the road, they hadn't traveled far when they spotted a rider approaching. His easy slouch in the saddle showed him to be an experienced cowboy as he casually galloped toward them. A very young brown and white calf was slung across the horse's neck.

"Hello, the wagon!" he hailed.

"Hello!" Sam called back.

The cowboy came to a stop in a cloud of dust beside the team of horses. "Can I help you folks?" He was a young man with curly brown hair and sun-darkened skin. Boyishly handsome with an honest, open face, he tipped his hat to the ladies in the back of the carriage as they looked out the windows.

"Yes, we're—" Sam started.

"I am Prince Johann Kessler," Johann interrupted excitedly. "We are here to see my ranch!"

The young face clouded. "Yeah? We didn't expect you here 'til next week." His tone implied that even next week would have been too soon. "And it's *half* yours."

"Yes, that is what I mean."

"Well, the part you're sitting on belongs to my father, Carl Tyson. My name's Boone."

Johann quickly introduced everyone. Boone nodded politely, but he obviously wasn't looking forward to sharing his father's ranch with anyone, especially foreigners.

Sophia asked abruptly from the window, "Where is *our* land?"

Boone stared at her a moment, then gestured west toward the bluffs of the plateau rising in the distance. "Back that way."

"I am accustomed to being referred to as 'Highness,' or 'Princess.'"

"Good for you, ma'am."

Sam and Katy both had to cover their smiles.

"How impertinent!"

"Sophia!" Johann warned. "We are guests in this country."

"We *own* part of this country—we are not *guests!*"

Sam said quickly, "Boone, would you mind showing us the prince's land?"

"We will find it ourselves, Mr. Bronte!" Sophia pouted. "Drive!"

"No, we won't find it ourselves. We could pass right by it and not know it. That's why we need Boone here to lead us."

"You were hired to follow orders!"

"Sophia, please!" Johann said fretfully.

Katy, sitting behind the princess, had had enough. "We were hired to guide and protect. We're not your servants!"

"How dare you speak to me that way!"

"Ladies, if I may—" Johann began.

Katy smiled at Boone and said, "Boone, would you please take us there?"

Boone, who'd been watching the bickering with amusement, had to smile back at Katy. "Yes, ma'am. I'll take you there."

"Thank you. And please, don't call me ma'am—I'm not much older than you."

"Yes, ma—I mean, OK." Glancing at Sam, he said, "It's about three miles to the main house. I'll need to drop this calf off to his mother along the way." The calf had begun to struggle against Boone, who was keeping him on the horse with effort.

"Lead on, my good man." Sam had to admire the boy's maturity in the face of a spoiled adult. But his guarded attitude with the new owners only could have been learned from Carl Tyson, his father, and Sam was afraid the reception would be less than cordial.

In the carriage, Sophia cast a dark glance at Katy before moving to the other side. Wilhelm, too, stared at Katy sullenly, and she suddenly realized that Wilhelm cared for the princess with more than friendly feelings. The signs had been there all during the trip, but Katy hadn't put it together until now. He'd always kept an eye on Sophia, offering to get her water or checking to see if she was comfortable. Katy wondered if Sophia knew, and then wondered if Johann, Wilhelm's best friend, knew.

———————

Dos Culebras consisted of a large main house, a smaller and older house a bit farther away on a rise, a bunkhouse for the ranch hands, and a huge barn. Beside the barn was an expansive corral with twenty or so horses inside, and next to it was a cookhouse. Flowing beside the whole property was a ten-foot-wide stream, an offshoot of the Concho River.

As they came in sight of the house, Boone spurred his horse into a sprint to tell his father of their visitors. Cowboys standing near the corral turned and gazed curiously at the carriage as Sam stopped the horses near the house. Boone and his father emerged from the house.

Carl Tyson was in his forties, with light brown hair that was receding rapidly from his forehead. The points of his thick mustache were greased in an upward spiral, and his dark eyes were filled with self-assertion. A small boy of eight with brown, searching eyes came out of the house to stand next to Tyson.

"Welcome to Dos Culebras," Tyson said, "I'm Carl Tyson, and you've met Boone. This is my other son, Remy." He put a hand on the boy's head as he spoke.

Sam made the introductions as everyone climbed down from the carriage. Johann and Wilhelm shook Tyson's hand, while Sophia examined the ranch with a critical eye.

"This is a beautiful place, Mr. Tyson," Sam said.

"Yes—wonderful!" Johann agreed.

"Thank you. It's taken a lot of hard work. I've taken the liberty of setting you up in the house on the hill, if that's all right. It's stocked with food and supplies, but I don't think it's large enough for all eight of you."

"That's fine," Sam said, "I'll sleep in the bunkhouse."

"And so will Fritz and Otto," Johann nodded.

"Then the rest of you will be comfortable. Would the ladies like to get settled in?"

Sophia announced that she wished to take a nap. Wilhelm took her with Fritz and the servants to unload the carriage at the house.

"It is very kind of you to allow us the use of your house, Mr. Tyson," Johann told him, as the rest of them sat on the long porch. Remy and Boone headed for the corral.

Tyson said grudgingly, "Just until you get your own place built."

"It used to be your house?" Katy asked.

"Yes, until my wife died giving birth to Remy." His eyes followed his sons across the expansive yard. He was wearing a starched brown shirt buttoned at the collar, brown pants, and well-worn, cracked leather boots.

"I'm sorry."

"It was a long time ago," Tyson said, shrugging. "Eight years."

Katy didn't mention that she lost her mother in the same way, and not a day went by that she didn't regret not knowing her.

"Let's get down to business, Prince Johann," Tyson stated flatly. "Since I sold your uncle his share of the ranch, I've managed to scrape up some money. I'd like to buy you out."

Johann had been absently brushing lint off of his dark blue trousers when he looked up sharply. "Buy . . . ?"

"You out."

"Why, that is out of the question! I have traveled halfway around the world!"

"I'll make you a good price for it." Tyson's dark eyes didn't waver from Johann's stunned face.

Johann glanced at Sam, who shrugged and carefully studied the activity by the corral. Some men were saddling horses, and a bay colt was having none of it.

"I am sorry, Mr. Tyson, but I decline your offer."

"Now, you listen to me," Tyson said pointedly, leaning forward to place his elbows on his knees. His tolerant nature was gone, and though his tone wasn't rude, it was very close. "This ranch has been in my family for twenty years. My daddy and I built it with our own hands. Pa, Mama, and my wife are buried on this land. With all due respect, you're a foreigner with no idea of the history of this land. You haven't bled on it, or blessed it, or cursed it. I have. My boys have. We *belong* to the land, and it belongs to us."

Johann looked at Sam and Katy helplessly. He hadn't expected a fight on the day of his arrival, and to make matters worse, he understood what Tyson was saying and felt sorry for him.

Katy caught Sam's eye from her place on the other side of Tyson and inclined her head toward the ranch owner.

Sam shook his head almost imperceptibly.

Katy narrowed her eyes and lips and nodded again emphatically.

Sam cleared his throat. "Um, Mr. Tyson. Prince Johann has the deed to his share of the ranch, which you sold fair and square to his uncle. Now—"

"Mr. Bronte, do you know why this ranch was named 'Dos Culebras?'"

"No, I don't, and we were wondering how—"

"The first day me and my daddy walked on this spread and laid a claim, he got bit by a diamondback rattlesnake. We had an old Mexican cook at that time, and he tended to Dad while I went out exploring and got bit by another one." Tyson rolled up his sleeve and showed them an angry red swelling on his forearm. "See that? Swells up every year where that old rattler bit me. Now that Mexican cook, Rivera his name was, he told us that in the village he grew up in, it was considered good luck to get bit by a snake. It meant that all your bad luck was behind you, and only good luck was in the future. Me and Dad both thought he was crazy, since we were throwing up and shivering from fever at the time, but the next day we named it Dos Culebras."

Johann stared, fascinated. "But you said your father and mother and wife have died here."

"That's true. I didn't tell you that story because it was some sort of miracle, and everybody lives happily ever after. I told you because there's a *history* here. A Tyson history that I want to stay here."

"But you still have thousands of acres. Is that not enough?"

Tyson stared at Johann for a time, then sighed and leaned back in his chair. "Just what I thought. You wouldn't understand."

"I think I understand, Mr. Tyson," Johann said. "I just cannot do what you ask."

Tyson nodded curtly. He was silent for so long, Katy almost stood. Finally he spoke, and his tone was milder. "You know, I was ready to hate you, Prince Johann. I thought you would come in here and start throwing weight around like you owned the whole place. You're making it hard to dislike you, so I'll give you some helpful information."

"Please, call me Johann."

"All right. Then I'm Carl, to all of you," he nodded, glancing at Katy and Sam. "There's a fella that owns the property north of ours by the name of J. B. Flynn. He's land hungry and wants Dos Culebras bad. He's already tried taking your share away in the courts, claiming the sale wasn't legal to a foreigner, and I had to fight him for you."

"Thank you."

"Now, before you get all teary on me, understand that I'd rather be a neighbor to a lizard than Flynn. I fought him for my own reasons. After he failed at that, he tried damming a stream that flowed on to the ranch that I use to water the cattle. I had to get the judge in Abilene to slap his hand for it. Now he's making noises about getting this property any way he can."

"Such as?" Katy asked.

Tyson smiled faintly. "J. B. Flynn has no limits. The man that owned the ranch Flynn has now, the Box T, up and disappeared when he wouldn't sell to Flynn."

After a short silence, Sam asked the question that was on everyone's mind: "Did Flynn—get rid of him?"

"You tell me, Sam," Tyson said, his dark eyes expressionless.

———————

"Let 'er go!" Billy Mantooth called, and the two cowboys holding the bawling calf released their hold on its legs. Casting a distrustful look around at the cowboys, the calf trotted across the corral to its mother.

"*Ach!* That smell!" Sophia exclaimed to Fritz, choking, who nodded his agreement. They were sitting on a buckboard, watching the brandings. Waves of smoke, dust, and burning cowhide assaulted their noses repeatedly.

Two days had passed since their arrival. Katy, still a novice at horsemanship, was trying to get accustomed to the sorrel that Sam had chosen for her to ride. She'd asked him to stay close in case the animal bolted. The sorrel seemed aware that his rider was inexperienced and kept trying to see how far Katy would let him go with antics of throwing his head around, fighting the bit, and shifting his hooves.

The branding corral was a mile from the main house, strategically planted there just because of the horrible smell. Sophia had chosen to be driven in the wagon rather than ride a horse of her own. Johann and Wilhelm sat on the corral fence, dangling their feet and wearing Stetson hats that seemed totally out of place with their fine clothes but feeling like real cowboys.

"Anybody wanna give this a try?" Billy Mantooth called, raising the smoking brand after marking another calf. He was a tall, thin man with large ears and tanned, leathery skin. Carl Tyson might own the place, but Mantooth ran the show. They'd already seen evidence of his iron control over the cowboys. One of the ropers had missed snagging one of the calves, and Mantooth, shooting the man a thunderous glare, shouted, "If you can't handle that job, give it to someone who can!" The cowboy hadn't missed again.

"I will try it!" Johann called. He jumped down from the fence, lost his hat, retrieved it, and went to stand beside Mantooth with excitement lighting his features.

"Let's get this brand red hot," Mantooth said as he thrust the iron back into the fire. He handed Johann a pair of sweatstained leather gloves. "Put these on. Now don't press too hard with the brand—let it burn its way down naturally by applying a tiny bit of pressure. Got it?"

"Yes."

"Get another calf over here, boys."

Johann looked up at his companions with a huge grin on his face as the cowboys roped another calf. When the animal was by the fire being held down by two men, Mantooth removed the smoking iron from the fire and showed Johann how to place it. Johann saw that the brand was identical to the snakes on the sign they'd seen at the edge of the property. He took the iron and placed it against the calf's flank. A stinking smoke erupted from around the brand, but he managed to hold his breath as he applied pressure. Mantooth said, "That's good—ease 'er out!" Johann removed the brand, took a deep breath, and for a moment thought he was going to vomit from the sickening smell. When the feeling passed, he was very thankful—throwing up in front of these tough cowboys would have been the ultimate embarrassment.

"That was real good!" Mantooth exclaimed, slapping Johann solidly across his back.

Sam and Katy expressed their approval by clapping as Johann beamed.

"Anybody else?" Mantooth asked. "We've got about fifteen more that need to be marked."

After Sophia and Wilhelm declined, Katy summoned up all of her courage and took a turn. "What if I hurt him?" she asked Mantooth.

"Don't worry, ma'am. His skin's so thick he won't feel nothin'."

Despite his words, Katy's fear of burning right through the hide into the calf itself caused her to hold back from applying enough pressure. Mantooth stopped her, placed the brand in the fire again, and told her they'd try again when it was hot.

"Why is he wiggling if he's not hurt?" she asked worriedly. She was beginning to think this wasn't such a grand idea after all.

"They don't like to be held down, any more than you would," Mantooth smiled reassuringly. "He's just bawlin' 'cause we took him away from his mama."

When the brand was hot again, Mantooth handed it to her

carefully. He couldn't help but smile at her discomfort, and the way the huge gloves looked on her small hands.

"Go ahead, Katherine," Johann urged. "It is easy!"

Katy grimly tried again. This time the branding was so well done, Mantooth turned to Sam and Johann and with a wink said, "She'll be taking my job if I don't watch out."

Sam helped her back on the sorrel and whispered, "Very good, *Katherine*."

Katy made a face at him.

"Come on. Let's go for a ride."

"Now? The barbecue's only an hour or two away." Carl Tyson had arranged a barbecue for them, and she didn't want to be late.

Sam consulted his watch. "Exactly an hour and twenty-three minutes. Plenty of time."

The smell of sage floated through the hot air as they rode north. Sam started them off at a canter to let Katy get adjusted to the sorrel, then he gently urged them into a gallop. Katy was breathless from excitement and grasped the pommel with her left hand.

"When you get to the point where you don't hang on to that for dear life, you'll know you're a horsewoman." Sam was wearing only blue jeans and a brown leather vest, and Katy couldn't help but notice the fine sheen of sweat on his tanned arms and shoulders. With his long dark hair and deep bronze coloring, he could almost be mistaken for an Indian from a distance.

They rode a half mile, then Katy asked, "Did you bring me out here for a reason?"

"What do you mean?"

"I mean, this is the first time we've had to ourselves since we arrived. Were you trying to get me alone for a reason?"

"Do I need one?"

Katy playfully slapped at him with the end of her reins. "Will you stop answering questions with questions?"

43

"I got tired of standing in line behind Johann. Thought I was going to have to make an appointment."

"That's not funny."

"I was only *half* joking."

"Sam Bronte, don't tell me you're jealous!"

"Bite your tongue, madam," he said with his easy smile. "Let's walk for a while."

They dismounted and led the lathered horses to a stand of oak trees by a small creek. Redwing blackbirds took flight from the trees as they let the horses drink, and Katy watched a crow fly to the ground across the water and snatch up a grasshopper. The shade from the burning sun was more than welcome.

Sam took off his hat and splashed water on his face and hair. "We seem to have gotten ourselves into more than we'd bargained for with this Flynn fella. How do you want to handle it?"

"There's nothing to handle."

"Not right now, but in the near future, I'm sure there will be. Since I've been staying in the bunkhouse, I've heard some interesting stories about Flynn from the cowhands. A couple of them hired on with Flynn before Tyson, and they say Flynn's famous for his Irish temper and doesn't hesitate when he sees something he wants."

"What can we do except wait?"

"I don't like waiting around for someone to bushwhack me. Why don't we take the war to him?"

Katy knelt down and began pitching acorns into the slow-moving water. She saw a small fish dart by when the first one broke the surface. "Sam, first of all, there's no war. Secondly, why take the chance of starting trouble when nothing may happen anyway? You worry too much."

"Maybe so. But worrying has come in handy for us a few times—remember dynamite night in the railroad tunnel?"

"How could I forget?"

"So I think we should go have a talk with Flynn tomorrow. Just to clear the air. We *are* here to protect Johann, remember?"

Katy sighed. "I suppose you're right. But I still have a bad feeling about it."

"Tell you what—we'll take Fritz with us. He'd scare anybody."

"They probably won't let us in the door."

Sam stood and shook the water from his hair. "May I ask you something?"

"Sure."

"Are you all right? I mean, Johann's not bothering you, is he?"

"Of course not!" Katy said, a bit more defensively than she'd intended.

He held out his hands, palms facing her. "OK, OK, I was just asking. You two seem to be spending a lot of time together, that's all."

"We like each other's company, the same as you and me."

"If you say so."

"Sam, I appreciate your looking out for me, but I'm a big girl and don't need a big brother."

Putting on his hat, Sam looked at her, his bright blue eyes spiked with flint. "One thing I'm not, Katy Steele, is your big brother." He turned his horse and swung into the saddle. "I think it's time to get back."

"Now, don't go pouting on me." Katy tried to smile, but his face was stony.

"Are you coming?"

"Yes."

They hardly spoke on the way back to Dos Culebras.

CHAPTER FOUR

Dance of Anger

K aty took a quick bath after they returned from the ride,
vigorously washing off the horsey smell. She was still
disturbed about Sam's reaction. At times he could be so
sweet, and at others he was mocking, quick-tempered, and childish. *That's one thing about Sam,* she thought as she toweled off. *You
never know what you're going to get from one moment to the next.*
A smaller voice told her, *And that's what attracts you to him. That,
and the fact that he's caring, trustworthy, giving, and handsome
beyond belief. Right, Katy?*

"He's just a friend, nothing more," she said aloud. *Oh, really? That
sure was a friendly stare you had today when you were noticing his
arms. Weren't you remembering, just for a moment, the time he took
you in those strong, brown arms and crushed you to him? Tell the
truth, Katy.* "Well—it crossed my mind," she admitted, as she stepped
into her green dress. It was cotton, with a lace-trimmed bodice, and
the skirt had four flounces at the hem, also trimmed with lace. Just the
right touch for an informal barbecue.

The memory of Sam's kiss came back to her. He'd been teaching
Katy to dance, and at one point they'd found their faces inches
from each other. Truthfully, Katy wasn't sure who kissed whom,
but she'd felt a confused mix of emotions flow over her like a
wave: excitement, embarrassment—and hope. Sam had been the

one to pull away, and then her overriding feeling had been the desire for him to do it all over again. But she'd seen caution and surprise in his eyes, too, and the moment had passed. What made the situation more frustrating for Katy was that Sam wasn't a Christian and she was.

She sighed deeply and concentrated on getting ready.

Johann met her as she arrived. He was dressed in a royal blue suit, with vest, tie, and white shirt. His face was already sweating, and Katy scolded, "Johann! This was supposed to be a barbecue of beef, not of you. Why didn't you wear something cooler?"

"Forgive me, Katherine, but one of my many faults is ego. Something inside me insists that I look like a prince."

"I wonder why?" she asked, smiling.

Two long tables covered with white linen were set up behind the main house. Katy immediately spotted Sam, standing by a massive oak tree and talking to Wilhelm. He saw her, but his face remained carefully neutral. She put him out of her mind for the moment, taking a deep breath filled with the smell of barbecue and newly cut hay. "Let's follow our noses," she told Johann.

He looked at her questioningly but said nothing.

They crossed the big yard, greeting and thanking Tyson as they passed him, and found the huge, stone-enclosed cook fire. On the spit, a side of beef was being turned slowly by a short and stocky man, about sixty, with high cheekbones and black, square-cut hair. To Katy, something seemed out of place about his appearance; then she noticed the blue eyes underneath the heavy brow structure. Apparently he was only part Indian.

"This smells wonderful," Katy said.

He watched them with no expression for a moment, then turned to look behind him. Not many people acknowledged he even existed, much less struck up a conversation with him—other Indians included. "Thank you, miss." His smile revealed stark white teeth against his coffee-colored skin.

Johann stepped forward. "I am Prince Johann Kessler. This is Katherine Steele." He offered his hand and was surprised at the man's reaction. He looked at Johann's outstretched hand, frozen with indecision, then quickly wiped his hands on a rag attached to his belt and took it with a firm grip.

"Seth Moon. Very glad to meet you." He tipped his hat to Katy, and the crow's feet around his eyes grew deeper as his smile broadened. He tried to remember the last time he'd shaken a white man's hand, or *any* man's hand, and couldn't. Suddenly he was struck dumb, and he busied himself by taking a small brush from a pot of sauce and adding a layer of the thick, crimson liquid to the beef.

Katy inspected the contents of the pan and asked, "What do you put in your sauce to make it smell so good?"

Moon smiled again. "Secret recipe. Just between me and the Lord."

"Are you a Christian man, Mr. Moon?" Katy asked, surprised.

Moon looked at her quickly to see if he'd offended her. When he saw genuine wonder and pleasure in Katy's face instead of accusation, he nodded, "Yes, I am—converted last year."

"That's wonderful! I'm a Christian, too. How did you come to God?"

His face turned serious for the first time, then he looked around uncomfortably. "Are you sure you want to hear?"

"Of course! Why?"

"Well—not many people want to talk to me, and—"

"*I* want to talk to you. Don't you, Johann?"

"Yes, very much. Please tell us."

"Um—all right. I'd been wandering all my life. There's not much chance of a home when you're a half-breed—don't fit in anywhere." The statement was made matter-of-factly, with no bitterness that Katy could detect. "Fell in with a bad bunch during the war."

"Who was that?" Katy asked.

"The Yankees called them Quantrill's Raiders."

"Oh, my. I've heard of them. Weren't they—um—kind of—?"

Moon snorted and finished for her: "A pack of murderers and thieves? Yes, they were. And I was just as guilty as anyone." He shifted his feet nervously and didn't meet their eyes when he said, "There was an—incident in Lawrence, Kansas, that was pretty horrible, even for a war."

"Yes, I remember," Katy said softly. She'd read in the papers of a massacre that had included women and children. By seeing Moon's haunted face, she could tell that he would be tortured by the event for quite a while, if not for the rest of his life.

"I left the outfit and landed in a small church in San Angelo, not far from here. God spoke to me one night in a service. It was the most peaceful feeling I'd ever had in my life when I asked him into my heart." He shrugged, and the bright smile returned. "So now I serve him."

Katy turned to Johann. "You see? God works in all our lives."

"God's love is the greatest thing that ever happened to me, Prince Johann," Moon said simply.

"Then perhaps we should accompany you to a service," Johann suggested, and after only a brief hesitation, Moon nodded.

"This Sunday," Katy agreed. "If that doesn't work out, then soon." As they turned to join the others, Katy sighed happily. *Perhaps this would give Johann a glimpse of her beliefs.*

At dinner, Katy found herself sitting between Johann and Remy, who smiled shyly at her when they started eating. "How old are you, Remy?"

"Eight."

"That's a good age to be."

"Why?"

Katy took a bite of beef and moaned softly. "That is *so* wonderful!"

"Why?" Remy asked persistently.

"Why what? Oh, yes—eight is good because you've got your whole life ahead of you. You can be anything you want and do anything you want. You don't have to worry about money or girlfriends—*do* you have a girlfriend?"

"No."

"Good. You're too young."

Remy took a small bite of potato and chewed thoughtfully. "I want to be a doctor."

"Really? I've had some medical training. Why do you want to be a doctor?"

"So I can save women from dying when a kid's born."

Katy looked at him quickly, but he was concentrating on cutting his meat. "That's a very noble idea, Remy. Did you know my mother died when I was born, too?"

He stared at her, his liquid brown eyes huge. "No foolin'?"

"No foolin'." Katy watched him absorb this, and she suddenly wanted to take him in her arms and hug him. "You still miss her, don't you?"

Remy nodded slowly as he studied his plate.

"Well, Remy, there will always be a part of you that misses your mother. I won't lie to you. It's not natural to never have a mother's love. And do you know that for a long time I was mad at mine? Like it was her fault that she died and I never got to love her?"

The small head whipped around. "You felt that way, too?"

"Sure did."

"And—and—do you still?"

"No, and do you know why?"

Remy shook his head.

"Because it wasn't her fault that she died." Katy placed her knife and fork on the table and turned to face him fully. "I'll tell you the same thing my father told me when I was about your age. Do you know what that was?"

Another shake of the head, with a breathless look.

51

"He said that my mother would have wanted nothing more than to love me and watch me grow up. But she couldn't. Her body wasn't strong enough. So she went to live with God. And when we finally go home to God, we'll have a wonderful surprise waiting for us! We'll be able to see our mothers. Won't that be great?"

Remy's lower lip began to tremble, and he looked away quickly to wipe his eyes with his napkin. Katy glanced over his head and saw Fritz staring at her. She'd thought he couldn't understand English, but a ghost of a smile came to his lips before he continued eating.

"Pa says I'm too big to cry," Remy said with a nasal tone.

"Do you think *I'm* too big to cry?"

"But—you're a girl!"

Katy leaned toward him and wiped a spot of barbecue from his mouth. "And you're a little boy that has feelings, too. Feelings hurt sometimes, and I say you can cry if you want to."

"Really?" he beamed.

For the rest of dinner, Katy made a point to include Remy in the conversation. Through their private talks, she discovered that he was a very lonely little boy who didn't receive nearly enough attention from his father and brother. Katy resolved to spend more time with Remy.

After dinner, she was talking with Tyson and Johann, when she felt someone touch her arm.

"Can we talk for a minute?" Sam asked.

"Of course."

They walked around to the front of the house. The moon was nearly full and lit their way easily. Sam stopped by a rose bush with bright yellow blossoms and turned her to face him. "Katy, about this afternoon—" He was stopped by her fingers on his lips.

Katy said nothing. Smiling into his eyes, she shook her head slightly. He took her fingers in his hand and squeezed them gently. They stayed there for a while, smelling the sweet scent of roses, with no words needing to be spoken.

After dinner, Carl Tyson announced that there was a dance the next night in the small town of Fargo, twelve miles north of the ranch. He invited everyone, apologizing about informing them of it so late. Katy and Sam believed that he'd had no intention of inviting the prince and princess until he'd discovered that Johann was an extremely likable man. But that didn't matter. Sam found out that J. B. Flynn would likely be there, and it would give them a natural atmosphere in which to talk to him.

On the following night, they all rode in the carriage to Fargo. The dance was held in a pavilion at the southern edge of town. The Texas and Confederate flags hung from the rafters in the center, drooping heavily in the humid air. Forty or fifty citizens crowded inside on the dance floor, while a small band played a wide range of music from simple jigs to amazingly well-done waltzes. Punch was served, along with cakes and pastries. Outside the pavilion and off to the side was a group of serious-looking men, obviously discussing politics or national policy. An unidentified jug was passed among them.

The prince and princess were the stars of the evening. Rumors had been circulated for some time about the foreign half owners of Dos Culebras, and every eye was upon them as they stepped down from the carriage. Johann was handsome in a resplendent red Austrian military uniform, complete with medals and saber. Sophia wore a royal blue silk dress, with an upright collar that produced a shawl effect, decorated with pearls and Persian lamb. Many women gasped when they saw the dress that probably had cost more money than they would see in a year.

A few brave souls walked directly up to them and introduced themselves, and before long Johann and Sophia were receiving a long line of people. Fritz stood behind them, eyeing everyone. He wasn't accustomed to every male citizen carrying a firearm, and it made him nervous. In Austria, the practice was considered gaudy. He'd never had to defend an attempt on their lives, but his mentor, the emperor's bodyguard, had warned Fritz of the suddenness and savagery of such things.

Katy and Sam asked Tyson if Flynn was present, and after peering at the men passing the jug, he shook his head. Sam and Katy helped themselves to some punch and watched the band and crowd. A grizzled old man suddenly appeared beside them, grinning. "Howdy," he said cordially, and they could smell whiskey fumes from three feet away.

"Howdy," Sam returned.

"You see that strange-lookin' platform over thar'?" He gestured to the far side, where a separate structure had been built outside the roof. Two thick posts supported a third that ran between them.

"Yes, I see it," Sam said with amusement. The man was noticeably weaving and had an unsteady grip on the edge of the punch table with a bony hand.

"Be *r-e-e-e-a-l* careful you don't do-si-do your gal thataway. That thar's the town gallows. We done had to hang seven men from it since this town's incep—inshep—since this town was built. That trapdoor ain't never give way without a yank on that lever, but you never know!"

"Thank you for that information," Sam said. "It's also nice to know that we're only yards away from the site of all those grisly deaths."

The drunk took a while to digest this, unsure whether an insult had been issued his way. His red-rimmed, watery eyes focused somewhere below Sam's chin. Finally deciding that Sam was sincerely thankful, he belched heartily and said, "Think nothin' of it. You got any questions, you just look me up, y'hear?"

"I'll do that."

The harmonica player struck up a slow, sad rendition of "Dixie," and the crowd stopped their chatter and turned to the Confederate flag. In the hushed silence, the lilt of the Southern anthem flowed through the summer air, and by the time he'd finished, there was more than one person weeping openly. Katy felt her own eyes tearing when she spotted a boy of about twenty leaning on a crutch, one sleeve of his coat and one trouser leg pinned up in a show of stark vacancy. The wounds of the war were still open and bleeding, and no family had gone untouched by the carnage that had fractured a nation.

The mayor walked to the front of the crowd and announced: "Ladies and gentlemen, thank you for coming. I'm sure you're all aware that we have some new neighbors from Europe with us tonight. Please stop by and give them a warm Texas welcome." He prattled on about local interests and business, and then: "Let's show the prince and princess how we fandango!" The band started playing a lively tune, and dancers moved onto the dance floor and began to dance with hopping steps.

"Care to try it?" Sam asked Katy, whose attention was somewhere behind him.

"I would, Sam, but I think our man just rode up with his own army."

Sam turned and saw about twenty riders coming down the street at a walk. In the lead was a middle-aged man, with a graying, well-trimmed beard, penetrating eyes, and erect bearing. They dismounted, and Sam noticed the way the crowd gave him plenty of space as he walked to the pavilion.

"That's him," Carl Tyson said, suddenly appearing beside Katy. "Him and his hired thugs."

Flynn spotted Tyson from across the floor and without hesitation made his way directly through the dancers with three of his men in tow. Sam found Johann, Wilhelm, and Fritz beside him, and briefly thought that this already looked as if battle lines were being drawn. Every person, both inside the pavilion and out, whether dancing or not, was managing to watch the confrontation while seeming not to.

"I thought we were just going to have a little talk with Flynn—just you and me," Katy whispered.

"Apparently we weren't the only ones anxious to introduce ourselves." He started to say something to the rest of them, but then Flynn was directly in front of them.

"Tyson," he nodded.

"Flynn."

"And this must be our prince," Flynn said in a surprisingly soft voice, as he nodded to Johann. "Aren't you going to introduce us? Or does he not speak our language?"

Without hesitation, Johann took a half step forward and bowed. "I am Prince Johann Kessler." He introduced Wilhelm and Princess Sophia, who'd appeared from nowhere, and Fritz. Johann looked stately and professional in his uniform, but Flynn seemed not to notice.

"Your English is impressive. I was afraid we were going to have communication problems." Flynn hooked his thumbs through his suspenders and looked at Sophia. "And this is your—wife?"

"My sister."

"Ah." Flynn nodded, quickly. "I've never met a princess before, and I must say you look exactly as I'd imagined."

"Thank you," Sophia said, inclining her head.

Sam was watching a thick, bull-necked man beside Flynn, who was carefully looking Sophia up and down. His nose was flat and wide and had obviously been broken in the past. An unpleasant smile came to his red lips.

"See something you like, partner?" Sam asked him. Fritz had seen the man's look, too, and stepped forward threateningly.

The man's eyes shifted between them, showing no sign of alarm. Of Sam he asked, "Are you talking to me?"

"Gentlemen, gentlemen," Flynn said calmly, showing surprise.

"Nobody wants any trouble here, do they? This is a social event, B. B., nothing to get excited about."

Despite Flynn's protests, Sam detected a hidden smile in his voice, as if he was secretly pleased with the confrontation. Sam was left with the distinct feeling that the whole thing had been choreographed; therefore, he couldn't resist setting his own little flame under Flynn. "J. B. and B. B? How quaint."

Flynn's eyes narrowed. "And who might you be, friend?"

"Sam Bronte, and this is my partner, Katy Steele."

"And your business for being here is . . . ?"

"None of yours."

"Wait," Katy said quickly, "can we just start all over again? This is ridiculous."

Flynn raised his eyebrows. "Brains as well as beauty. I like that. I won't keep you long—I'm sure you came here to have a good time like everyone else. However, I'm a businessman, and I've come here to make a final offer for Dos Culebras." To Johann and Tyson he named a sum that made Katy gasp. "I *do* mean final offer. This is a one-time-only proposal."

Tyson said stubbornly, "You can offer twice that and I wouldn't take it."

"A generous offer," Johann stated, "but I must decline, also."

Flynn looked as if he'd expected no less, and after gazing back and forth between the two men, he sighed and shook his head sadly. "That's too bad. I was hoping that the amount would entice you to see reason, but I'll just have to come up with another figure—or another *way.*"

"Is that a threat?" Tyson asked.

"Why, no, Carl, it isn't! The last thing I want to do is intimidate anyone."

"That's not what I hear."

"Then you've been misinformed."

"You can put on a show for the prince, but you don't fool me, Flynn. Not at all."

"Carl," Flynn said, tapping his lower lip with a crooked finger for a moment, "I sense antagonistic feelings coming from you. Why is that?"

"Good night, Flynn."

With an innocent look and an I-tried-didn't-I-shrug to Johann, Flynn touched the brim of his hat to Sophia and Katy. "Until next time, ladies. What is it you say in Austria, Prince Johann? *Auf Wiedersehen.*"

B. B. and Fritz had been eyeing each other like two bulls ready to do battle over territory during the exchange. With a sarcastic grin at Sam, B. B. followed Flynn with a self-assured gait.

"Well, that was a pleasant conversation," Sam said sardonically.

"He did not seem that bad a fellow," Johann maintained.

Tyson chuckled emptily. "You only saw the face he wanted you to see, Johann."

"What does that mean?" Johann asked.

"It means," Tyson answered, his eyes boring into Flynn's back, "that the next time Flynn makes an offer, it won't be nice, and it won't be money."

Johann shook his head blankly.

"It'll be with guns, Johann," Sam said grimly. "Or something worse."

CHAPTER FIVE

Bait

Carnicero caught a passenger steamer for America in Amsterdam. Actually, he'd had to board a small boat in the port city for transport to the steamer that waited patiently and majestically at the mouth of the North Sea. Despite the summer season, a cold rain beat at his face as he stood in the rear of the boat, away from other passengers. He was prone to seasickness and had found that if he pinched the lobe of one ear tightly for the first few hours of riding the water, his chances of getting sick were reduced considerably. It worked most of the time, but not all of the time, and therefore he stayed close to the railing in case the worst happened.

As the boat docked beside the French steamer, *Napoléon,* Carnicero was shivering uncontrollably. His light coat was no comfort from the biting rain, but he'd managed to keep his breakfast down. As he boarded and found his cabin, still pinching his earlobe, he reflected on his sudden self-loathing. Carnicero hated weakness. He'd seen most of his victims reduced to begging, slobbering remnants of humanity when confronted with their inevitable deaths. Even as he despised them for it, the thrill of his power over them caused him immense pleasure. But when a weakness was found in himself, that was another matter entirely.

Carnicero had been born with an innate terror of horses. He'd avoided the animals at all costs until he was ten, when his mother had beaten him with a broom handle until he'd had no choice but to mount a horse. His mother, too, despised weakness in him and insisted that he conquer his fears. He supposed he'd learned his perfectionism from his mother, since his father had been a harmless and unambitious bookkeeper. Carnicero didn't dwell on this disturbing trait of his mother's; he only concentrated on making of himself the best he could be at his profession, and as far as he could tell, he'd done just that. But the seasickness was a problem that he couldn't totally overcome, and he felt like putting his fist through the small porthole in frustration.

A sharp knock on the door brought Carnicero out of his brooding, to his feet, and beside the door with a wicked-looking knife in hand. Before he could ask who it was, a man called something in Dutch. *Another weakness,* Carnicero thought, gritting his teeth. *I can't speak Dutch.*

Cautiously opening the door and finding a small, elderly man dressed in ship's uniform, he swung open the door while keeping the hand that held the knife behind it. With snobbishness characteristic to the French language he spoke, Carnicero asked, "Pardon me, but isn't this a *French* vessel?"

"Of course, sir," the man answered, switching expertly to French.

"Then why are you using that barbaric language when speaking to me?"

"My mistake, sir. I know you've just boarded from Amsterdam, and—"

"And you assumed I was Dutch. I would think that assumptions in your line of work would get you into trouble."

"I—er—"

"Tell me, do I look Dutch to you?"

The rheumy eyes regarded him, totally flustered.

Carnicero knew that he looked nondescript and could be any fair-skinned nationality in the world, but he was enjoying the man's discomfort.

"Um—no, sir, you don't look Dutch—absolutely not." He looked pleased while putting himself in the same category as Carnicero—two men who obviously detested the Dutch.

"Why not?"

"I—uh—beg your pardon, sir?"

"Why do you think I don't look Dutch? Are you prejudiced against the Netherlands people?"

"Absolutely not!"

"Do they have some sort of telling feature that causes you to immediately designate a man Dutch and therefore hold him in contempt?"

"No, sir, I swear it!"

Carnicero suddenly smiled. The man was so lost he didn't know whether to bolt or stay. His short, stubby fingers worried at the tickets in his hand. "What do you want, my good man?"

"Um—ticket," he mumbled, his eyes untrusting. "I need your ticket, please, sir."

"Well, why didn't you say so?" Carnicero reached inside his coat pocket and produced a rainsoaked ticket. "There you are."

"Thank you, sir. Good day."

"Oh, and one more thing."

The ticket-taker stopped, and his face was like that of a man who faces a firing squad.

"Would you have any French-to-Dutch translation books?"

"I'll be glad to ask the captain, sir."

"Thank you."

Sheathing his knife, Carnicero again sat on the small bunk and pinched his earlobe painfully. The trip would be long and tedious, with plenty of time to read.

He might as well cancel out a weakness while he sailed.

———⸭———

"The first thing you need to do," Carl Tyson told Johann, "is buy your cattle. You *are* going to raise cattle, aren't you?"

"Yes." Johann looked around Tyson's office, unable to hide his awe. A massive room, fully thirty feet long, it was decorated with a huge oak desk, comfortable chairs with red leather seats, and a bear rug spread on the hardwood floor. A glass-fronted guncase with seven rifles and shotguns stood against one wall. Johann looked at none of these things, however; his eyes were on the mounted trophies high above their heads. Deer, elk, wolf, coyote, bobcat—even a tiger—stared with glassy eyes from their wooden-backed mountings. Above and behind Tyson's desk coiled two rattlesnakes, fully five feet long, with trunks as big as Johann's arms. Their fat bodies entertwined as they stared at each other with open mouths, revealing hooked fangs over an inch long.

Sam, too, was studying the snakes with severe discomfort. He'd been bitten by a water moccasin as a boy in Tennessee and had almost died from it. The memory of his painful sickness was coupled with that of the sharp piercing of the fangs into his calf. He shuddered. "Excuse me, Carl, but—are those real?"

"No, they're dead," Tyson answered with a straight face.

"I mean—"

"Yes, I know, Sam," he finally grinned. "They were found right on this spot actually. I had them stuffed. Impressive, aren't they? Can't even see the bullet wounds on the one I shot, and the other's head was cut off by a hoe. Can't see that, either."

"Mmmm. Very impressive," Sam mumbled through numbed lips.

Katy, sitting across from Sam and to the side of the desk, watched him carefully. His normally tanned face had lost all color, and his bright blue eyes were stark as he stared at the snakes. She'd never seen Sam with even the shadow of fear on his face, but right

62

now he appeared ready to run—or faint. She knew why and asked, "Sam, are you all right?"

"Me? Of course. Why?" The sweat on his face reflected the light from one of the windows.

"Nothing."

Tyson asked Johann, "You did—um—bring money, Johann?"

"Yes, many dollars. I have—"

Tyson held up a hand. "Don't tell me how much; I don't want to know."

"Very well."

"You need cattle, and if you buy them now, at the end of the summer, you'll need to buy healthy ones so they'll make it through the winter. That'll run up the price a little, but you'll be sure to have a herd at springtime."

"Do you wish to sell any of yours, Carl?" Johann asked.

Tyson looked at him sharply.

"I am sorry if I offend. I thought we could . . . how do you say? Cut out the middleman? That is, if you were planning on selling some before winter."

Tyson's face relaxed. He was still finding it difficult to suppress the hard feelings he'd had for so long regarding the faceless Austrian prince. But now, to know Johann was to like him. "No offense taken, Johann. And you're right. I was thinking of selling a few head to get us through the winter, and I don't know anyone I'd rather sell them to. I can also save on the auctioneer's fee."

"How many were you thinking of selling?"

"Oh, about a hundred head or so."

Johann's face brightened as he turned to Katy and Sam. "Did you hear that? I will own *cattle* soon!"

Katy smiled at his enthusiasm. "You still need to negotiate a price, Johann."

"Ah, you are right." Johann's eyebrows came together as he put on a businesslike scowl for Tyson. "How much, Carl?"

"Well, the way it works is, you need to make me an offer."

"Yes, yes." Johann looked at Katy and Sam. "How much?"

They both shrugged. "I have no idea what cattle is going for," Sam said helplessly.

The door burst open, and Remy flew inside, noisily bang-banging a wooden toy rifle. He stopped instantly when he saw that the room was occupied. A short lariat dangled from one shoulder.

"Remy!" Tyson bellowed, vaulting from his chair. "How many times have I told you to play outside? What do you think you're doing?"

"Shootin' Injuns, Pa," came the soft reply. His eyes were round, and he noticeably cringed at his father's harsh tone.

"Get outside, boy! Don't you have chores to do?"

"Finished 'em."

"Then go split some wood for Moon."

"He don't want my help. I already—"

"We're conducting business here, Remy," Tyson said, calming down a bit. "Go outside, please."

Katy watched Remy turn and go, looking as if he'd received a caning. She looked at Tyson and momentarily saw guilt and regret pass over his features before the usual iron control came back. "Sorry about that, folks. That boy never had a ma to train him in house rules. I've done the best I can, but I'm a busy man."

"He seems like a sweet little boy," Katy commented.

"I suppose so," Tyson said absently. "Now, Johann—" Tyson continued their conversation about cattle as if the interruption hadn't occurred. He told Johann a current fair market price per head of cattle, and Johann agreed to buy his first stock.

Outside, Katy and Sam found Remy sitting on a stump at the side of the house, his head down, throwing dried corn to a rooster one kernel at a time. His wooden gun and lariat lay on the ground by the stump amidst a cluster of daisies and dandelions.

"Now if that's not a lonely sight, I don't know what is," Sam observed.

"I feel sorry for him."

"Me, too. He sort of reminds me of me, when I was a boy. No one to play with, nothing to do. Let's go talk to him."

Remy didn't look up when they approached, even though he was sure to have seen their shadows, and the rooster carefully strutted a few feet away.

"Hey, Remy," Sam greeted. "Who's your friend?"

"He don't have a name."

"Well, I think he needs one, don't you?"

"No," Remy said sullenly.

"How about General Lee? He looks important enough to have a name like that."

The boy shook his head, still without looking up. "I don't think that'd be a good idea. Pa thinks a lot of General Lee; he prob'ly wouldn't like a rooster to be named after him."

"Then how about Stonewall?"

Remy looked up. "That might be all right."

"Stonewall it is, then."

Stonewall the rooster wasn't concerned about his glorious new name—he just scooted closer to Remy for more corn and was rewarded with another kernel.

"Don't you have any friends to play with, Remy?" Katy asked.

"No. I mean, yeah, but they live too far off, and Pa won't let me ride that far alone."

"So you'll be glad when school starts, huh?"

"Kinda."

Sam said, "How about you and me go fishing sometime? Just the two of us?"

"Really? D'ya mean it?"

"Sure I mean it. I haven't been fishing in a few months. You know the last time I went, Katy went with me. It was her first time, and she caught the biggest fish."

Remy looked at Katy with new respect. "How big?"

Katy spread her hands a foot apart. "About this big. It was a bass."

"There's catfish in a pond over that way, by the west herd."

"How about today?" Sam asked. "You don't seem to have anything to do."

"Naw, there's nothin' to do around here. It's so boring, I wish something would happen."

"Be careful what you wish for," Sam advised with a smile. "I wished for that when I was a boy in Tennessee, and a tornado blew up and took our roof."

"Oh."

"Come on, let's go saddle the horses. Do you have one?"

"Yeah, his name's Albert."

"Get up a minute," Sam told him, and when the boy did as he was told, Sam tipped over the stump and dug through the rich black dirt underneath. Fat worms appeared, then desperately tried to dig out of sight again. "Here's our bait. Go get a jar, while I keep Stonewall away."

"Cain't he have one?"

"Oh, I guess we can spare one." Sam plucked a wriggling gray body out of the dirt and tossed it to the waiting rooster. "Now, he'll love us forever."

"I don't know," Remy said uncertainly, watching Stonewall feast on the treat. "He don't love anybody, I don't think."

"Sure he does. He just has a hard time showing it—like a few other people around here."

"What's 'at mean?"

"Never mind. Go get that jar."

Remy took off, and Katy touched Sam's arm. "That was sweet."

Sam shrugged. "I want to go fishing, too."

"Don't make light of it. Why don't you want anyone to know you're a nice guy?"

Sam mumbled something and looked away.

"Don't worry," Katy said with a smile. "I won't tell anybody."

Katy went back to the house and found Sophia and Fritz in the kitchen. The bodyguard was wolfing down a beef sandwich while Sophia sat at the table filing her nails. As Katy entered the room, Sophia was saying, "I told her no. The *idea* of a common peasant coming to my wedding was enough to—hello, Katy—was enough to turn my stomach!"

"Princess," Katy said, nodding. "Hello, Fritz." The silent man nodded while chewing. The fact that he couldn't talk seemed not to faze Sophia in the least.

"I was just telling Fritz about the time I almost got married."

"Oh, really? I didn't know that."

"Yes, to a Bavarian duke."

"What happened?"

"He was killed in a duel. You know how those Prussians are. . . . If they do not have a war to fight, they fight each other."

"That's terrible!" Katy exclaimed, horrified.

Sophia casually waved a well-manicured hand. "I never even met him. The marriage was arranged by my father."

"But, still—"

"I am glad, really. I had heard he was old and fat."

Katy felt her lips draw into a straight line. *The woman is so callous!* Glancing at Fritz disbelievingly, she saw him staring at her with no expression. Apparently he was accustomed to the princess's searing comments; either that, or he was a better actor than Sam.

"Where is Sam?" Sophia asked casually, as she studied her nails.

"He's going fishing with Remy." Katy saw Fritz look at her

sharply and stop chewing, while Sophia glanced at him. "Do you like to fish, Fritz?"

"I do not believe 'like' is the right word," Sophia said. "It is what he *lives* for."

"Then why don't you go with them? They probably haven't left yet."

Fritz's dark eyes went to Sophia with an almost comical look of eagerness. "Oh, go on, Fritz. I do not think I need protecting with all these big, strong cowboys around."

"Sam's probably still at the stables, Fritz," Katy said.

For the first time since Katy had known him, Fritz smiled. Starting for the door, he stopped and considered the half-eaten sandwich in his hand, looked for a place to put it down, didn't find one, and crammed the whole thing in his mouth on his way out. Katy watched him from the window as he jammed his hat on his head and hurried down the hill toward the stable.

"Men," Sophia remarked, her voice tinged with disgust, "they are so simple. What possible fun could it be to fish?"

"Have you ever been?" Katy asked, hearing the sharpness in her own voice.

Sophia heard it also, and studied Katy before answering, "Yes, I have been. It was cold and boring."

"I like it. Sam took me while we were in California. Maybe you were bored because you didn't catch anything."

"I was not even fishing. I went along to make my uncle happy."

Katy thought, *Yes, and I bet you were great company.*

"Fish are smelly and slimy creatures. I prefer hunting."

"Deer?"

"Yes. It is much more exciting and rewarding."

Katy sat down across from Sophia and took a sugar cookie from a full plate of them. Anna had baked them the night before. "I could never kill something so beautiful."

"They are not that beautiful up close. They have ticks, and they smell bad. But not as bad as fish."

"Have you ever killed one yourself?" Katy had the idea that Sophia had just followed a pack of hounds around and called that hunting. Sophia's answer suprised and alarmed her.

"I have killed more than a dozen. I am an excellent shot, you know. Most of them I brought down with one shot, but a few I had to finish off."

"Finish off?" The cookie became a sour paste in Katy's mouth.

"Cut their throat. Their brains are so small, it is too easy to miss with a head shot. Did you know their brains are only about the size of a small apple?"

Swallowing with effort, Katy placed the rest of the cookie down on the table. "No, I didn't. Thank you for the information, though."

"I am surprised you did not know that. Johann mentioned that you were some sort of amateur scientist."

Katy looked for some sort of smirk on the princess's face, but found only a casual interest. "I wouldn't call myself a *scientist* exactly. My uncle was one—a very successful one—and I learned an appreciation for it from him."

"Johann talks about you quite often," Sophia went on, as if she hadn't even heard Katy's explanation. Then she paused.

Katy didn't know what to say to that, so she was silent. Outside, a group of cowboys rode by, their voices loud and raucous.

"He has taken a real interest in you, Katy."

"He's a nice man," Katy said neutrally.

"He is a *rich* man. Comparatively speaking, that is."

The cowboys' shouts faded, replaced with the fading thunder of hooves. Katy kept her eyes locked with Sophia's, waiting for the next comment.

"What are your intentions concerning my brother?"

"I have no intentions."

"Really?"

"Really. What are you trying to say?"

Sophia broke eye contact and picked up a cookie of her own. Studying the sparkling granules on the top, she commented, "My brother had been arranged in marriage, too. It would have joined our family with one of the richest in Russia. But Johann refused, and my father backed down. I have *never* seen my father give in to the wishes of someone else, before or since." She took a small bite of the cookie and chewed slowly. "Do you know why Johann refused this marriage?"

"I have no idea."

"Perhaps Johann should tell you."

"I really don't think it's any of my business." Katy wanted out of this conversation and was glad to see Sophia stand up.

"I have a feeling it *is* your business," Sophia said with a smile. "You should ask him about it. I think his answer will surprise you."

Katy watched her leave and had no intention of taking the bait that had been dangled in front of her.

CHAPTER SIX

A Short Count

The two o'clock afternoon sun had already dropped behind a bluff that rose beside the pond. Oak trees surrounded the water, along with a few cedars and one lonesome weeping willow, whose branches rained a green curtain over a spread of lily pads. Sam, Fritz, and Remy stopped beside a huge cedar tree that rose to tower in the air. Its spiked, blue-gray berries covered the ground, and Sam took his knife and carved away a strip of bark to let the sharp, pleasant scent permeate the air.

Remy had his hook baited and in the water before either man had unraveled his line. "Pa says there's a *b-i-i-i-i-g* catfish hole over there under that weepin' willow. But I ain't ever caught any there."

"Don't say 'ain't,'" Sam told him, as he tucked the cedar bark into his vest pocket and began tying a small pebble on the end of the line for a weight. "So, where have you caught them?"

"Well—I *haven't* 'zactly caught *any* since I've only been here one time. But Boone's caught a bunch. He wouldn't tell me where, though. Said a man's spot was his own business and no one else's. It ain—I mean, it's not fair!"

Sam clucked his tongue. "I hate to be the one to tell you this, Remy, but your brother's right."

"Why?"

"It's an unwritten rule of fishing. A man works hard to find a spot, maybe takes days, and he figures he's earned exclusive rights to it."

"But I'm his *brother.* It's not like I'm gonna go tell the whole state of Texas!"

"I had a little brother, too. I wouldn't have told him."

"You *had* a brother? What happened to him—he get kilt or something?"

Sam watched Fritz move down the bank a few yards and cast out his line. A look of supreme pleasure was on his face, and his mouth was set with unmistakable determination. Sam finished hooking one of the worms and cast. The pebble landed with a *plop!* and sank out of sight. "I don't know why I said 'had.' I guess I still do."

"Don't you ever talk to him or see him?"

"Not since I left home at fourteen."

"Why'd you leave?"

Sam had forgotten that young boys were full of questions. His little brother had been the same way, and Sam had hated it. "That's a long story, believe me."

"What was his name?"

"Who?"

"Your brother."

"Obadiah James Bronte."

"Land sakes! That's a fancy name! Do you have one like that?"

"Mine is Samuel Matthew Bronte."

Remy whistled. "Your ma or pa must've really liked the Bible."

"My father wanted our first names to be from the Old Testament, and our middle ones from the New."

"Obadiah's the shortest book in the Old Testament."

Sam looked at Remy sharply. "That's right. How'd you know that?"

"I study the Bible with Seth Moon. Well, I don't really study it—he tells me lots of stories that are in there. He just told me about

72

Obadiah not too long ago, how he was a prophet that warned some folks that they were gonna get it 'cause they turned their back on God's people who lived in—in—"

"Judah."

"Yeah, in Judah. And these sorry folks in—in—"

"Edom."

"Right, in Edom—they were in *b-i-i-i-g* trouble!"

Without thinking, Sam suddenly quoted in a booming, fire-and-brimstone voice, "'For the day of the Lord is near upon all the heathen: as thou hast done, it shall be done unto thee: thy reward shall return upon thine own head. For as ye have drunk upon my holy mountain, so shall all the heathen drink continually, yea, they shall drink, and they shall swallow down, and they shall be as though they had not been.'" *Not been, not been, not been* echoed over the pond and off the bluff wall. Remy and Fritz were staring at him with round eyes, and he just grinned. For the passage to come to his mind so easily had surprised him, too.

"Sakes alive! Did you hear that, Fritz? That was really somethin', Sam! Where'd you learn to preach like that?"

"Well, I'm not a preacher, but my father was."

"You're joshin' me! So that makes you a Christian like me, then, huh?"

"I—um—suppose so."

"That's great, that's really great!"

In the silence that followed, Sam felt the weight of guilt crushing down on him. He'd hated his father, a habitual family beater, and therefore had rejected everything that he'd believed in. Sam had been literally forced by his father into a confession to Jesus that meant nothing, except to further Sam's hostility toward him. He'd been only five years old, and the confession was forced from him before a congregation of fifty people. He was less than sure that he was a Christian—*you know you're not, and you're fooling yourself* and *the boy* a small voice told him—and he was ashamed that he'd answered Remy so quickly.

Remy continued, chatting happily, "Seth says that being a Christian is the most important thing in the world, and the most *fun* thing, too. That's because we don't have to go through life afraid of dying like other folks. Ain't that right, Sam?"

Keeping his eyes steadily on his line, Sam answered uncomfortably, "Don't say 'ain't.'"

"Sorry." Remy stared at his own line, too, suddenly quiet.

"Are you afraid of dying, Remy?"

"Not any more. Don't have to be. Seth says that since I'm a Christian, I've been delivered from bondage—it says so in Hebrews—and that other folks have to worry about going to . . . that hot place, but I'll be with Jesus, and everyone'll be happy, and I'll get to see my ma. That's what Miss Katy told me. Do you think so, Sam? Will I see her?"

Sam realized his hands were shaking. The fishing line trembled so much he imagined he could hear it humming with sound. *What's the matter with me? Katy's talked to me about this before, but I didn't start sweating like I am now.* He looked at Remy, who was calmly waiting for an answer. The boy had an unnervingly direct stare, with big brown eyes that searched inside Sam's mind for reassurance he couldn't give. Remy's matter-of-fact faith was disturbing for some reason. Wiping the sweat from his hands one after the other on his pants, Sam knew he had to say *something,* or Remy would question him more about his own faith—or lack of it—and Sam wanted to avoid that at all costs. "Without a doubt, I think you'll see your mother, Remy. And you'll both be happy."

Remy smiled contentedly and, to Sam's relief, had no more questions.

At the edge of his vision, Sam saw Fritz abruptly jerk his fishing pole. The thick oak rod bent at a sharp angle, the line became tight, and Fritz struggled to bring in the fish. Soon a fat catfish was flopping at his feet, and before Sam could make his way over to him, Remy dashed by excitedly.

"Hey, that's a big one! Be careful of the fins!"

Fritz, his face shining with pride, looked at the boy uncertainly.

"Ain't you ever caught a catfish before?"

Fritz shook his head.

"You gotta watch out for the fins, 'cause they'll stab you. See those sharp things?" Remy pointed at the dorsal fin, where a thick, thornlike form rose at the front, camouflaged amidst the ridges. "If one of those stabs you, your hand'll swell up like from a bee sting. I always take the hook out like this." Placing his foot on the fish, Remy reached down and tugged out the hook and line while keeping the catfish still. Then he grasped the fish by its lower lip and lifted it into the air proudly.

"Couldn't have done it better myself," Sam observed with a smile.

Remy threaded the cat onto a stringer and promptly ran for his own pole. Before Fritz had had a chance to cast again, Remy had already placed his baited hook in exactly the same area that Fritz had caught the fish.

"That's Fritz's spot, Remy," Sam said.

Remy's face fell in disappointment.

Fritz waved his hand to get Sam's attention, then nodded his head in an "it's all right" gesture. Sam said to the boy, "But Fritz says you can fish there."

"Thanks, Fritz!"

Altogether they caught eight catfish, none of them larger than the first one Fritz had snagged. Remy only caught one, but he couldn't have been prouder. His face beamed, and Sam and Fritz heard the story over and over from first nibble to exotic dehooking, right up until they left.

The late afternoon sun was hot on their backs, especially after the relatively cool shade by the pond. Dos Culebras's west herd of cattle had moved into the road they'd taken on the way out. Sam admired the healthy brown-and-white cattle, which were thick with muscle and meat. They lazily grazed on grass dotted with daisies and dandelions.

"Hey, this ain't right," Remy muttered.

"What do you mean?"

Remy searched the wide, sprawling prairie around them as if looking for something. His scowl brought his blonde eyebrows together under his hat brim. "Some of 'em are missing."

"*Cattle* are missing?"

"Yeah."

"Are you sure?"

"Well, I ain't counted yet, but it sure looks like less than fifty, don't it? Pa divvies up the herds into fifties."

Sam did a quick count and came up with thirty-five. He recounted, and the number was the same. Fritz had been looking around while he'd counted, and he caught Sam's eye, put his palms together, then slowly spread them. Sam said to Remy, "Fritz thinks they just separated for a while."

A solemn shake of the small head. "Uh-uh. They *never* do that." The boy's face was so serious that Sam had no choice but to believe him.

They found the trampled grass showing the direction from which the herd had come while they'd been fishing. After following for about two miles, they came upon the herd's last grazing area, evidenced by close-cropped grass and the telltale absence of prairie flowers.

Fritz suddenly pointed, and Sam stood in his stirrups and gazed after the thick finger. More trampled grass, this time not as wide as the one they'd been following.

Just enough for, say, fifteen head or so, Sam thought grimly. The trail led north—straight toward the ranch of J. B. Flynn.

From her seat on a porch swing at Hill House, as Katy had heard Tyson refer to it, she smelled smoked turkey, thought about Seth Moon, and observed some interesting things

The turkey came to them courtesy of Seth Moon, who'd killed it on his way home from church the previous Sunday. "It deserved to die," Seth told Katy solemnly.

This seemed a strange thing to say, so Katy asked, "Why in the world do you say that?"

"Turkeys live in the hills and forests. They are very hard to find because once you do, the slightest noise will send them flying. That is why a hunter must practice his turkey call enough to sound like the real thing." Seth let loose a piercing, *"Gobble, gobble, gobble!"* that startled Katy so much she took a step back. "If your call is good enough, they'll come to *you*."

"I'll try to remember that," Katy said with a smile. "But why did this one deserve to die?"

Seth waved a hand contemptuously at the huge bird that probably weighed eighteen pounds. It sat sprawled on the kitchen table in a bed of its own brown, white, and black feathers. "Because this one was on the prairie—sitting right by the road—and didn't try to flee when I came by. He's too stupid to have lived so long. I believe he is a gift from God." Katy must have looked at him strangely, for he said softly, "No, I'm not loco, Miss Katy. I really *do* think that God sends me an animal every once in a while. It helps me keep my job. Mr. Tyson doesn't like me much, and I think he's always looking for a reason to fire me." He indicated the turkey again. "This is God's way of keeping me employed."

On the porch, Katy stopped swinging for a moment and inhaled the aroma of the turkey in question being baked by Anna. Katy still thought Seth was slightly fanatical, until it dawned on her: *Of course, it made perfect sense. And why shouldn't God send Seth a turkey or deer? They're his to make gifts of, if he wants to.* She wondered why Tyson didn't like Seth and reminded herself to ask him the next time she saw him.

Sophia's baffling revelation concerning Johann's rejection of marriage gnawed at Katy—probably just as Sophia had intended. *Why did she tell me that? Why did Johann break it off? What does it have to do with me?* Katy liked Johann; he was polite, sweet, kind, honorable, and had shown no signs of taking advantage of her. The ultimate fear of Katy's life, drilled into her by her Aunt Agnes, was that some man would charm her into falling in love with him, completely and totally, then, like a beggar throwing off an old coat for a new one, would cast Katy aside at a whim of his nature. As Katy had grown older, and since she'd been away from her aunt's warnings and met many different men, her conclusion was that Aunt Agnes was a lonely, dour old woman for a reason: She was wrong.

Let me clarify that, Katy told herself, *she was wrong about the vast majority of men. I think. As far as I know.* It was hard to imagine, but Katy had been away from her aunt for less than a year. It seemed much longer, because Katy had grown so much in mind and personality. Just as she would convince herself that her aunt was completely crazy and paranoid, Katy remembered Cole Price.

An extremely handsome and charming man, Price had been an engineer on the Central Pacific Railroad. He'd befriended and courted Katy, who couldn't understand his interest in her. She began to think that she *did* have something to offer a man, that she *was* attractive and worth getting to know. Then, to Katy's horror, she discovered that he'd been the one behind all the sabotage and murder and that he was only staying close to her in order to keep tabs on what she and Sam knew.

It had taken Katy a while to get over that. In fact, she was *still* getting over it.

Katy's eyes had been stuck on the far horizon while she was

swinging. A magnificent cloud cluster hovered over the hills at the very edge of her vision, promising a storm. From her position, she had a view of every building on Dos Culebras. A movement caught her eye behind the stables, and she turned that way.

Sophia and Wilhelm were talking, with Wilhelm waving his arms emphatically. Sophia started to walk away, but he suddenly spun her around, took her in his arms, and kissed her. Because the distance was too great, Katy couldn't make out Sophia's facial reaction. She didn't, however, seem surprised or upset. She stood before him, his hands grasping her upper arms, listening to him say something. Then he kissed her again. After a moment, Sophia pushed him away, or attempted to. Wilhelm's hands went around her waist, and Sophia slapped him so hard that Katy imagined she could hear it from the porch swing. Sophia stalked off, but Katy had a strange thought: By the set of Sophia's shoulders, or the way she held her head, or *something,* the princess had secretly enjoyed the confrontation. Wilhelm watched her receding back, frozen where he stood.

Katy bit her lip. So her earlier suspicions were confirmed: Wilhelm's interest in Sophia went beyond friendship. Katy couldn't help but wonder what that meant for the royal party. And, yet again, she wondered if Johann knew of his friend's feelings.

It's not my problem, Katy thought. *And I wish I hadn't seen that.*

"What are you doing out here by yourself?" Johann asked as he came outside. He'd been taking a nap, and Katy noticed that one side of his blonde hair was sticking up and his eyes were sleepy.

"Oh, hello, Johann." Katy cast a quick glance to the rear of the stables and was relieved to see that Wilhelm had disappeared. She didn't want to lie to the prince about his best friend's unusual posture as he stood behind the barn. "I'm just sitting here, thinking."

"About me?" Johann took a seat beside her on the swing and at once looked at her face closely.

"What's the matter?" Katy asked, a hand automatically smoothing her flowing hair.

"You are very beautiful in this light."

"I am?"

"Yes. And your blush only adds to your radiance." Johann took her hand in both of his. "Please do me the honor of going for a ride with me. I wish to see more of my ranch, and I can't think of a better companion."

"You mean now?"

"Why not?"

"Well—I—it's late, and it'll be dark soon." Katy was flustered by his suddenly amorous advances. Up until this moment, he'd been polite and vaguely interested—nothing like the bold man that was beside her now.

"How about tomorrow?" Johann persisted. Then, as if reading her mind, he said, "You must forgive my audacity. I slept very heavily, and had a dream that my ranch could be one of the finest in all of Texas. And you were in it."

Katy attempted to distract his advances, which had come out of nowhere. "When you dream, is it in German or English?"

The prince's setback was only a brief second. "This one was in English, which is unusual, because most of them are in German." He squeezed her hand. "Maybe it was because you were in it. How about tomorrow? Will you go?"

"Yes, I suppose—"

"*Ausgezeichnet!* That means 'excellent.' Would you like me to teach you German? Some say it is an ugly, barbaric language, but I ask you—was Mozart barbaric? Or my namesake, Johann Wolfgang von Goethe?"

"I don't—Goethe?" Katy had never heard of him.

Johann quoted, very softly:

Kennst du das Land, wo die Zitronen blühn?
Im dunkeln Laub die Gold-Orangen glühn,
Ein sanfter Wind vom blauen Himmel weht,
Die Myrte still und hoch der Lorbeer steht—
Kennst du es wohl?
Dahin! Dahin
Möcht ich mit dir, o mein Geliebter, ziehn!

Katy listened to him, her eyes locked on his lips as he spoke. She could see how the language could be interpreted as harsh and gutteral, but Johann's rendering was caressing and loving. His gentle tone washed away the coarseness and sang the majesty of his native language. It was the most beautiful thing Katy had ever heard.

Johann stared at her, not smiling now, and leaned toward her with his eyes on her mouth.

Snapping out of her hypnotized state, Katy asked quickly, "That was wonderful, Johann. Or should I say, *ausgez—aus*—how do you say 'excellent' again?"

"Ausgezeichnet," he whispered, unable to hide his disappointment that she'd broken the mood.

"Yes—*ausgezeichnet."* From Katy's mouth it sounded awkward and sloppy, and she laughed. When he only smiled faintly, she felt ashamed at her own hesitance. Placing her other hand over his, she said, "That *was* wonderful, and it sounded very romantic, but for all I know you were talking about the weather. What does it mean?"

"It translates: 'Know you the land where the lemon trees bloom? In the dark foliage the gold oranges glow; a soft wind hovers from the sky, the myrtle is still and the laurel stands tall—do you know it well? There, there I would go, O my beloved, with thee!'"

Katy felt her heart skip a beat. Now *she* had the urge to kiss *him.*

"That was Goethe—a German poet." Johann leaned toward her again, and this time Katy met his lips.

81

"Oh, excuse me!" Sophia called from the bottom of the porch steps. "I did not see you two! I'll come back later."

Katy jerked back quickly at the first sound of her voice and immediately pulled her hands from Johann's and clasped them together in her lap. Hard.

"It is all right, sister," Johann called cheerily, as if they'd been discussing politics. He turned back to gaze at Katy with a secret smile. "You won't bother us."

That's what you think, Katy thought darkly, feeling the blush finally leaving her face.

Sophia was watching her with a smile fixed on her face and a trace of lightning in her light blue eyes. She raised the hem of her long skirt and started up the steps. "I was not watching where I was going and did not see you until the last moment. I am terribly sorry."

"Where is Wilhelm?" Johann asked.

"He is back there somewhere," Sophia answered, with a vague wave of her gloved hand. "I have not seen him for a while."

The princess's lie gave Katy answers to her earlier questions and more confidence in herself. *Yes, you caught Johann and me,* she thought with satisfaction, *but you've also been caught and don't know it.* She smiled sweetly at Sophia, who suddenly looked uncertain.

"How long have you two been here?" Sophia asked innocently.

"*I've* been here for half an hour," Katy remarked. "I never knew that a ranch was so . . . busy! All sorts of things going on." She deliberately switched her gaze from the princess to the fine view of the stable. Sophia followed her eyes, and when she looked back at Katy, her face was cold and wary.

Johann, missing the two ladies' fiery looks, commented, "I must admit that I did not, either. There is so much to do to keep it running."

"I am going to check on dinner," Sophia said lightly and, with one more withering look at Katy, went inside.

At that moment Sam, Fritz, and Remy came riding in at a gallop. They passed Hill House, and when Sam saw them on the porch, he waved for them to follow. Billy Mantooth and three other cowboys heard the thundering hooves and came out of the barn to investigate. By the time Katy and Johann reached Tyson's house, the whole group had gathered, and Tyson emerged from the house with his usual stern look. Taking one look at Sam's face, he asked pointedly, "What's happened?"

"They stole some cattle, Pa!" Remy sang out.

Tyson looked down at Remy, who'd jumped off his horse excitedly and stood on the steps holding Albert's reins. After a moment, Tyson said, "I was talkin' to Sam, boy. Go wash up for supper."

"But, Pa!"

"Don't make me tell you again!"

Remy looked at Sam quickly, his face full of hurt, and raced inside the house.

"Now, Sam, what's this about?"

"Your son was right, Carl," Sam stated, and Katy could hear an edge to his voice. Sam obviously disapproved of Tyson's handling of Remy and was having a hard time hiding it. "It looks like someone made off with about fifteen head of the west herd. That is, if you had fifty out there like Remy says."

"There were fifty," Tyson said tightly. He looked at Mantooth. "Where's Boone?"

Mantooth shrugged and glanced at the other cowboys, who shook their heads. "Ain't seen him, sir."

"Blast!" Tyson exploded. "That boy—!" He cut off his sentence by biting his lower lip and looking off in the distance. "I told him to work with you, Billy. You haven't seen him at all?"

"Saw him saddling his horse early this mornin'. Not after."

Tyson shook his head sadly and muttered under his breath, "All right . . . all right." To Sam he said, "Did you have a look around? Notice anything?"

Sam nodded. "We found a spot where it looks as if they were taken."

"Which direction did they go?"

Sam hesitated. "North."

"Billy—you boys get your rifles and saddle up."

"Now, wait a minute, Carl—" Sam began.

"You comin', Sam?"

"I don't think this is a good idea," Sam debated, his hands patting the air to try to settle Tyson down. "I think we ought to think about this before we react. Maybe it's not what it seems."

"Fifteen head of cattle don't just leave their herd and walk off."

"I know, but why just fifteen head? Why not the whole herd? A man can be hanged for stealing fifty head just as easy as fifteen."

Tyson considered this, and in the silence they heard more horses.

Mantooth said, "That'll be Jasper and Legs, comin' in from the south herd."

Three men rode in instead of two, and one of them was Boone Tyson. He wouldn't meet his father's eyes.

One of the men called breathlessly, "They's been some cattle stole, Mr. Tyson! 'Bout twenty head outta the south."

Tyson ignored this. "Boone, where you been? He been with you, Jasper?"

Jasper didn't answer. He looked at Boone, who stared at the back of his Appaloosa's head while his face burned.

"I'm talkin' to you, boy!" Tyson roared.

"I went to town, Pa."

"Town! Didn't I tell you to work with Billy today?"

"Yeah, you did, but I didn't feel so good, and—"

"Get in the house with your brother!" Katy had never seen Tyson so angry. Veins stood out on his neck and forehead. "Now!"

Boone looked at the people gathered around and found some bravado. "Now, hold on there, Pa! You can't talk to me like that in front of—"

"I'll talk to you any way I want! Now git!" Tyson pointed to the house and stood out of the way, sure that Boone would obey.

Boone's lips disappeared in a thin line as he handed Mantooth his reins and stormed inside.

Tyson watched him go, daring him to say anything else, then turned to Mantooth. "Get those horses saddled, and mine, too. I wanna see those tracks before it rains." He looked up defiantly at the thunderhead that Katy had noticed earlier, which had spread toward them. "Jasper, I really don't need to ask this, but which way were those cattle taken?"

"East, sir."

"East?" Tyson glanced at Sam, who nodded.

"See? Why don't we investigate, before we go burn Flynn's house down?" he asked sarcastically.

If Tyson heard the dry tone, he didn't let on. To Katy's surprise, he turned to her and Johann. One side of his mustache trembled slightly. "What do you think, Johann? You've got a say in this, because now I may not be able to sell you those cattle we discussed."

Johann looked at Katy, who saw his confusion of American ways and said, "I think Sam's right. We shouldn't just accuse Flynn without solid evidence. He's dangerous enough as it is."

"Yes," Johann agreed, "that is what I think, too."

Tyson stared at them, his dark eyes going from one to the other. Katy wasn't sure, but she didn't think that Tyson was very happy about a woman helping make decisions on his ranch. But he nodded slowly and said, "All right. We'll try it your way."

Sam looked at Katy, smiled, and nodded almost imperceptibly.

"But I warn you," Tyson continued, raising a finger and sweeping it over the group. "If Flynn *is* behind this, there'll be a range war. And, with all due respect, Johann, I don't think you and your sister want to be around when that happens. I don't know how you settle your differences in Austria, or if you even *have* any like this—but you might want to rethink your decision on staying here. 'Cause you ain't seen *anything* like an American range war."

CHAPTER SEVEN

A Father's Confession

On the fourth day of Carnicero's voyage, he received a shock.

The Dutch lessons he taught himself had gone well. In fact, they'd gone so well that he boldly joined in a short conversation with a young couple at the dining table next to him that fourth night who were speaking the language. He made up a false past, talked about the weather, and learned that they were going to America to open a general merchandise store and start a farm with money the young man had inherited from his father. Discreetly, Carnicero inquired as to how much money. He was always in need of cash. He was by no means a poor man, but being a man on the move all over the world prevented him from carrying a large amount.

The young Dutch couple, to Carnicero's mirth, had received some very bad advice as to how much money they would need in America to fulfill their dream. The amount was pitifully low—so miniscule that Carnicero knew he would never take a risk on stealing it. But keeping a straight face, he assured them they would be fine and wished them well in their new life. Just before he turned back to his dinner of lobster, shrimp, and potato, Carnicero gave them one last piece of advice, to which the eager, smiling young husband listened intently: "Beware of thieves—a man just can't be too careful these days."

"Thank you," the young man said, "but I can spot a man of dishonest reputation at a glance. Just as I can tell you are a man of unusual moral character. That's as rare as thieves are plentiful."

Carnicero was still smiling as he made his way to the gentlemen's salon on the promenade deck after his meal. The salon was extremely small, with only two tables stocked with cards and poker chips, a six-foot bar, and a monkey dressed in a small glittering vest and hat. The animal was lightly chained to a thin metal rod that ran the length of the bar, leaving it free to scamper. At the moment, it was turning incredibly quick backflips for two men playing darts and one sitting at the bar nursing a drink.

Carnicero's smile vanished immediately when he saw the man at the bar. With an involuntary gasp, he spun out of the doorway to the main deck and stood with his back to the outside wall of the salon, breathing heavily. A half-moon on the horizon spread a long reflection to the ship, like a shimmering walkway. The cool, salty air was thick with moisture. He imagined the briny mixture coating the inside of his lungs, clogging up his bronchial passages.

The only man that Carnicero had ever felt fear or respect for was on the same oceangoing steamer, in the middle of the Atlantic, ten days from land.

Gonzalez Bilbao.

The name made him grit his teeth.

Realizing Bilbao could walk out of the salon at any moment, Carnicero went to the rail, pulled his derby down tighter against the wind, and watched the ocean fight against the ship's side. Dizzily, he recalled their first encounter. . . .

General Juan Prim led a revolutionary uprising against Queen Isabella II of Spain. In the midst of all of the political upheaval and unrest—not to mention treachery—the need for Carnicero's violent talent had been great. Carnicero himself had no political ties or preferences, but Isabella paid more than the rebels. His ultimate goal had been to assassinate Prim, but the circumspect general kept himself well guarded at all times. Not even the skillful Carnicero could find an opportunity.

One of Isabella's generals, Victor Sardonia, had secretly commissioned Carnicero to hurt General Prim in the next best way: assassinate his son, Colonel Antonio Prim. Maybe the elder Prim would reconsider his foolish liberal views if he were forced to pay a dear price for them.

The casual guard around Antonio had proved easy to circumvent, and Carnicero hanged Colonel Antonio Prim, the eldest and most favored son of Juan Prim, from a eucalyptus tree on the bank of the Guadiana River.

The killing itself had been easy. But Carnicero was spotted as he rode away by Antonio's chief bodyguard, Colonel Gonzalez Bilbao. Thinking Bilbao would chase him for a few miles only, Carnicero rode north for France.

Carnicero had been seriously mistaken about Gonzalez Bilbao's determination. He fled all the way to Genoa, Italy, and disguised himself as a fisherman on a boat to Corsica to escape Bilbao. He hadn't even had time to collect his pay from Sardonia for his work.

Three months later, Carnicero cautiously had gone back to France, only to discover that a price was on his head not only from Prim but from Queen Isabella herself. It seemed that Isabella didn't approve of General Sardonia's order for a personal attack against Prim. In order to appease Prim and save her own family from retaliation, Isabella had Sardonia beheaded and offered a huge reward for Carnicero's head, too.

Carnicero, despite his independent nature, had fallen in love with a *señorita* in Madrid before the whole affair had begun and decided to return for her, and together they would leave Spain for good. It was an extremely dangerous undertaking.

The industrious Bilbao had foreseen Carnicero's move and

posted a lookout at the *señorita's* villa. As Carnicero and the girl were leaving, Bilbao was ready with armed troops. The *señorita* was killed in the ensuing fight, but Carnicero managed to escape again.

By the ship's railing, Carnicero shivered. And now, here was Gonzalez Bilbao on the same ship as he.

Coincidence?

Carnicero didn't believe in coincidence.

A plan began to form in his mind.

The easterly tracks Jasper had seen extended five miles. By that time the massive thunderhead was directly over the heads of Tyson, Sam, Katy, Johann, Billy Mantooth, and three other cowboys. Tyson stopped the party and glanced up when a roaring peal of thunder cut the air.

"Looks like the tracks go as far as we can see, Mr. Tyson," Mantooth remarked. He took advantage of the break to roll a cigarette.

"Mmmm," Tyson grunted noncommitally.

Katy shuddered in the suddenly cold wind that whipped her blue wool jacket at the waist. As she'd done on the railroad case, Katy had taken to wearing loose-legged riding breeches and colorful Western blouses. This day her blouse was a rich red.

"What should we do?" Johann asked Tyson.

"I'm gonna ride this trail out. You people are going back home."

"Now, wait a minute," Sam cautioned, "you don't know what's out there, Carl. It may have been professional rustlers, or even Indians." Sam was nearly shouting to be heard over the escalating wind.

"Look over there," Katy pointed, and they all turned. To the south hovered a particularly dark and ominous cloud. Lightning threaded through it like cracks in smokey glass.

"We can't stay out here much longer," Mantooth yelled. The cowboys beside him looked ready to bolt at any second. "I think we ought to mark those cattle off to Injuns, Mr. Tyson."

While following the cattle trail, they'd kept a careful eye out for horse tracks but had found none. The rustlers had somehow either erased their tracks or stayed in front of the herd. While everyone looked at the thunderstorm cloud, Sam had wandered farther along the trail. "Wait a minute!" he yelled back to the group, pointing to the ground. "Look at this!"

The party rode forward and gathered around.

Sam said grimly, "I guess this answers our questions. They weren't Indians." The two hoofprints were clear enough to reveal that the horses were shod. Indians didn't shoe their horses.

Mantooth started to reply, was drowned out by another crash of thunder, then said, "Indians could've stolen white men's horses."

Without hesitation, Tyson withdrew his Sharps rifle from its scabbard and checked to see if it was loaded. "I'm going on."

"I'm going with you," Sam declared immediately.

Tyson shook his head. "Not your fight."

"I'll make it mine."

"Thank you, Sam, but I'll take Billy with me."

"You need Billy to run the ranch." Sam shrugged casually and secretly winked at Katy. "I don't have anything better to do."

Tyson stared at him for a moment, then asked, "Can you shoot?"

"I generally hit what I'm aiming at." His stomach rolled as he remembered Grat Cummings. A gunfighter for hire in the Central Pacific case, Cummings had drawn on Sam instead of giving up a valuable piece of evidence that Sam and Katy had needed. Sam, despite his leisurely and nonchalant manner, had always possessed extremely quick reflexes. Grat Cummings had been the first man he'd ever shot. And the first he'd ever killed. Cummings's death had hit him hard, and Katy had been instrumental in helping Sam come to terms with it. However, he didn't look forward to drawing on anyone again.

Fat raindrops began falling, and everyone reached for the yellow slickers that Mantooth had provided before they'd left. Tyson buckled his slicker, gave Sam a long look, then told Mantooth, "Billy, see to the ranch. Sam's right, and I know for sure I can't leave the responsibility to Boone." His face tightened as he spoke.

"May I go?" Johann asked. His blue eyes were shining with excitement.

"I'd rather you went back, Johann," Sam said. "Let Carl and me handle it."

"Be careful," Katy told Sam.

Sam nodded, and as the two groups split off in opposite directions, the rain began coming down in torrents.

Seth Moon placed Remy's plate of grilled venison in front of him and sat down at the main kitchen table in Carl Tyson's house.

Sophia, sitting between Fritz and Wilhelm at the other end of the table, couldn't hide her surprise. To Boone she asked, "You let him eat with you?"

Boone looked from Sophia to Moon to Sophia in confusion. "Seth? 'Course he eats with us. When Pa's not around, that is."

"Your father will not let him?"

Remy spoke up. "Why are you talkin' about him like he's not here? He's sittin' right there."

A ghost of a smile crossed Seth's mouth. He wasn't surprised at the princess's indignation; he'd heard worse than her ill-concealed protest in his lifetime. His smile was for Remy, who in his youth and innocence hadn't quite grasped the concept of prejudice.

Boone continued, "Pa don't have anything against Seth personally. He just doesn't want any of the hired help having an excuse to eat with us. If the cowboys saw Seth with us, they'd raise a stink."

"Who cares what they think?" Remy asked bluntly.

"That's enough, Remy," Seth said quietly and turned to Sophia. "If it'll make Your Highness feel better, I'll leave."

Sophia was momentarily flustered and unfolded her napkin as she spoke. "Well—that is up to Boone. I just never have had a servant at the same table before."

"He ain't a servant!" Remy argued.

"Remy, that's enough!" Boone thundered. "The princess is our guest, and you'll treat her with respect!"

"Sorry," Remy mumbled.

"Don't tell me, tell her."

"Sorry, Princess."

Seth was still waiting for an answer from Sophia, who was whispering to Wilhelm. He had a feeling that the subject they were discussing had nothing to do with him, so he asked Remy, "Would you like to give thanks?"

"Sure." Putting his hands together, he prayed, "Dear God, thank you for what we are about to receive. Thanks for keeping us safe through another day." Then, in a barely discernable whisper, "And thanks for the fish I caught today. Amen."

When Remy looked up, Sophia and Wilhelm were looking at them in wonder, while Fritz favored him with a secret smile.

They started eating their venison, and despite Sophia's disagreement with having Seth at the table, she couldn't help complimenting him. The deer had a distinctly different taste than the ones in Austria—wilder and sharper, but not unpleasant. An idea popped in her head. "Who shot this deer?" she asked the other end of the table.

"Seth did," Boone replied.

"What did you kill it with?" she asked Seth.

"A bow and arrow, ma'am."

"Do you people really shoot that well with those items?"

Seth grinned. "I do."

93

Wilhelm and Fritz perked up. "Would you teach me?" Wilhelm asked. Fritz nodded and pointed to himself.

"Of course, sir. I'll be glad to teach both of you."

"Wilhelm, why in the name of heaven do you want to learn that?" Sophia cried. "I can understand Fritz; he loves anything that shoots or fires."

"Simple. Because I don't have anything *else* to do." His tone was coarse as he glared defiantly at the princess. The rest of them were slightly startled at his rudeness. "I came over here with you and Johann because I thought we would have our own ranch. We don't even have our own *house!*"

Sophia carefully dabbed at her mouth without looking at him. "Wilhelm . . . you are talking in 'we's' and 'our's.' What are you implying?"

Wilhelm's face reddened, and he put down his pure silver knife and fork less than gently. "I imply nothing! Why do you do this to me, Sophia?"

"Whatever are you talking about?" Sophia asked innocently.

Remy was staring openly at them, and he felt Seth's hand gently pat his arm. When he looked at him, Seth nodded to Remy's plate. Remy continued eating but kept an eye on the two Austrians.

"You know what I'm talking about," Wilhelm countered. He seemed ready to say something else, but instead he cut his meat some more and pushed it around his plate.

Sophia acted as if nothing had happened. "So, Boone. When do you think your father and my brother will be back?"

"I really can't say, ma'am. Depends on how far those tracks go."

"What becomes of the ranch when your father dies?"

Complete silence. Not even the *tink* of silver on china.

Boone's mental answer was *none of your business!* But what he said was, "Um—I believe it goes to me and Remy."

"Do you think you're capable of handling it?"

"You bet I am!" Boone answered sharply.

Seth glanced at the princess warily. She seemed to enjoy causing conflict, and Seth had, as a rule, avoided such people all his life. They were only interested in satisfying their own twisted desires of making other people react to their statements. Sophia suddenly looked directly at him, and he averted his eyes. He wanted no part of this woman.

Boone's youth and quick temper couldn't be denied long, however. "Why you askin' me all this?"

Sophia shrugged and looked at him with wide, innocent blue eyes. "I am just making conversation."

"My father dyin' ain't much of a dinner conversation, if you don't mind my sayin' so."

Placing a hand to her throat, she said fervently, "I apologize to you, Boone. You must understand that in my country, we have very open conversations. Nothing is considered secret."

Across from Seth, Fritz was staring at him as he chewed his food. Seth had seen such blank eyes only once. A captain in Quantrill's Raiders had had colorless gray eyes that seemed to look right through Seth. He'd proven to be as heartless a killer as his emotionless eyes promised.

Fritz's black eyes, however, weren't killer's eyes. Seth had no doubt that Fritz would defend the prince or princess in any way necessary, but the emptiness in *his* eyes was of a guarded contemplation. His were the eyes that missed nothing, that took in every detail of his surroundings in the time it took another man to absorb one object. At the moment he seemed to be trying to tell Seth something that Seth couldn't understand.

Sophia's answer satisfied Boone to a certain extent. "Well, we ain't used to discussin' death at the dinner table. If you don't mind," he added grudgingly.

"No, I do not mind at all."

Remy wasn't ready to dismiss the conversation. He asked Fritz, "Fritz, y'all really talk about *anything* at the dinner table?" His face reddened when he realized his mistake. "I mean, I know *you* don't talk about nothin', but do other people?"

Fritz was surprised to be addressed directly. After giving Seth another peculiar look, he shrugged his wide shoulders.

"Fritz does not listen to other people's conversations," Sophia commented. "At least, he's not *supposed* to."

"How can he help it?" Remy asked.

Fritz now had his eyes locked on his plate.

Sophia answered in a lofty tone that made Remy feel as if he were four years old. "Fritz is a very highly trained bodyguard. He can ignore any unnecessary conversation or events in order to concentrate on threats to me or my brother. Do you understand?"

"Yeah, I'm not stupid."

"Remy," Seth warned. In order to change the subject, he said, "Allow me to invite all of you to my church this Sunday. They're actually going to let me preach a small sermon. Of course Reverend Smalley is taking a chance on no one showing up, but he's a man that follows his heart instead of traditions."

Neither Wilhelm nor Sophia spoke.

"I may be preaching to a one-man congregation."

"We will see," Sophia evaded.

They all heard the horses and went outside to meet the party. The thunderstorm hadn't reached the ranch, but they still wore slickers that glistened in the lamplight. Boone saw that his father wasn't among them and asked, "What happened? Where's Pa?"

Billy Mantooth took the reins of Katy and Johann's horses after they'd dismounted. "He and Sam went on and followed that easterly trail to see where it leads."

"Just the two of them? Why didn't you go with them, Billy?"

Mantooth looked uncomfortable. "He wanted me to come back and see to the ranch."

"Well, I can do that," Boone reasoned. "He needs your help more than I do." No one spoke, and Boone looked at all the cowboys as they averted their eyes. Suddenly, he understood. "Oh, I get it. He don't think I'm capable of it, is that right?"

"Boone," Katy began.

"Is that right, Billy?" Boone nearly shouted. "Well, I'll show him. Someday this ranch'll be *mine!* He's gonna hafta let me start runnin' the show sometime. You fellas get some sleep, 'cause it's gonna be a hard day tomorrow! And *I'm* in charge, Billy." He spun on a heel and stomped back into the house.

"Is Pa gonna be all right, Miss Katy?" Remy asked.

"He'll be fine. Sam will help him."

Remy gazed off into the east at the dark, turbulent clouds, his forehead wrinkled with worry.

Sam and Tyson rode as fast as they could in the driving rain, hoping to find the end of the trail before all signs were washed away. On the dark horizon to their front, stars winked as if teasing them. However, they couldn't outrun the storm directly overhead in time.

After crossing a shallow arroyo, the prairie grass gave out and they were left with red, sandy mud that revealed no tracks. They separated and searched north and south, but to no avail.

"What do we do?" Sam asked Tyson. The slap of raindrops on their slickers and hats was loud in their ears.

Tyson hung his head for a moment. He was tired and cold, not accustomed to riding so far for so long. For the first time in his life he fully felt his forty-three years. "We go back, I guess."

"It has to be two o'clock in the morning, Carl. Why don't we bunk down for a few hours before we head back?"

Tyson squinted up into the rain. "In this?"

"I think I saw a natural shelf in that arroyo bed to the north. We could take cover under that."

"If we don't get washed away in the flood."

The shelf was a natural haven. The overhang was at least twenty

97

feet deep, but some rain had blown into the shelter. They spread their slickers on the damp ground to sit on.

Tyson cut a chunk of jerky, handed Sam half, and as they chewed gratefully he said, "I don't know, Sam. Losing thirty head puts a serious dent in my finances, no matter *who* stole them." He studied the small stream in front of them that had swollen with the thunderstorm. "I guess you know that I had some money troubles a while back. That's why I sold half the ranch to Anton Kessler. Now, just when I was starting to get my feet back under me, I lose more money."

Sam didn't know what to say. Having grown up on a farm, he knew the value of livestock and felt bad for the man.

"I'm trying to build up a decent ranch for my boys. I know I won't live forever, and with Boone's wildness and irresponsibility, I don't know how much more time I have left with him. He may just up and join a circus—or something worse, like a band of outlaws."

Finished with his jerky, Tyson withdrew a remarkably dry cigar from his shirt pocket, offered it to Sam, who refused, and bit off the end. After spitting the wad into the stream, he said something that Sam couldn't hear.

"What was that, Carl?"

"I said, 'That boy hates me, I think.' Both of 'em, maybe."

"They don't hate you, Carl."

"You think boys aren't capable of hating their fathers?"

Sam felt a chill as he remembered that he did, indeed, hate his own father. But even with Tyson's obvious shortcomings when it came to being a father, he wasn't nearly as bad as Jacob Bronte had been to his boys. "Maybe so. But those boys don't hate you. They might be disappointed in the way you treat them sometimes, but they don't hate you."

Tyson shook his head. "Sure hope you're right, Sam."

The rain finally slacked off, and they were left with the sound of the water dripping from the roof of the shelf into the stream. In a matter of minutes, a swollen moon and the stars were again shining brilliantly overhead, as if the storm had rejuvenated even them.

"Can I ask you a question, Carl?"

"Sure."

"Don't think I'm nosey or anything, but why are you so hard on those boys?"

Tyson looked directly into Sam's eyes for the first time since they'd taken shelter. The dim glow from the moonlight outside the arroyo shelf reflected his wet face and mustache. "Kind of a personal question, ain't it?"

"If it's none of my business, just say so. But you're the one that brought your boys up. If you're concerned about their feelings for you, I was just wondering . . ."

"You was just wonderin' if I don't have anybody to blame but myself, like I'm drivin' 'em away all by myself." Tyson nodded, then he sighed. "Fair enough, I guess."

Sam didn't look at him while he pondered the question, thinking it would be easier for him if he didn't. The wait was a long one.

"I loved their mother. Guess I loved her as much as a man can love a woman. Gave her everything she asked for, and more. We were as close as this." He entwined his index and middle fingers. "Heck, I enjoyed her company more than my best friend's. There was nothing we couldn't tell each other, nothing we couldn't do together. You know, I took her to all those horse and cattle auctions, and she loved it. I went to church with her, though I'm not really a God-fearin' man, but I liked it 'cause she liked it."

Sam nodded, but said nothing.

"Then, when Remy was born and she died, I thought very seriously about joining her, do you know what I mean? I couldn't see me living the rest of my life without her. You see, she had become my only reason for living anyway. You know how you see a pretty painting of a girl, and everything else in the picture is just there to support the girl? Well, Carrie was like that. Everything else was just scenery." He took a deep breath. "After I got over my mournin', I was left with a lot of resentment. First of all, she left me. It wasn't her fault, but she left me. Second, she left me with two boys that I had no idea how to raise by myself. And third, God help me, one of those boys killed her, just as sure as murder. Or so I thought for a long time."

Sam had thought something like that was Tyson's problem, but hearing the man admit it made it seem much worse. He tried to imagine how he would feel if something like that happened to himself. He wanted to think that he was stronger and more understanding than that, but Sam had never felt that way about a woman. About anyone, as a matter of fact.

"So," Tyson continued, "I let Boone run wild, 'cause I didn't want to take responsibility for raisin' him, and I was real hard on Remy. Real hard. I ain't proud of this, you understand. Just how things turned out. Once I got over bein' mad at the boy, it seemed like it was too late to do anything about it."

"I'm sorry, Carl, but I think you're wrong. It's never too late."

Tyson's head whipped around. "What do you know about it, Bronte? You ain't even got a wife or kids!"

Sam didn't respond, he only nodded his head and bit back a retort. Unfortunately, Tyson was right.

"Let's get some sleep," Tyson said curtly, as he smoothed out his slicker and lay down with his back to Sam.

Sam, despite feeling a deep weariness in his bones, stayed awake for a long time. He thought that Tyson did, too.

CHAPTER EIGHT

Unwelcome Intuitions

Boone Tyson woke before daylight, determined to run Dos Culebras that day and prove his father wrong. Not just wrong—beyond that. *Unjustly wrong,* he thought, with a nod of satisfaction at his vocabulary. The two words floated through his head as he dressed, brushed his teeth, and made coffee. He would surprise Billy and the other cowboys by waking them up. *Loudly.* Hammering on a tree saw should do the trick.

Boone had grown up a loner. Having no friends within miles of Dos Culebras, he'd tagged after his father until he learned that he wasn't wanted. Then he adopted cowboys as his new playmates. They proved to be remarkably patient with him, but they were too busy most of the time. His father had seen Boone's loneliness and bought him an Irish setter that, after days of consideration, Boone had named "Rainbow." After all, he *was* Irish, and he *was* redheaded, so-to-speak, and since he made Boone so happy, the boy considered him his own personal pot o' gold at the end of the rainbow. Boone was very proud of his reasoning.

Boone and Rainbow had spent nine years together and were almost inseparable the whole time. They went hunting, fishing, for walks, played and slept together, and sometimes, if Boone could get away with it, ate together. Boone talked to the dog as if he were simply another boy. He shared his frustrations and joys with Rainbow so well that the dog could recognize Boone's mood on sight. Boone didn't know it, but the dog couldn't replace a human being completely; Rainbow could never tell him when he was being unreasonable and selfish, or give him encouraging words when he was down. Whatever Boone wanted to do or say was just fine by Rainbow.

Just after Rainbow turned nine, he suddenly stopped eating and drinking. He would disappear for long periods of time—much unlike the dog that waited for Boone every morning to find out what was in store for the day. Boone told his father about the unusual behavior, and five years later Boone could remember every detail of Carl Tyson's face at that moment, because it softened. The muscles around his eyes and mouth loosened in a sad image of remorse. The only other time Boone had seen his father become so emotional was when Boone asked about his mother.

"He's got rabies, son. I'm sorry."

"What's that mean?"

"It means he's got to be put down."

Boone had known exactly what "put down" meant. His father used the expression when he or one of the cowboys had to shoot a horse because of a broken leg. Tears filled the thirteen-year-old Boone's eyes at once and spilled over his cheeks. "No. I ain't gonna let you." It had been the first—and last—time that Boone had ever told Carl Tyson no.

But Carl had felt sorry for his son and hadn't admonished him. "We don't have any choice, Boone. If he runs loose, he could spread it to the cattle. Then we'd lose Dos Culebras. You don't want that, do you?"

"I don't care about this ol' ranch! I wanna keep Rainbow!"

"I'm sorry, son."

That had been the end of the argument, and the end of Rainbow. Carl had offered to buy Boone another dog, but he had refused. There would never be another Rainbow—ever.

For all his years after that incident, Boone swore never to become affectionate toward an animal. His overcompensation spread to horses, and Billy Mantooth had once asked him why he treated his mounts so rough and disrespectful. "'Cause I want to, and it ain't none o' your business, Billy," was Boone's sullen reply.

"Boone, if you don't respect your horse, he won't respect you. That's mighty important, you know."

"Then why don't you go give your horse some respect right now and leave me alone, if it's so important?"

Boone would have been very surprised to learn that his father wondered if his sons hated him. For Boone, he could no more hate *or* love his father than he could a complete stranger. There had been too many absences and a magnitude of words unspoken for that. Boone only thought of his father as someone to impress, a man who held considerable power over Boone and Remy's futures.

Boone didn't think on these things as he walked out the door to the bunkhouse. His main concern was bluffing Billy Mantooth into thinking Boone knew what he was doing—not an easy task by any means.

Heading straight for the barn to get the tree saw and hammer, Boone stopped abruptly when he saw a lamp lit inside. *What . . . ? How . . . ?* Boone wasn't allowed to carry a pistol. His father had told him at one time that he could when he turned eighteen, but on the very eve of Boone's eighteenth birthday, another boy the same age had been gunned down in a saloon in Abilene, and Carl had heard of it. "Let's wait another year, Boone," his father had said. Once again, Boone lost an argument with his father.

Before Boone could decide whether to go back inside the house and retrieve a shotgun from Carl's study, Jasper walked outside and pulled up short when he saw Boone. "Mercy, Boone! Shouldn't sneak up on a man like that in the dark!"

"What are you doing, Jasper?"

"We're saddlin' up. What are *you* doin'?"

Boone couldn't exactly tell Jasper that he was coming to wake them all up when they were already saddled and ready to go, so he chose to ignore the question. "Where you goin'?"

Billy Mantooth appeared in the barn door. "Mornin', Boone."

"Why you saddlin' up, Billy?"

Mantooth looked bewildered. "Goin' to work."

"What were you plannin' on doin'? I told you last night I was in charge."

"We always get up at this time, Boone. We can't just lay around in the bunk and wait for . . ."

"Wait for me? Is that what you were goin' to say?"

"Well . . . yeah."

"Why didn't you tell me what time to get up?"

Mantooth nodded to Jasper. "Go get those ropes out of the storage shed, Jasper."

"Right." Jasper ambled off in his peculiar, lopsided gait.

"I'm waitin', Billy," Boone said testily. "Why wasn't I told?"

Mantooth moved directly in front of Boone. He stood a full head taller, but he didn't look down on the younger man. Instead he looked at the lightening sky in the east over Boone's shoulder. "That's my point, Boone. I shouldn't *have* to tell you when we get started around here."

"But that's—"

"Now, hold on, Boone, hold on. Let me say my piece." Mantooth's dark eyes locked with Boone's, not unkindly. "I've worked for your daddy for as long as you are old. We practically know what each other's thinkin' before the other one thinks it. That's called *trust,* and it's a needful thing between a ranch owner and his head wrangler."

"But *I'm* a ranch owner, too!" Boone didn't like the whining tone in his voice, but it was too late to take it back.

"No, you *ain't,* Boone! You don't know the first thing about ownin' a ranch. Just standing around *announcin'* to everyone that you own one won't do it! It takes hard work and hands-on care. You're too busy runnin' around, goin' to town, and doin' whatever pleases you." Mantooth's voice softened when he saw Boone look away with hurt in his eyes. Mantooth and Boone had never had cross words. Mantooth wasn't stupid, and he knew that he'd been more of a father to Boone than Carl had ever been. At the moment, he resented his boss more than ever for putting him in this position.

Billy continued, "Your daddy and I ain't always agreed on everything, but I know he's the boss. What he says goes, no questions. He told me to run this place 'til he gets back, and that's what I'm goin' to do—do you understand?"

"Oh, yeah, I understand all right," Boone said sullenly. "I understand plenty." He turned and started back toward the house.

"Now, don't go swellin' up on me. I need your help today."

"Get someone else to do it, Billy. Someone more *able.*"

<hr />

At that moment in the Atlantic Ocean, five days from Cuba, Gonzalez Bilbao was finishing his breakfast. The smoked salmon omelet had been excellent. Belching appreciatively, the second-most-powerful man in the Spanish political structure was already looking forward to joining the early morning patrons of the gentlemen's salon.

On his first extended voyage, Bilbao had discovered that the ship and its passengers had evolved into a semblence of a small town or village. Despite various nationalities, the people behaved no differently than their land-based counterparts the world over. Rumors were whispered, odd mannerisms were exposed, and since the passengers felt freer among strangers, personal lives were less hidden.

One man, undoubtedly from the coast of some country and a bit strange, would always take extra bread from the dining table every morning and feed seagulls that weren't there. Breaking off bits of the bread, he would toss them in front of him over the railing, smiling into the empty air with pure pleasure. The bread would be ripped from his happy fingers by the wind, only to fly behind the ship and land in the ocean for fish food. Bilbao had spoken to him the first few mornings, but the man was in his own little world, where the hungry gulls were plentiful.

Marital discord rose to the surface like cream to the top of fresh milk. From open fighting to sullen distancing to blatant affairs, Bilbao was continually amazed as the private practices of couples were heedlessly unmasked.

Bilbao had always been a people watcher and enjoyed every minute of his voyage. He considered his habit of studying people an asset in his line of work. Security of important political figures involved not just stopping an attack when it happened; the important thing, at which Bilbao humbly believed that he excelled, was spotting the attack before it happened. An assassin usually gave himself away with telling personal habits, either right before the attempt or in his previous work. Bilbao had a detailed file on every assassination attempt in Europe, successful or not. The only professional he'd been unable to figure out was The Butcher. Carnicero.

His failure left a barb in Bilbao's soul.

Realizing he'd been staring at the dining table blankly as he thought about the ship's peculiarities, Bilbao suddenly stood and stepped into the narrow aisle, feeling his arm connect with another person. Turning, he watched in horror as a small, stooped old man with a cane tumbled over a chair to the floor with a feeble cry. "I'm terribly sorry!" Bilbao cried as he rushed to the man's aid.

Looking more stunned than hurt, the man muttered in American-accented English, "I'm all right—I think." His white eyebrows were thick and bushy, just like his mustache. A very pale face with many moles stared back at Bilbao in a combination of anger, embarrassment, and fear.

Switching from Spanish to halting English, Bilbao said frantically, "Here, let me help you up." He reached for the man's arm, but he jerked away.

"Young man, if your helping up is as beneficial as your knocking down, I'll assist myself, thank you very much."

Bilbao stood by, his hands inches from the man should he take a spill trying to stand. Slowly, painfully, the old man grasped his cane with one pale hand and the seat of the chair with the other and managed to rise to his feet. Bilbao repeated, "Please—I apologize again—very—how do you say? Clumsy of me."

The old man cocked an eye at him. Bilbao noticed an unfortunate hump high on the man's back. "You're as dangerous as a New York City hack driver—they don't watch where they're going, either."

Bilbao said the first thing that popped in his mind. "Please let me buy your breakfast to make amends."

"What kind of offer is that?" the man asked, his voice cracking. "Our meals are paid for—included in the fare. Besides, I've already eaten."

"Yes, yes, you are right—*estúpido!* Stupid me!" The old man started for the door, and Bilbao snapped his fingers and made one last attempt. "A drink then! In the gentlemen's salon."

"It's raining out there! Do you want me to catch my death of cold?"

"Of course not! I have an umbrella—you won't feel a drop."

The remarkably clear eyes studied Bilbao again for an uncomfortably long time. "You always drink this early in the morning? What are you—Russian?"

"No, I am from Spain."

The man waited. "And?"

Bilbao looked confused. "And what, *señor?*"

"I asked you two questions, and you only answered one."

"Ah! Um—oh, *sí,* I have one drink every morning. But only one. Mostly I go to watch the monkey. Have you seen the monkey?"

"Monkey? Are you sure you only have *one* drink?"

Bilbao laughed. "No, *señor,* there really is a monkey in the salon. *Por favor,* allow me to show him to you." He extended his hand. "My name is Gonzalez Bilbao."

The old man inspected the outstretched hand for a moment, then gave it a short, limp shake. "William Pruitt. Let's go. I'm tired of standing here arguing about it."

High winds buffeted them as they made their way to the salon. They met no one on the promenade deck; the bad weather apparently discouraged people from leaving their cabins. Despite Bilbao's promise of keeping Pruitt dry, the old man's coat was completely wet by the time they got there. Pruitt didn't mention it, however.

The gentlemen's salon was empty except for the attendant, and they sat at the bar while Bilbao introduced Pruitt to the monkey, whose name was Aubergine. "He loves eggplant," the French bartender explained, "and eggplant is *aubergine* in French." Aubergine watched Bilbao and Pruitt with bright eyes. His tiny black beret was perched on the side of his head in a cocky manner and held in place by a tiny strap under his chin.

Bilbao and Pruitt talked easily. Pruitt ordered a glass of goat's milk, while Bilbao had his usual drink. Bilbao told the old man that he was traveling to the United States to establish a better relationship for the new government in Spain. Pruitt listened attentively, then divulged that he was a banker returning from an important business transaction in Switzerland that had needed personal, hands-on treatment.

Pruitt asked, "So, your only mission is to strengthen ties with America? Nothing else?"

"My dear *señor,* is that not enough of a task?" Bilbao chuckled. "Why do you ask?"

"No reason," Pruitt answered shortly, and Bilbao saw a strange smile on the pale face.

After talking for an hour, Pruitt declared, "I must go to my cabin and rest. It's been an exciting morning."

"Let me help you. The wind may still be gusting."

The ship again seemed deserted when they went outside. The rain had slacked off, but the wind was still high. Pruitt looked all around them, then told Bilbao, "Come to the rail. You have to see one of our banking investments, one that I feel is a waste of good money."

"What is it?" Bilbao asked curiously.

"The painted name *'Napoléon'* on the side of this ship is special. It's supposed to resist saltwater forever, but I noticed yesterday that it's already beginning to fade."

Bilbao followed the stooped figure to the rail and leaned over to see where he pointed. After scanning the side for a moment, he suddenly realized that the ship's name was on the *other* side. "Excuse me, *señor,* but the other side is where you—" Bilbao broke off, startled. The old man stood next to him, doubled over, as though in pain. Bilbao felt a feeble hand grasping at his pants leg.

"*Señor,*" he began in concern, "Are you—"

He suddenly felt his leg held in an iron grip.

"Bilbao, I've waited long for this moment."

The Spaniard stared, horror filling him. The old man's features changed before his eyes. Gone was the feeble, pained expression. White teeth flashed as the man sneered up at Bilbao.

"Carnicero!"

In the same heartbeat as this whispered realization, Carnicero straightened, his hand firmly grasping Bilbao's leg, and heaved him over the railing.

At the last moment Bilbao flailed out, managing to grasp the rail with one clinging, desperate hand. The metal was slick with rain, and very cold. Strong wind gusts tore at his coat and slammed him against the side of the ship. He knew he couldn't hold on for long.

Carnicero glanced around once more, saw no one, and shouted in Spanish, "You were good, Bilbao, but not good enough! Remember me on your way to the bottom of the ocean!" With deliberate ease, he tore Bilbao's fingers from the slick rail, waving to the white, terrified face of the man who plummeted toward the water.

Bilbao felt himself falling and screaming, hoping to the last that someone would hear and come save him. But he slammed into the cold, churning water, and the impact knocked the breath from his lungs. The current sucked him beneath the surface, and by the time he was able to draw a breath he was ten feet under the Atlantic Ocean. Unintentionally, he fulfilled Carnicero's last demand.

His final thought was of the man called The Butcher.

<hr />

Katy paced nervously, her boots pounding the porch in a steady rhythm. "They should be back by now."

Johann watched her from the porch swing of Hill House. He was dressed in a maroon jacket, snow-white shirt and black riding breeches with suede on the inside of the thigh. He'd finally gotten Katy to agree to go riding with him, but her worry over Sam and Tyson had increased to the point that she insisted on waiting for their return before they left. "You worry too much, my dear. I am sure they can take care of themselves."

The pounding boots stopped, and Katy gave him a sour look. "Don't you ever get upset? Are all Austrian princes so calm?"

"Actually, we carry the weight of the world on our shoulders, but we have a remarkable ability to hide it," he said, grinning.

Katy didn't return his smile, only shook her head and resumed pacing.

"You are lovely when you are worried." This time, Johann saw a brief secret smile on her lips before she turned to the other end of the porch. She stopped at the railing twenty feet from him and gazed over the western prairie. Never in his life had he seen a woman wearing pants; to Johann, it only added to her personality and charm. He let his eyes run over her rich, thick, ash-blonde hair. A warm breeze from the west blew it back from her neck, and he caught a glimpse of her soft jawline before her locks again settled on her shoulders. He always found himself wanting to run his fingers through it, slowly and deliberately, as if experiencing hair for the first time.

Johann had never been in love before. Every day spent with Katy confirmed the fact that he'd never really *cared* for anyone before, either. Tearing his eyes away from her, he fingered the riding crop in his hands and unconsciously pursed his lips. He was so smitten he was unsure how to proceed. Though he joked about his composed manner, he'd been extremely proud of his ability to take matters as they came and shun worries. Johann took his birthright seriously and knew that someday he would be making important decisions for a whole nation. His father was a rash, emotional man who had let poor judgment interfere with his decisions, and Johann had worked hard to refine his own sense of serenity and judgment.

"There they are," Katy pointed.

Johann looked up from his riding crop to see Sam and Tyson riding in from the south. Even from where he was sitting Johann could see the two men were tired. He followed Katy as she walked quickly, almost *ran,* to the barn. All the cowboys were out on the range, but Boone and Remy came running out of the house.

"What happened, Pa?" Boone shouted before he reached the riders. "Did you find 'em?"

"Nope. Rain washed away the tracks." Tyson and Sam dismounted slowly, the way men do when they've been in the saddle for a long time. Johann heard a few bones popping with relief.

"Are you two all right?" Katy asked.

Johann couldn't help but notice that she looked directly at Sam when she said this, and then went to him and grasped his arm with both hands. A dark jealousy washed over him, but he fought it away with effort.

"We're fine, Katy," Sam answered. The morning sun had baked away the thin layer of mud on the prairie, and he and Tyson were covered with a thin layer of red dust that loosened itself with their every move and swirled in the air.

Boone took the reins of his father's horse. "You know it was that rat Flynn, Pa! Why are we messin' around here, when we should go up there? He's probably got 'em in his corral right now."

"No, we *don't* know that. Those tracks led everywhere *but* north."

"'Course they don't! He planned it that way!"

Tyson surprised everyone by gently placing a hand on Boone's shoulder. The movement was hesitant and awkward, and no one was more shocked than Boone himself. Tyson said, "We need to settle down and let Sam and Katy handle it. I've already decided that."

"What! How can *they* help?" Boone ducked under the horse's head and began loosening the saddle.

Sam led his horse into the barn, nodding at Katy and Johann to follow. They went to the far end, as far away from the hotheaded Boone and private conversation as they could. Johann helped Sam unsaddle the horse, and then Sam told them quietly, "Tyson figures we'll have a better chance of finding the stolen cattle than he will, because nobody knows us." He looked at Johann. "We can refuse, if you want. We work for you, after all."

"By all means, go ahead."

"Thanks. Now, I'm going to get some sleep. Long night."

Thirty minutes later, Katy and Johann were riding along a narrow ridge above an empty arroyo bed. The smell of wild onion filled the air, and the grass was covered with rosy purple fireweed, cactus dahlia, and a few sunflowers. The heat wasn't as oppressive as it had been, and Johann thought to himself that the flowers weren't the only ones glad for the brief thunderstorm.

Seeing Katy shift uncomfortably in her side saddle, Johann suggested, "Would you like to walk for a while?"

Katy nodded gratefully and slipped from the saddle.

Johann dismounted, picked a fluffy dandelion, and handed it to her. "You are awfully quiet, Katherine. Is something wrong?"

"No. I'm just feeling sort of melancholy today, I suppose."

"Is there anything I can do?"

"Thank you, but you're probably giving me what I need—fresh air and sight-seeing." Katy blew on the dandelion and watched the delicate white petals float away on the wind. The dandelion stem, naked and forlorn now, only made her more depressed.

"Would you like to talk about it?" Johann asked

Katy had slept fitfully during the night, worried about Sam. For some reason she was concerned about his soul. The dangers were plentiful on the prairie, just as they had been when they'd been searching for a killer on their previous case. But she had been so wide-eyed and harried on the Central Pacific case that she hadn't had time to worry about *anything*. Now, in the relatively calm surroundings of Dos Culebras, she found herself thinking of Sam and Johann and all the others who, if not Christians, were probably on unsteady ground. *Am I a strong enough witness for you, Lord? Am I doing all I can to bring more people to you?*

Along with this uncertain thinking, Katy felt a strange foreboding. The last time she'd been aware of the feeling had been the day she'd kissed her father goodbye on the final day of his life. In the past few days she'd felt a heaviness inside her; whenever someone rode into Dos Culebras, she could feel herself tense up, as if her mind was readying itself for bad news. Katy didn't care much for intuition. Her mind was mathematical and scientific, with a clear sense of right or wrong, straight or crooked, clear or obsure.

Intuition had no solid grounding or explanation, and therefore baffled and disturbed her.

"Katherine?"

"Yes?"

Johann took her arm and stopped her. Their horses, a bay mare and chestnut colt, touched noses and stamped impatiently. Turning Katy to face him, Johann's eyes were full of concern as he said, "What is *wrong?*"

Suddenly tired of cloudy and formless fears in her life, Katy asked, "Johann, what's your relationship with God?"

"What?" He gave a small, uncomfortable chuckle.

"Do you consider yourself a Christian?"

"I am Catholic, Katherine. I was baptized at birth."

Katy nodded and looked over his shoulder at blue bluffs in the distance rising against the clear sky. She came to a decision. "Johann, I'd like to tell you about being a Christian. . . ."

CHAPTER NINE

Accusations

The morning after Katy and Johann went for their ride, Wilhelm Kesselmeyer stepped from his room, which was on the second floor of Hill House. For as far back as he could remember, even to the days as a young boy in Anschluss, he'd always been an early riser. During his education at the University of Vienna, he'd never been able to claim any athletic prowess as could most of the other boys. He was short, fat, and slow-footed but remarkably intelligent. All the other students knew better than to go into a chess match thinking they would win against Wilhelm. The other trait that was admired the most about him was his ability to function on little or no sleep. No matter how late studying, talking, partying, debating, or *anything,* Wilhelm was wide awake at 5:00 A.M.

Wilhelm went downstairs to drink coffee and watch the cowboys stir from their bunks as he did every morning. Boring, boring, boring. He'd had a much more exciting view of America: saloon girls batting their eyes at him every night, Indians attacking at all hours of the day, gunslingers walking around with dark, predatory stares, looking for an excuse to start shooting.

When Johann had asked him for help in running his ranch in Texas, Wilhelm had accepted immediately. Then came the long

115

voyage of constant seasickness, and now the flat, dusty, hot plains of Texas. And no saloon girls.

To Wilhelm's surprise, Sam walked through the front door. Wilhelm hadn't seen him coming as he'd stared out the window into the early dawn. Sam's eyes were puffy, and he yawned a good morning.

"What are you doing up so early?" Wilhelm asked, slightly wary. Had they been fifteen years younger, he was sure that Sam would be one of the athletic boys that rode Wilhelm unmercifully. His easy self-confidence and good looks caused Wilhelm to be on guard for any insult, real or imagined. A real man's man—the kind to which Sophia was attracted.

Sam strode directly to the kitchen counter. "Oh, good, you've got coffee." As he poured from the pot he answered, "My sleeping's all messed up after being awake all last night. Slept all afternoon, then went back to bed at two, and now I'm up again." He shook his head. "Can't wait to see what tonight brings."

Wilhelm watched him pour the coffee and take a sip, secretly grinning inside. *Wait until he sees how Austrians make coffee! It's so strong he'll choke!*

But Wilhelm was disappointed. Sam sipped, breathed an "Aaaah!" and sat down across from Wilhelm contentedly. "That's good—you make it, Wilhelm?"

"You *like* it?"

"Sure. Why shouldn't I?"

Wilhelm shook his head. "No reason."

"Why are *you* up so early?"

Wilhelm explained his habit of getting up at the same hour every morning.

Sam whistled. "That must get pretty tiresome."

"Never," Wilhelm proclaimed proudly.

Sam lifted his cup in a salute. "Here's to you, then."

Maybe he's not so bad after all, Wilhelm thought. He had an honest, open face and seemed genuinely interested in the people around him. Wilhelm had seen Sam's attempts to be a father to the boy, Remy, and his tolerance of Sophia's barbs. *Speaking of Sophia . . .*

"What do you think of the prince and princess, Sam?" he asked casually.

Sam's eyes locked with Wilhelm's, as if sensing a trap. Then the look was gone, and he pulled out the chair next to him and rested his booted foot across it. Massaging his thigh, he answered, "Who *wouldn't* like Johann? He seems to be a genuinely good man. Hard to find that sort in a powerful position."

"And the princess?"

"She's . . . a princess, I suppose."

Wilhelm grinned, showing the prominent gap between his front two teeth. "Nicely evaded."

"I'm sure she's a nice woman once you get to know her—*if* she lets anyone get to know her." He raised one eyebrow and ended the sentence in a rising, questioning tone.

Wilhelm acted as if he didn't understand and ignored the implied question. "And Miss Steele? Are you concerned about her relationship with the prince?"

"You're very direct, aren't you?"

Shrugging, with a guarded look, Wilhelm said, "It's one of my faults."

"Mmm. Or strengths. Katy goes her own way, just as I do."

Wilhelm nodded, then stood up in surprise when Sophia appeared in the doorway. "Sophia!"

"Bad night for sleeping, I guess," Sam commented as he stood, too. *"Guten Morgen,* Highness."

"Gentlemen." She wore a rich royal blue robe tied at her tiny waist. Her long, freshly combed blonde hair swirled to her shoulders brilliantly, and the effect was stunning. "Please, sit down. It's too early in the morning to be jumping to your feet for ladies."

Wilhelm offered to get her coffee, but she declined. As she sat down in the chair beside Sam, he noticed with amusement and surprise that she was barefoot. When she crossed her legs, her robe fell open to reveal a slim white calf. With a tiny smile at Sam's inspection, she slowly covered it. Sam smiled back gallantly.

Wilhelm asked, "Did Johann find a place for our house yesterday?"

"He was sort of vague about it. Actually, he seemed upset about something." She turned to Sam. "He was with Katy, you know. I hope it was not a lover's quarrel."

Sam shrugged. "It happens."

"Does it? I have never been in love before."

"That doesn't surprise me."

"Have *you*, Sam?" Sophia let the barb pass—for now. "Been in love?"

"Hundreds of times."

"Oh, really? You are a heartbreaker?"

"On the contrary. I'm a heart *giver*—but, alas, a dainty foot only grinds it into the dust every time. 'By heaven, I do love, and it hath taught me to rhyme, and to be melancholy.'"

"Shakespeare. But the play escapes me."

Sam sat up straighter in his chair, impressed. *"Love's Labor's Lost.* I didn't know you were an admirer of The Bard."

"Nor I you. When we were learning English, our teacher insisted on us reading Shakespeare." She looked at him with new respect. "Where did you learn him?"

As Sam told them of his stage experience and life as an actor, and how he'd come to love Shakespeare, Wilhelm was wondering how he'd been excluded from the conversation. Sam was trying to include him, but Sophia's attention was fixed on Sam. He injected "Mmmm"'s and "Oh, really?"'s into Sam's story in an attempt to let the princess know he was still present and breathing. He'd grown accustomed to Sophia's insults and arrogance, but when she blatantly ignored him, it was still difficult to take.

When Sam finished, Sophia clapped her hands excitedly. "Quote another one."

"Give me a subject."

"Ummm. Royalty!"

"'Uneasy lies the head that wears a crown.'"

"No, no, *everyone's* heard that one. Another one."

Sam took a sip of coffee while he thought, found it cool, and went to refreshen it. Suddenly he turned back to them from the counter and quoted:

> 'Tis not the balm, the scepter, and the ball,
> The sword, the mace, the crown imperial,
> The intertissued robe of gold and pearl,
> The farcèd title running fore the king,
> The throne he sits on, nor the tide of pomp
> That beats upon the high shore of this world—
> No, not all these, thrice-gorgeous ceremony,
> Not all these, laid in bed majestical,
> Can sleep so soundly as the wretched slave,
> Who, with a body filled, and vacant mind,
> Gets him to rest, crammed with distressful bread;
> Never sees horrid night, the child of hell.

Sam grinned at them. "I thought that would be appropriate, since everyone's having trouble sleeping."

"You must have been very good," Wilhelm said in admiration, despite his jealousy.

"So the peasant sleeps better than the king," Sophia pondered. "Why is that?"

Sam sat down with his coffee. "Not as many worries, I suppose. At least Shakespeare thought so." He chuckled. "His kings and princes were full of worry, always wandering the night, seeing phantoms, hearing plots against themselves. I'd be afraid to go to sleep, too. Might wake up with my throat cut."

Sophia was inspecting him closely, her bright blue eyes hooded. "I can see you living back then. Sword fights, damsels in distress, chivalry . . ."

Wilhelm was on the verge of leaving the room. This was too much.

"Please, Highness," Sam said, holding up a hand, "don't condemn me to that time. Shakespeare's world was extremely dark and eerie. I'm very happy in the nineteenth century."

"I would have *loved* to have lived in that time," Wilhelm stated, looking defiantly at Sam.

"You probably would have fit in perfectly, Wilhelm." Sam nodded, then squinted his eyes at him in scrutiny. "I'd say you would've made a good statesman or advisor to a king."

Wilhelm narrowed his own eyes. He'd pictured himself a tortured Hamlet or Austrian Othello, not some common politician. "Why is that?"

"Because you seem to be a quick thinker, a behind-the-scenes sort of man. The brains behind the crown, if you will."

Wilhelm smiled with satisfaction and glanced at Sophia to see if she heard the compliment directed at him. Sophia was gazing at Sam.

"And who would I be?" she asked Sam.

Sam shook his head. "That'll take some thought. I'm not very quick on my feet at five in the morning."

The front door burst open, and Carl Tyson and Billy Mantooth rushed in. "Is Boone here?" Tyson asked without preamble.

They all looked at each other in momentary confusion, and Sam said, "We haven't seen him."

Tyson turned to Mantooth with a grim expression. "That's it. Get the horses saddled."

———◦•◦———

J. B. Flynn finished his ham and eggs and belched heartily. He enjoyed his breakfasts alone, planning his day and life each morning. He'd never married, preferring to have only himself to worry about, and he'd never regretted it. The company he enjoyed the most was that of his dog, Oscar, a bloodhound that could track a mouse across the state of Texas.

Flynn threw a piece of ham fat to Oscar, who was sitting patiently at his feet. Oscar's sad eyes said thank you. "You're welcome," Flynn replied. "See? You and me communicate better than any married couple I know of."

Oscar thumped his thick tail on the wooden floor in agreement. "A fine specimen of a companion you are, Oscar. Fine specimen."

Oscar let it be known that they were in complete harmony on that statement also.

Flynn took out his pocket watch, noticed it was getting on nine o'clock, and began to rise. Oscar let loose with one of his deep-chested bark-howls that never failed to startle the daylights out of Flynn. He opened his mouth to admonish the dog, then realized it was Oscar's warning bark-howl and automatically turned to the front door to see who was coming.

B. B. Easterling entered without knocking. He was smiling, exposing his yellow, uneven teeth, and said, "You gotta see this, boss."

Flynn, despite the fact that B. B. was his head wrangler, detested the man but found him indispensable. Nevertheless, he couldn't resist taking him down a notch. "How many times have I told you to knock, Easterling?"

"Sorry," the wrangler mumbled. His dark eyes lit up with mischief again. "You ain't gonna believe this, Mr. Flynn. You just ain't gonna believe it!"

"All right, Easterling. Oscar, come on." Oscar followed the two men outside into another warm, sunny day. Flynn said, "What have you found, Easterling, a two-headed calf?" He stopped dead when he saw a young man on his horse with his hands tied behind his back, surrounded by grinning cowboys.

"I think this may be better than a two-headed calf, don't you, boss?"

The boy was watching Flynn with a contemptuous stare.

"Who is he?" Flynn asked.

"Why, that's Boone Tyson. One o' Carl's pups."

Flynn strode to the edge of the porch, his eyes never leaving Boone. "Don't leave me hanging, B. B. Why is he here?"

Easterling was almost jumping with excitement. "Caught 'im messin' with the herd this mornin'. Claims we stole some o' his daddy's stock."

"What exactly does 'messin' mean?"

"I was checkin' brands," Boone broke in, his eyes flashing defiance.

"So he claims," Easterling said airily. "Could be he was gonna rustle 'em."

Flynn raised his eyebrows. "That true, boy?"

"You stole some of our cattle, so don't deny it."

"That's a mighty serious accusation, son," Flynn said dangerously.

"I ain't your son."

Flynn ignored him, walked down the porch steps, and stood beside Boone's horse. "Looks like you should be apologizing to me instead of trying to rile me."

"Apologize! What for?"

"For trespassing. Judge Simpkins in Fargo doesn't look too highly on trespassing and criminal intent. You could do jail time if I want it."

"I ain't apologizin' to you, Flynn," Boone spat out. "You sayin' you didn't rustle our steers?"

"I have no idea what you're talking about."

"Then you're a black liar."

Flynn's cheeks grew crimson with anger, in stark contrast to his well-trimmed gray beard. In a low, hoarse voice he ordered, "Get him down off that horse, boys."

Three cowboys dismounted and went to Boone, who started kicking at them to no avail. They managed to get him down and stand him up in front of Flynn. Boone stood an inch or two taller and did his best to look down on the older man. He was working his wrists in the rope to try to loosen the knot.

Flynn said, "You're about to find out that I don't like being called a *liar*"—his fist shot out and connected solidly in Boone's stomach, doubling him over—"and a *thief*"—Flynn's knee came up flush against Boone's nose. Boone fell flat on his back. "And I don't like trespassers on my land."

Boone moaned in agony, blood gushing in a fountain from his nose. He hadn't seen either blow coming.

"Easterling, take him to Tyson's land and dump him." Flynn leaned down close to Boone's face. "I don't want to see you again. You understand?"

Boone looked at him through a red haze, but found he couldn't answer.

As Flynn turned to go back into the house, he heard riders approaching and turned. Carl Tyson, that smart-aleck Bronte, and five other men rode in. One of them was the thick, brutal-looking gorilla that was with the prince's party. Flynn's men had them outnumbered, but the looks on the riders' faces made his stomach turn for an instant.

Tyson began dismounting before the horse had stopped, and ordered, "Billy, help Boone up on his horse."

"Your son seems to have had an accident, Carl," Flynn said with concern.

Tyson strode toward Flynn, but Easterling stepped in front of his boss. In a silver blur Tyson whipped out his pistol and brought it across the side of Easterling's head with a dull thump. Easterling dropped in a small cloud of dust and didn't move. Flynn, alarmed that Tyson now had a gun in his hand, backed up a step and drew his own. But while he was doing this, Tyson just as quickly holstered his pistol and with a roundhouse right connected solidly with Flynn's right eye and cheek. Flynn fell flat on his back. The three cowboys who'd gotten Boone off his horse grabbed Tyson.

Sam, still sitting on his horse, saw Flynn's mounted cowboys nervously reaching for their pistols. Before any of them could draw, Sam's .44 was in his hand, and he shouted, "Whoa, there, boys! This is between them, so keep those hands clear!" A few of them considered ignoring him but thought better of it.

"Let me go!" Tyson roared, shaking himself loose from the ranch hands. Tyson stood over a stunned Flynn and stuck a finger in his face. "Don't you *ever* touch my boy again! If you do, I'll kill you! Do you understand?"

Flynn's eye was already swelling shut, but he stood and watched Tyson wheel and mount his horse. "You're finished, Tyson! You hear me? Finished! I'll run you out of this country, you and your little royal family!"

Sam still held his gun in the direction of the mounted cowboys, but looked at Flynn. "Maybe you've already started trying."

"What's that mean?"

"I think you know what I'm talking about."

"Let it be, Sam," Tyson growled. "This coward's not gonna own up to something he did. This is a man that likes to beat up boys, as long as he has ten men behind him."

Flynn was livid, and spittle flew from his lips as he screamed, "Get off my land! Now!"

Tyson pointed a finger at him again, in no hurry to do as he was told. "If I find any evidence that you stole my cattle, there won't be any judge to help you like the one that stood by while you took

over this ranch here. It'll be just between you and me!" Not waiting
for a reply, he wheeled his horse and led his men back to Dos
Culebras.

Easterling began stirring at Flynn's feet, and Flynn kicked him.
"Get up, B. B."

"What d'ya wanna do, Mr. Flynn?" asked a cowboy.

Flynn watched the men riding off, seeing Bronte looking back
at him, still holding his pistol as it hung loosely by his side. The
man's arrogance and confidence made Flynn want to smash him—
in any way. Flynn's head throbbed in earnest now, and his eye was
swollen shut. He glanced at Easterling, unaware of how similar
their faces appeared. "I want you to assign a man—"

"What? I can't hear outta this ear so good."

Flynn stepped close and shouted, "I want you to assign a man to
watch that place. I want to know their habits—where they go, what
they do. Did you hear that?"

"Yessir."

Flynn turned back to watch the riders, but now they were only a
cloud of dust. Anger, coupled with swelling, twisted his features
horribly. "I'm going to plan a nice surprise for Mr. Carl Tyson and
his litter."

———◆———

"What'd you think you were doing, Boone?" Tyson shouted as they
rode home. "You could have gotten hurt a lot worse than you did."

Boone held a bloodsoaked kerchief to his nose. No matter what
he did, it wouldn't stop bleeding. He answered in a nasal twang,
"I'm all right, Pa. Besides, *somebody* had to do something." He
looked at his father with barely hidden disdain.

"Don't you look at me that way, boy. What you did was stupid
and irresponsible. You didn't have proof, and we'll probably never
get it, now that Flynn's on his guard."

"He stole 'em! You know it, and I know it!"

"Did you see 'em?"

"Well, no, but—"

"Then we *don't* know it! Why don't you use your head, Boone?"

Boone threw the sopping kerchief to the ground. Sam offered him his, and Boone gave him a grateful look.

Tyson continued, talking more to himself than Boone, "Now there's no telling what Flynn'll do. Billy!" Mantooth rode forward. "I want the herd together at all times for a while. And I want guards, every night."

"Yessir."

"And you"—he pointed at Boone, his dark eyes blazing—"you stay home. You don't go to town, you don't go out on the range, nothing! You hear me?"

"But, Pa—"

"Not a word! I'll tie you down like a calf if I have to! If you're gonna act like an irresponsible kid, I'll treat you like one."

Sam, riding beside them, noticed for the first time how much their profiles were alike. Then he realized that it was only the anger on their faces. Both exhibited a tightness around the mouth and eyebrows that came together fiercely. Sadly, Sam realized that father and son were similiar in anger, but in nothing else.

———

Carnicero hated New Orleans. Its loud music, boisterous crowds, and blistering heat combined to motivate him to find transportation to Texas as soon as possible. When he found out how far he was from his destination, he was surprised and appalled. He'd been to America once before—New York—and though he'd had the wide expanse of the Midwest described to him, he hadn't appreciated the image until the stagemaster told him that Abilene was twenty days away. Carnicero had sailed across the huge Atlantic Ocean in that time!

With no other choice, Carnicero purchased a ticket for a stage that left the next morning. He checked into the St. Louis Hotel, planning on an early dinner and bedtime. He walked to Galatdire's on Bourbon Street, a small, marble-fronted restaurant that boasted interior walls lined with mirrors, which gave the impression of pure size. He ordered an exquisite dish called trout *marguery,* which turned out to be generous portions of trout, shrimp, and scallops covered with a rich white sauce.

His thoughts turned to his mission while he ate and observed the other restaurant patrons. First, he would have to buy suitable clothes. He'd seen a shop close to the hotel that carried western wear, and that was his destination after dinner.

Second, he had to decide on his plan of killing: long-range rifle shots? poisoning? knives? accidental deaths? The choices were endless in Carnicero's line of work, and he sighed deeply. His usual manner was to dispatch the victims in the quickest and most convenient way possible. But his curiosity was piqued. This was royalty—people on which a nation would depend in the future. What sort of people were they? Were they pompous and disdainful, as Isabella II had been? Or were they like regular citizens, with hopes and dreams and failures and faults? And the princess—did she *look* like a princess? Was she beautiful, ugly, or merely plain looking?

Carnicero shook his head as he finished his meal. This particular mission was much too inviting to his inquisitive and singular nature. How could he pass up this opportunity? He would not kill them. Not right away. There was too much to be learned first.

In the dress store called Vittorio's, Carnicero found with relief that only one other customer was present, a large, heavyset man who arrived at the same time as Carnicero, and the shopkeeper was alone. Carnicero was tired and ready for bed, and he managed to confront the shopkeeper an instant before the heavy man did. "I'm interested in dress for the plains. What would you suggest?"

"Goin' west, huh?"

"Yes."

The heavyset man spoke up beside Carnicero. "Now, that's a coincidence. Me, too." He turned to the shopkeeper. "You Vittorio?"

"At your service, sir."

"I think we'll be needing the same type of clothes, but as you can tell, different sizes."

Carnicero tried to cover his disappointment. Now that he was on the American continent, he preferred to remain as inconspicuous as possible. He didn't plan on anyone making a connection with Vittorio's in New Orleans with the death of a prince and princess, but one never knew.

The man spoke to Carnicero again: "My name's Rorke, Jack Rorke. I write for the *Times-Picayune*." He held out a beefy hand, which Carnicero accepted.

Luckily, Carnicero was prepared with a name that he would use during his visit, one that satisfied his love of irony. "Paul Goodfellow."

"Are you?"

"Am I what?"

"A good fellow!" Rorke laughed. "Bet you've heard that one a thousand times."

Carnicero smiled. "This is the first, actually."

"You're not serious!"

"Oh, but I am."

Rorke looked for signs of a joke on Carnicero's face, found none, and turned to Vittorio. "Can you help us?"

By the time they left, Carnicero and Rorke had each purchased enough clothing for a week in the hot summer plains of the Midwest. As they were leaving, Rorke asked him if he would care to have a drink with him.

"No, thank you. I've an early appointment."

Rorke shrugged. "So do I. Got a stage to catch."

"Really? Going where?"

"Some ranch in Texas called Dos Culebras. There's supposed to be a prince and princess that bought a piece of it and are settling in. The *Times-Picayune* is sending me to get the story."

Carnicero felt himself stop breathing. It took every ounce of effort to keep his face mildly disinterested instead of shocked. His mind worked at a blinding rate of speed at this information. "Er—do they know you're coming?" he asked, more to gather his thoughts than for information. But the information solidified his thoughts.

"We've sent a letter to Carl Tyson, the owner. They're expecting me."

With true delight, Carnicero smiled at Jack Rorke, his best friend in the whole world at the moment. "If you don't mind, I think I *will* have that drink with you, Jack. May I call you Jack?"

"Of course."

The Butcher took the big man's thick arm and led him away.

THE NEW ORLEANS TIMES-PICAYUNE
AUGUST 31, 1868

Jackson Simms Rorke, a reporter with the *Times-Picayune,* was found murdered in an alley off of Decatur Street in our city early this morning.

Police say Rorke was stabbed many times in the chest with a knife that was not found at the scene. There were no witnesses to the senseless crime, and police are conducting an intense investigation in the French Quarter. . . .

CHAPTER TEN

Fritz

T he week following the violent incident at the Box T was a tense one at Dos Culebras. Tyson was sure Flynn would try something immediately, since he possessed such an aggressive nature. However, the guards Mantooth posted over the cattle reported no trouble, and life went on as usual, except for Tyson becoming more anxious as each day passed.

One day Sam could stand Tyson's nervousness no longer. "You're driving yourself crazy over something that may not even happen, Carl."

"Oh, it'll happen."

"Maybe Flynn realized he bit off more than he could chew with you. Maybe he's given up."

Tyson, who was saddling his horse to ride out to the herd, as had become his daily custom, looked at Sam with patient, knowing eyes. "You don't know Flynn. He's up to something—we just have no way of knowing what it is."

Sam helped him cinch the saddle. "If that's true, then he's won half the battle. You're so tensed up, you're going to have a heart attack just from worrying."

Meanwhile, Johann had picked out a suitable area in which to build his own ranch. His first choice had been beautiful but impractical. Tyson had pointed out Johann's need for water availability and grazing, and with that in mind the prince finally found a spot two miles to the west of Tyson's house. The site chosen, he set about hiring some men from Fargo to begin construction.

On the following Saturday morning, Seth Moon and Remy were studying the Bible as they sat on thick oak stumps outside Moon's small cabin by the smokehouse. Stonewall the rooster strutted nearby, waiting for Remy to produce some dried corn. Moon was nervous as he prepared his sermon for the following day, and Remy could tell something was wrong by his serious and quiet nature.

"What's the matter, Seth?" Remy finally asked. "You're actin' funny."

Moon looked up from the book of Ephesians. "Am I?"

"Yeah. You're mumblin' to yourself."

Sighing and shaking his head, Moon said, "This is a big, scary thing I'm doing tomorrow. I don't know that there's ever been a half-breed stand up in church like this. I'm afraid."

"You? Afraid? I ain't *never* seen you afraid, Seth."

"Everyone gets scared sometimes."

"What are you scared of?"

"Well, people rejecting me, I guess. Nobody showing up, Reverend Smalley getting in trouble, my mind or lips freezing up—things like that."

Remy watched him for a moment. "Why don't you pray for God to help you not be scared?"

"I have."

"So why are you still scared? I thought you said that whatever we ask in God's name, he'll give us?"

Moon flashed his white teeth. "I did say that and it's true, but I'm just feeling a little short on faith today. It's *my* fault I'm still afraid, not his." He looked up to see Fritz walking from the bunkhouse to Hill House. Fritz was looking at them as he strode along, and Moon waved him over. Fritz waved back. Moon waved more expansively, and after Fritz checked over his shoulder to see if Moon was gesturing at someone behind him, he joined them with a curious look.

"Fritz, good morning."

"Hi, Fritz," Remy said.

Fritz nodded at them with a very small grin.

"Would you like to join us?" Moon asked, holding up his Bible. "We were preparing my sermon tomorrow."

After a pause, Fritz shook his head.

"Got somethin' else to do?" Remy asked, squinting up at him through the morning sun.

Fritz turned to Hill House, and looked back at Remy and nodded.

"That's all right," Moon said. "Can you come to church tomorrow? I'd really like you to be there. I'll need all the friends I can get."

Fritz studied Moon in the same unnerving fashion as at the dinner table. The dark eyes were blank as he pondered his answer. Finally, he made writing motions with his hands and pointed to a small school blackboard and chalk beside Moon. Moon used the board to take notes in his studies.

Uncertainly, Moon handed Fritz the blackboard. "I can't read German, Fritz."

Fritz ignored him and wrote on the board.

Remy watched, fascinated and breathless. Fritz was about to speak!

Fritz finished and showed them the board. In small, childlike English letters it read: *If it is good with my prince.*

"You can write English!" Moon breathed. "That's—that's—"

"Great!" Remy finished for him.

"Where—how did you learn, Fritz?" Moon asked, handing him a cloth to erase his earlier writing.

Fritz erased, then wrote, *My prince let me learn.* Moon nodded, and Fritz quickly erased that message and wrote, *Please not tell my princess. Prince asks it.*

"That's fine, Fritz," Moon answered, and asked Remy, "Do you understand, Remy?"

"Sure I do. I can read, Seth."

Moon didn't know why Sophia was kept in the dark concerning Fritz's knowledge, but he had a good idea. The concept that a common servant or bodyguard could read and write might be too much for a princess such as her to take.

Fritz handed the board, chalk, and cloth back to Moon, who said gratefully, "I'm glad you're coming, Fritz."

Fritz shook his head and looked sideways at him.

"I mean, I'm glad you *want* to come, if Prince Johann lets you."

Fritz nodded, gave a nearly imperceptible smile, and walked to Hill House.

Reverend Benjamin Smalley of the Baptist Church in Fargo, Texas, was a young, blonde man with high ideals and a slightly liberal view of the way things should be done around his church. He didn't stomp and rant and rave as was the way of his predecessor, J. Middleton Calder. J. Middleton had been known to scare women and small children with his devil-hating, hellfire-is-waiting-for-you-sinners frenzies. Chester Donovon had suffered a heart attack during one of these tirades but had lived to assure everyone that he'd been having strange chest pains for days and the attack had just happened to occur at that time. Chester had been known to tell a tall tale every once in a while, and no one believed him. When Chester died six months later of a massive stroke, the congregation of the First Baptist Church shook their heads and knew that the Reverend J. Middleton Calder had killed Chester, just as sure as if he'd shot him.

J. Middleton hadn't been able to understand why his flock suddenly treated him like a leper. There were no dinner invitations any more, a certain coldness in attitudes, and—heaven forbid—a few had actually been spotted at the Methodist church on the other side of town. This was too much for J. Middleton to take, so one Sunday he announced he was taking his pious self and his pious family on to Missouri. His pious work was done in Fargo. The congregation, like the good Baptist Texans they were, managed to avoid applauding when they heard this.

Enter Ben Smalley. He was a breath of fresh air to the people of the church with his ever-present smile and an ear that would always listen. The older men of the church even agreed that the young pup even knew a little bit about the Word of God and what makes men tick. And by golly, they said, wasn't his little wife, Ruth, just as cute as a newborn colt? The people took them into their homes, told them of their dreams and failures, and accepted them as their own, even though they *were* Yankees. It helped that they didn't talk funny, most people said.

The love affair between Ben and Ruth Smalley and the First Baptist congregation lasted until Ben up and did a strange thing: He asked a half-breed to preach a Sunday morning service. Not a special Tuesday or Thursday night service, where everyone could conveniently come up with an excuse not to attend; not even a Wednesday night, when most of the families had a hard time making it into town. No, Ben Smalley had made it a Sunday morning service, which put the congregation in a serious alibi-less position. Seth Moon was barely tolerated sitting in the same pews with them, much less preaching a sermon at them. What would they do?

As it turned out, most of the people had grown to trust Ben enough to grudgingly attend that Sunday morning, much to Seth Moon's dismay. Standing around the corner of the little church with Ben and Remy, Moon watched the wagons arrive one after the other and said, "I wasn't sure if *anyone* would show up." He clutched his Bible tightly in his strong brown hands.

"You'll do fine, Seth. These people aren't the lions of Rome, and you aren't being thrown to them. Just let the peace of the Lord help calm you." Ben squeezed Moon's shoulder. "Say, that must be the people from Dos Culebras. What sort of contraption is *that?*"

The ponderous royal carriage rolled toward them, and Moon strained to see who was inside. Although Katy, Sam, and Johann had promised to attend in addition to Fritz, Moon had prayed that nothing would happen to keep them from being there, such as a busted axle or an emergency on the ranch. He sighed with relief to see them all step out of the carriage, along with Boone and, surprisingly, Princess Sophia. Reverend Smalley greeted them, then left to welcome the other worshipers.

"I'm so glad you came," Moon told his friends. "And thank you, Highnesses."

"Our pleasure," Johann returned.

"Please come inside."

The church was roomier than it seemed from the outside. Eight rows of pews divided into two sides were almost full. All four large windows were open, but a hot mid-morning breeze had the ladies fanning and the men wiping the sweat from their faces with handkerchiefs. Every eye was on Moon as he went to the front row and sat down.

Reverend Smalley stepped up to the pulpit and announced, "Good morning! Thank you all for coming. I know that God will bless you for coming to his house to worship today." Ben smiled broadly at Moon after favoring the congregation with eye-to-eye contact. "Stand and turn in your hymnals with me to page 122, 'All Hail the Power of Jesus' Name'!"

The song service was halfhearted, with everyone frequently glancing to the back of Moon's ebony hair instead of the words in the hymnal. Katy, sitting with the rest of the party three rows behind Seth, saw the looks of distrust and wished fervently that she had sat beside Seth after he'd entered. But she hadn't wanted to cause a scene since everyone had been seated by the time he came in—or so she'd told herself. She knew the real reason was pride, and she willed her feet to move even now, but they were nailed to the floor. Glancing up at Sam beside her, she found he was looking at her strangely, as if reading her mind. She attempted a smile, but it fell flat.

Sam leaned down and whispered, "I'll go first if you want me to." Before she could answer, Sam moved out into the aisle and started forward.

Stunned, Katy woodenly followed him while her ears registered the sudden drop in the volume of the singing. Her face burned as she rounded the front pew and went to stand beside Seth, whose face reflected the shock that she felt at her own audacity. Stubbornly, she pushed the embarrassment to the back of her mind and continued singing. After a moment, Fritz, Remy, Boone, and Johann appeared and filed in front of them to stand on the other side of Sam. When she turned to smile at Seth, she found unabashed tears pooling in his eyes. But he was smiling with confidence.

After singing two more songs, Reverend Smalley told everyone to sit down, then introduced Seth without hesitating. "Ladies and gentlemen, today we have a special message in store for us. I've heard Seth Moon's testimony, and I was deeply moved as you shall be. The Lord has—"

"Preacher Smalley!" cried a big, burly man, who ponderously rose to his feet.

All eyes turned to him as Ben asked, "What is it, Brother Burns?"

Burns wiped his nose and chuckled. "Well, Preacher, I didn't really think you'd do it. I really didn't." He glanced around him and received a few nods of encouragement.

"What's that?" Ben asked, knowing what was coming.

"Why, put that half-breed up in front of a God-fearin' white congregation! They's a darkie church for him over at—"

"Brother Burns, do you believe the teachings of our Lord and

Savior Jesus Christ?" Smalley still held his genuine smile, looking as calm as if he'd just asked Burns if he had the time of day.

"'Course I do, Ben, but—"

"Do you believe that God's only Son would lie to us? Mislead us?"

Burns shifted his considerable weight to his other foot while his confident smile trickled down his face. "Why, no! No, he wouldn't do that, it's just—"

"Did he or did he not say 'Come unto me, all ye that labor and are heavy laden, and I will give you rest'? Did I read that wrong all those years ago?"

"No, he said that—"

"Did he *really* say 'Come unto me all ye *white people* that labor and are heavy laden, and I will give you rest'?" Smalley looked down at the Bible in his hands in confusion. "Did I get another one wrong? 'For God so loved the *white people* that he gave his only begotten Son, that any *white people* who believeth in him shall not perish, but have everlasting life'?"

"Now, wait a minute, Ben, that's not—"

"Did our Lord say, 'I am come that you *white people* should have life—'"

"All right, Ben, that's enough!" Burns roared and turned to an equally plump woman and three children sitting near him. "Come on, Edna. Let's go."

"Please stay, Brother Burns," Smalley pleaded. "I'm not picking on you; I'm talking to *all* of you who are against this man speaking today. If you don't want Seth Moon coming to your house, that's your business and your right. But this is *God's* house, and *he will turn no one away!* No one!"

Smalley's voice rose to a throaty bellow that he'd never imagined he'd possessed. A few of the congregation gasped openly as they feared they had another J. Middleton Calder on their hands. But J. Middleton's voice hadn't vibrated the rafters as the meek

Ben Smalley's did now as he continued, "You people appointed me your pastor, to lead you in God's will. I have never had the Lord speak to me so plainly as to tell me to *let this man speak!* Seth Moon has a message for one or more of us in this room and, God's will be done, he *will* speak!"

Katy stared in shock, just as did the rest of the congregation. Chills coursed through her, and she looked down at her arms to find goose pimples, despite the stifling heat of the building. She'd never heard a more powerful voice in her life.

Brother Burns, after finding himself rooted to his spot in awe, quickly sat down. The pew groaning under his weight was the only sound in the church. Even Ruth Smalley was gaping at her husband in astonishment.

Eerily, Ben's face returned to the normal Ben. Gone were the cherry-red face and the blazing blue eyes. The horrible pointing finger that seemed to single out every person in the room disappeared behind the pulpit. Ben looked at them calmly and said, "Brother Seth Moon will come forward now."

Moon snapped himself out of his own trance and stepped forward to shake Ben's hand before replacing him at the pulpit. His hands were shaking as he opened his Bible. He couldn't look at the congregation, and he chastised himself for not wiping his tear-stained and sweating face. He grasped both sides of the pulpit, head still down, and said, "Uh." But nothing else would come. He felt like he could stand before them for an hour saying "Uh," but he didn't think that was what the Lord wanted him to do. *The Lord,* he thought suddenly. Then he remembered the words of Ben Smalley outside the church. *Send me your peace, Lord. Calm me with your peace and speak through me.*

"Preach it, Seth," he heard whispered, and he glanced up for the first time. Remy was leaning toward him on the front row, his brown eyes shining. He jerked his head in the direction of the people behind him. "Tell 'em! Just like you tell me." Though Remy was whispering, the silence of the hall allowed his voice to carry. Moon saw the rest of the Dos Culebras row smile, then, amazingly, a few people behind them. Sam held up a clenched fist in front of his chest and nodded to him firmly. Fritz raised his massive head high, and though a smile touched his lips, his eyes said, "I am here as you asked. Let me hear you."

Seth Moon straightened his back to his full height and heard it crack. Taking out his handkerchief, he wiped his face and began looking every person in the eye as he said, "I have two stories to tell you. They are brief, for I am no speaker—I only say what's in my heart and leave the preaching to Brother Smalley."

The people Moon faced had ceased all movement. No fans stirred the air around the women, the men were grudgingly attentive, and even the children had stopped fidgeting. "The first is about a man named John Newton. He lived most of his life in the century past. He was a womanizer, a debaucher, a brawler, a slave trader in Africa, a murderer, and an infidel. He cursed a God he didn't believe in, he cursed men he both hated and liked, and most of all he cursed himself. He found himself despicable and unforgivable."

Moon let this settle over the congregation like a layer of soot. Some of the women covered their mouths in horror. The men glared at him for listing such terrible sins in front of their wives. Ben Smalley continued watching Moon with anticipation and expectancy. Katy smiled at him yet again, unfazed by his graphic descriptions. Sam and Fritz were granite faced and totally attentive.

Moon said, "Please take out your hymnals again and turn with me to page one. Join me as we sing." In a remarkably smooth baritone, Seth Moon began singing:

> *Amazing grace! how sweet the sound—*
> *That saved a wretch like me!*
> *I once was lost but now am found,*
> *Was blind but now I see.*

Moon could only hear himself, Ben, and Katy at first. Then, slowly, a few others joined in. Eventually the whole crowd was singing, though looking around in confusion as to why the sermon had been interrupted for another song service.

As the last notes died down, Moon closed the hymnal and smiled. "Thank you. 'How precious did that grace appear the hour I first believed.' Isn't that wonderful? No wonder that's the first hymn in the book." Grasping the sides of the pulpit, Moon realized that his palms were no longer slippery as before, and he wasn't holding the wood in a death grip to keep from shaking so badly. "That song was written by John Newton. The very same John Newton that seemed beyond redemption in his own eyes. He finally realized that the amazing grace of God could overcome any sin. Newton went on to become a pastor loved by his congregation, even preaching until he was eighty years old and quite deaf and almost blind. He wasn't considered a great preacher, but do you know what was said about him after his death? That he was more remarkable for his goodness than for his greatness. What a wonderful way to be remembered, and I think Newton himself would have appreciated that more than anyone."

Reverend Ben Smalley nodded and smiled. A woman behind him and to his left moved her head up and down once, and Moon felt a chill. *Maybe they're really listening!* With renewed confidence, he went on to tell of his own life and tie his story together with Newton. A horrible sinner with no point to his life, drifting from saloon to saloon, job to job, and ending up in an unimaginable destructive war against men, women, and children, he'd found God's grace one night.

"I couldn't believe that God could still love me and want me to be his after all I'd done. And I didn't even have to *do* anything to be saved except ask for it in faith, believing. 'For by grace are ye saved through faith; and that not of yourselves: it is the gift of God: not of works.'" Moon paused and scanned the faces in front of him.

Frown lines had disappeared and open interest had replaced them. His eyes landed on Fritz, who was staring at the floor between his feet, the only one not looking at Moon. *Have I lost him? Does he not understand?* With difficulty, he brought his attention back to the expectant crowd.

"So you see, we have nothing to lose and everything to gain: forgiveness, a relationship with the Almighty, and everlasting life. What more could you ask for?" Moon looked questioningly to Reverend Smalley, who gestured for him to continue and give the invitation. Moon felt himself beginning to panic; he hadn't planned on performing this important step. Breathing a silent prayer, he said, "Would you stand and sing 'What a Friend We Have in Jesus' with me? Anyone who wants what I've talked about, please come forward and accept Jesus as your Savior."

The congregation stood, and Moon felt foolish. *This is ridiculous! No one wants to respond to a half-breed. Who am I to give an invitation?* He held his Bible in one hand and tried his best to keep his eyes on the crowd, when all he wanted was for the song to be over so he could step down from the pulpit. Suddenly he thought, *Forgive me, Lord, for only thinking about myself at a time like this.* Bowing his head, he began to pray for the lost souls in the church. At the beginning of the third verse, he heard the singing falter noticeably but avoided looking up to see what was happening. After a moment, he felt a tug on his sleeve.

Fritz was standing in front of him, impossibly short, but Moon realized that he was still on the pulpit. In Fritz's eyes was a deep combination of fear, pain, and wonder. He held a piece of paper in his hand. Moon quickly stepped down and embraced him in pure joy. In Fritz's ear he whispered, "Thank you, Fritz. Thank you for your courage."

Fritz had tears in his eyes as he held out the paper to Moon, who took it and read, *I have done many bad things. I want to be forgiven for them and be saved by Jesus. Will you say the right words for me?*

Seth Moon wept openly over the words and embraced the solidly built man again. When he was able to speak, he told Fritz, "My friend, you are already saved—just by having these words in your heart. But kneel down here with me. I'll pray *with* you."

Through Seth Moon, Fritz was able to vocalize the words he longed to speak to his Maker.

And it was enough.

CHAPTER ELEVEN

A Fierce Thunder

Twenty miles from Dos Culebras, on the day after Fritz's conversion, the man called Carnicero became Jackson Simms Rorke. In Carnicero's mind, he didn't just *become* the man, he transformed himself *into* the man. Throughout Carnicero's career, he'd had to change his identity for certain cases many times. Each identity was different, with its own mind, idiosyncrasies, and personality. Sometimes he made them up, and other times he assumed the role of real people that had gotten in his way or become a convenient disguise. Such as the unfortunate Jack Rorke.

Carnicero knew four things about Rorke: He'd been large in stature, friendly, trusting, and inquisitive. All four had led to his death. He'd been too slow and ponderous to ward off Carnicero's sudden, vicious attack in the alley. His need to make conversation had led him to a killer. He'd shown no surprise or distrust while he was led down a dark, deserted alley. Most of all, his inquisitive nature had led him to the career choice of newspaper reporter that proved to be a convenient disguise to a desperate man.

So Jack Rorke had died due to his fateful choices in life.

Carnicero was a firm believer in fate and was beginning to see the close ties between fate and coincidence. Maybe he'd been wrong all these years concerning coincidence.

As he rode into the town of Fargo, Texas, on the bay gelding he'd purchased at the last stage layover, Carnicero smiled. Here was where his identity would become that of Rorke. Rorke had smoked cigars, so Carnicero would buy cigars and take up smoking. Rorke's hair had been trimmed short; Carnicero would trim his to the exact length. Rorke had had a mustache, and during the long trip Carnicero had grown one. He had no idea if anyone at Dos Culebras ever had met Rorke before. It was a big risk, but Carnicero had no choice. He frowned as he remembered the big man's bulk, but there was nothing to do about that.

After his haircut, Carnicero walked to the general store. The hot Texas wind tore at his new clothes, but he took no notice. Inside, he ordered cigars and asked the proprietor for directions to Dos Culebras. After he'd received them, he chatted with the man for twenty minutes. He was very friendly, trusting, and inquisitive.

Jackson Simms Rorke walked out of the general store, lit a cigar, mounted the bay, and turned northwest for Dos Culebras.

"So Fritz just—just—*walked* right up to the front and did it!" Sophia told Wilhelm in a breathless voice.

They were having a picnic along with Johann, Katy, and Sam beside the creek that flowed through the ranch. The Monday after Fritz's conversion found the princess no less shocked than the day before.

Wilhelm asked through a mouthful of roast turkey, "Did what?"

"You know," Sophia said, gesturing impatiently, "was saved, or whatever you call it. I was so embarrassed."

"Why were *you* embarrassed?" Sam asked her.

Sophia looked at him in exasperation. "Because he is one of our party! It was as if *all* of us went up there!"

"Maybe we should have," Johann observed quietly.

"Johann!"

To Katy, Johann said, "I was more surprised than anyone. I had no idea that Fritz was even *thinking* of such things. I mean, he is Catholic like the rest of us—why would he feel the need to do that?"

Katy didn't reply, choosing to let him work it out for himself.

Sophia looked at Wilhelm, her lower lip pursed in a pout. "And they just *left* me there all by myself while they changed seats!"

"You could have followed us," Sam said absently, as he watched Moon, Remy, and Fritz practice with their bows and arrows behind the house. Fritz had become quite good at the craft.

Wilhelm, unable to tear his eyes from Sophia's full lower lip, declared, "I wouldn't have left you alone."

"But you were not there. You and your silly accounting books are all you think about."

"No," he said quietly, "they are not *all* I think about."

"His face is different," Johann commented as he stared at the grass between them.

"Who?" Sophia asked.

"Fritz. He looks . . . different somehow."

"That's ridiculous, Johann. What is the matter with you today?"

Johann said nothing. A small cheer erupted from the archery competition, and they all looked to see Remy jumping up and down in front of the target, waving an arrow. Johann said, "He must have gotten a—what do you call it, Sam?"

"Bulls-eye."

"Yes, a bulls-eye. Why do they call it that?"

"I was afraid you were going to ask me that, and I don't have the answer."

"Why are you so quiet, Katherine?" Johann asked.

Katy looked at him quickly, then saw that everyone was waiting for her answer. "I don't know. Am I being quiet?"

"You have not said a word."

"Should we call the doctor?" Sam quipped.

Katy gave him a playful withering look. Truthfully, the feeling of dread simply would not leave her, despite the happiness she felt over Fritz. Something was coming. Something bad. Something that neither she nor Sam could stop.

"I want to walk, Wilhelm," Sophia announced.

"Of course." He dropped a bare drumstick, wiped his hands on a cloth napkin, and helped her to her feet.

After they'd gone, Katy, Sam, and Johann finished their lunch in silence until Katy said, "Sam, I've got this bad feeling."

"What's the matter?"

"Do you remember—well, of course you remember. A few days before the night of the tunnel—" she turned to Johann—"that's the night I told you about with the dynamite." Hesitating, she began to replace things in the picnic basket to busy her hands and decide if she wanted to go on.

"Katy, what is it?" Sam urged.

Suddenly slamming the lid of the basket down, Katy said, "For a few days before that, I felt strange. Like a black cloud was hanging over my head. Gloom and doom. That sort of thing." Again she hesitated.

Sam leaned toward her. "So?"

"I really hate to tell you, because it may be nothing at all. But I've been feeling that way for a few days now and . . ."

"And you think we're in for something bad."

"Oh, Sam, I don't know. I haven't wanted to say anything because I'd feel ridiculous if I got everyone all worked up and then nothing happened."

Sam frowned. "Why would you feel that way? When have I ever made you feel foolish for expressing your concerns?"

Frustration swept over Katy. Sam was right and she knew it, but she still felt like an overly emotional female. "I didn't say *you* made me feel that way!" she retorted, aware she sounded defensive and even more frustrated because of it. She stood abruptly. "Never mind, Sam. Just forget it, OK?" She spun and headed toward the creek, in the opposite direction of Sophia and Wilhelm.

"Katherine!" Johann called. Fixing Sam with a burning glare, he said, "She is scared, Sam. For some reason she wanted to tell *you* about it, though I cannot imagine why."

Sam returned his gaze steadily. "So why don't you go comfort her if you know her so well, *Prince Charming?*"

Johann bit back a retort, shook his head, and took off after her.

Just north of the picnic spot, on the other side of a small knoll, Wilhelm took Sophia's arm and stopped her. "We need to walk around that area. There may be snakes." He pointed to a hole in the ground a few feet from the creek that was about ten feet in circumference. "Billy Mantooth told me they like places like that near the water."

Sophia smiled gently, then walked straight to the hole, leaned over, and peered down inside. "Oh, *Schlange! Schlange,* are you there?"

"Sophia, stop it!"

"What are you afraid of, Wilhelm? A little snake?"

"They are big snakes in this country. Rattlesnakes that bite."

Turning to stand right in front of him, Sophia looked up and purred, "But you would protect me, no? From the big snakes?"

Wilhelm drank in her beauty with one long look and took her in his arms. He leaned forward to kiss her and, finding no resistance, did. As she'd done every time before, Sophia began to pull away after a few seconds. With great reluctance, he let her. "Why do you tease me, Sophia? You know how I feel about you."

With a small smile, she answered, "Yes, I know how you feel. I just do not know how *I* feel."

"I could make you so happy. You would never have to worry

about anything ever again. I know I'm not handsome and dashing and gallant like Sam, but I am *zuverlässig*—reliable. I would never leave you, no matter what."

Sophia looked away from his fervent proposal and began walking slowly. He followed her quietly. "I do not love you, Wilhelm. I am sorry."

"I don't care."

"But I *do*. Do you not see?"

"You would learn to love me."

Sophia stopped and turned to him. "But I do not *want* to learn to love! I want to be swept off my feet and charmed and romanced, like any other woman. I do not want a marriage of convenience—I could have had that in Austria."

Wilhelm hung his head. He was so tired of chasing a dream that seemed just out of his grasp.

"I must go back, Wilhelm. It is getting too hot." She passed by him, and when she didn't feel his presence behind her she turned back. He was standing in the same spot looking at the ground. "Wilhelm?"

With a short nod to himself, he went toward her with a determined step. His face was colder, more stony than usual. "Sophia, I apologize for making you feel uncomfortable. I'll not be asking for your hand again. That's a promise." He stopped beside her and offered her his arm. "Shall we go?"

Sophia took his arm and, with a strange feeling of loss, allowed him to lead her back to Hill House.

———※———

B. B. Easterling remembered to knock on Flynn's door before entering this time, though he was again bursting with good news. Oscar's predictable howl came right before Flynn's yell to enter.

Easterling entered, passed through the parlor, and found Flynn in his office behind his mahogony desk. Flynn removed his reading glasses and gingerly rubbed his eyes. His right eye still was not fully opened, and deep blue discoloring surrounded it. Easterling unconsciously touched the bruise on his own face.

"What is it, B. B.?"

"I think we got 'im, J. B."

"Who?"

"Tyson. Every mornin' he rides out alone to check on his herd. Before daybreak, even."

"Alone?" Flynn looked down at the papers scattered over his desk as he digested this.

"Yep. I saw him this mornin' myself. He just rides to the herd, gets off his horse, and . . . I think he talks to 'em."

Flynn looked up sharply. "Talks to them?" Realizing he was repeating back everything he heard like a parrot, he shook his head in irritation and asked the first thing that came to his mind. "About what?"

Easterling thought it was a silly question, but answered truthfully, "I don't know—couldn't hear 'im from where I sat."

"What about his boy, Boone? What does he do?"

"We ain't seen 'im. He must hide in the house all the time."

"Have any of you been spotted?"

"No, sir."

"You're sure?"

"I'm positive, J. B."

Flynn picked up a fool's-gold paperweight and watched the lamplight reflect from its many flat surfaces. The vision in his bruised eye was still blurry, and the light absorbed by that eye distorted the sharp rays of light into cloudy, disfigured prisms that only fueled his anger over the humiliation he'd suffered at the hands of Tyson and his son. "And Bronte," he whispered, running his thumb over the mineral rock.

"What was that, boss?"

"Nothing," Flynn said curtly, tossing the rock onto the desk. "The time has come, Easterling, to take what is rightfully mine. Here's what we're going to do. . . ."

That night Sam returned to Dos Culebras after a ride to the site of Johann's home being built. He'd watched the workers for a while, then pitched in and helped to raise the walls. His muscles were pleasantly tired from the unusual exercise, and he entered the bunkhouse with the intention of going right to bed.

The interior of the house was spartan. Two rows of cots lined the walls with a three-foot-wide space between them for walking. Over most of the beds were tacked worn, dog-eared pictures or drawings of loved ones. Browned newspaper clippings were in evidence also, speaking of birth or wedding announcements, personal feats, or heroes—events and people far from the lives of the cowboys of Dos Culebras but near to their hearts. Postcards, maps, and cattle-breeding charts were sprinkled amidst the disarray. The room smelled of stale smoke, unwashed bodies, worn leather, and coffee. The men talked, played cards, cursed, laughed, fought, sang, argued, and, those who could, read. They were lonely, yet strangely found comfort in the fact that the feeling was unanimous though never spoken. Most of them were barely in their twenties, but they were having the time of their young lives doing what most boys only read about in dime novels. They were comfortable with each other and took Sam and Fritz into their inner circle with no questions asked.

Sam nodded to them as he passed, careful not to let his eyes linger too long on what each man was doing at his bunk. The cowboys' cot and meager surroundings were the only part of the world they could call their own, and each man respected what little privacy was available.

When Sam and Fritz had come into their world, the cowboys had bestowed upon them an honor that neither man had recognized at the time: Their bunks were set up in a corner of the room with the slightest distance between theirs and the rest of the beds. Sam had thought the cowboys were making it a point to show the strangers that they were, and would remain, apart from the tribe of brethren. But one day Sam had mentioned the apparent snub to Seth Moon.

"They gave you two a corner?" Moon had asked with wide eyes.

"Gave? More like they stuck us there to keep from catching anything from us."

"No, no, Sam. That's quite an honor. Only the most experienced and best cowboys get the corners."

After that, Sam had treated the other men with renewed respect instead of returning the arrogance he'd felt he was receiving from them.

Fritz, propped up on his pillow against the wall, was reading his Bible. He smiled up at Sam as he threw his saddlebags on his bunk.

"Hello, Fritz. What are you reading?"

Fritz showed Sam the place he was reading.

"Matthew, huh? Chapter six? That's called the Sermon on the Mount."

Fritz nodded.

Sam sat down on his cot, pulled off his boots and socks, and massaged his toes. The low murmur of the cowboys was second nature to his hearing now, so he took no notice. He heard a scratching sound and looked up to see Fritz scrawling on paper with a stubby pencil.

You know the Bible?

Sam grinned. "Yes, I know a few things about it."

Are you a Christian, too?

Sam stared at the bold handwriting a moment. Fritz had been fishing with him and Remy that day when Sam hadn't denied being a Christian. Sam had thought that Fritz was listening that day and wondered if this was a test. Looking into Fritz's dark eyes he saw no duplicity, only interest. "I don't know," he said lamely.

Fritz studied him a moment, then wrote: *I pray you think more about it. It is important.*

Sam didn't answer, but asked, "What started you to thinking about it, Fritz? This seemed to happen sort of suddenly."

More scratching. *I had a hole in my heart with many bad things inside.* He watched Sam nod and wrote: *I did not know I could get rid of it until Seth told me how God removed his.*

"When did you and Seth talk about it?"

One day when he was teaching me the bow and arrow.

Sam propped his own pillow against the wall and unbuttoned his shirt. Slowly he asked, "And this hole . . . is it gone?"

Yes. No black anymore. Fritz smiled and shrugged his huge shoulders.

"That's good, Fritz. I'm happy for you," Sam said sincerely. Fritz kept his eyes on him, while Sam avoided his. One of the cowboys blew out all the lamps except the one between Sam and Fritz, making Sam feel as if everyone's eyes were upon him. The soft scratching came again.

Forgive me to ask. But do you have a black hole in your heart, Sam?

Sam sighed and shook his head. He was tired, and the last thing he'd wanted was to get into a discussion of the condition of his heart with another man, though Fritz meant well. In order to end the conversation for now and fend off any uncomfortable feelings inside himself, Sam stretched out his arms, cracked his knuckles, and said, "Fritz, my good man, there are a few ladies out there that would swear that I don't even *have* a heart."

Scratch, scratch, scratch. *I go deer hunting in morning. You come?*

"What time?"

Four.

Sam settled back and closed his eyes, more tired than he'd been in a long time. "You're on your own at four in the morning, Fritz. Try not to slam the door on your way out."

———◆———

At the grove of oak trees where Seth had told Fritz he might find deer grazing on acorns in the early morning, Fritz was surprised to find the whole herd of Dos Culebras. He'd never seen one thousand head of cattle before. In the gloom before dawn, he sensed rather than saw the closeness of so many animals. He could just make out white faces dotted among the sea of brown hide and restlessly shifting bodies.

Excited, he spurred to the nearest heavy-trunked oak tree and climbed up on the horse's back. Grasping a thick, low-hanging branch, he easily pulled himself onto the branch and tied the reins. Despite his bulk, Fritz nimbly scampered up the tree to the last branch that he could trust to hold his weight and looked out over the herd. All notions of hunting deer with his bow and arrow were forgotten for the moment.

Focusing his eyes on one spot in the middle of the herd, he began to detect swishing tails and a sensation of how small he was in the universe. To the massive Fritz, this was a thrill he'd never known. So much power in front of him!

A movement to his left away from the herd caught his attention, and he saw a shadowy rider approaching the cattle. The man was in no apparent hurry since the horse was held at a slow walk. Fritz couldn't imagine who else could be out this early, unless it was one of the guards that Tyson had assigned to watch over the stock. Maybe Sam had changed his mind about joining him, but it occurred to Fritz that he hadn't told Sam where he'd be.

The rider stopped near the herd, sat in the saddle and watched them for maybe a minute, and dismounted. As he walked toward the skittish cows, Fritz recognized the gait: Carl Tyson. What would he be doing out here so early in the morning? At the edge of the herd, he stopped and put his hands on his hips. Fritz could swear he heard the man murmuring to them.

Suddenly, the serene night exploded in sound and fire. Gunshots ripped through the air a half mile away, directly to the north of Tyson. Fritz saw the flicker of ignited powder from guns, then turned his attention back to the cattle in front of Tyson. He now saw that there were even more steers in the area than he'd thought when he saw their large backbones pop up from where they'd been lying down. As one, the herd nervously faced away from the incredible noise directly toward Tyson.

At once, Tyson sensed the danger and started for his horse at a run. As if that were the signal they were waiting for, the mass of beef surged right behind him. Fritz watched in horror as Tyson's horse didn't wait for him, but turned and ran before he could reach him.

Instantly Fritz clambered back down the tree, nearly fell twenty feet once, and finally jumped down on his horse with a grunt. The gunshots, which had ceased for a moment, erupted again, mixed with the new sound of fearful lowing from irritated steers. Fritz spotted Tyson running for all he was worth toward the oak trees. He was off to Fritz's left, and Fritz judged the angle of reaching Tyson before the cattle, which were now moving at a gallop—very close to breaking into a full run. Instead of running directly away from the herd, Tyson was veering toward safety at an angle that would cause the lower edge of the herd to gain on him even more. Without hesitation Fritz whipped the horse with the only thing available—the wooden shaft of an arrow—and urged him into a full run toward Tyson.

Tyson spotted him in the shadowy blue atmosphere of dawn and hesitated a moment when he thought Fritz was one of the gunmen. Then, sensing aid coming instead of harm, resumed his run. The cattle were gaining on him now, and Fritz saw with a sinking heart that Tyson wasn't going to make it.

Even if Fritz reached him.

Instead of stopping in futility and watching the man disappear under the brown mass, Fritz spurred even harder. The horse was beginning to falter when he saw where Fritz wanted him to go, but Fritz kept a firm hand on him and beat savagely with the arrow that had broken in half. *If* Fritz could reach Tyson, and *if* Tyson could time it perfectly to jump on behind him, and *if* the horse didn't fall down, they *might* have a chance. This was the only hope that Fritz could see.

The earth was rumbling and roaring as Fritz reached him. Tyson's eyes were wide open and staring as he struggled to draw enough breath to keep up with his run. As Fritz leaned over and offered his hand for Tyson to take, the terrified horse saw his chance as his burden shifted weight and bucked sideways, taking Fritz totally by surprise. He felt himself fly through the air and land flat on his back, the breath knocked solidly out of him. Instantly Tyson was over him, and Fritz saw him stare grimly at what must have been an awesome sight. Tyson drew his pistol and fired three shots in the air. The ground beneath Fritz was shaking so hard that he believed it was interfering with his ability to catch his breath.

Fritz made it to his hands and knees and looked up. A rolling line of fury was only seconds from them, and he watched as if from a dream as one, then two steers dropped down suddenly and disappeared beneath their fellows' hooves. Dimly Fritz became aware that Tyson had fired his last bullets and Fritz hadn't even heard them go off. The bullets had been as effective as trying to stop a train with a fly swatter. There was nothing else to do.

Stunned, Fritz thought in a brilliant, instantaneous flash that he was thankful that he'd seen the power of God work in his life before it was too late.

"Get down!" Tyson bellowed in his ear, and after pushing Fritz face down, fell flat himself. Both men clutched the ground and each other as they tried to make themselves as small as possible.

The world ripped in half in tumultuous, obscene thunder.

CHAPTER TWELVE

A Stranger and a Brother

T he double funeral was performed by Ben Smalley. To Katy it seemed that the whole town of Fargo turned out, and more.

As much as Katy longed to grieve for her friend Fritz, she was needed more by Remy. The boy had clung to her from the time Moon had broken the news to him, through the next day, and during the service. Katy was surprised since Remy seemed so close to Moon, but she wanted to help him in any way and moved into the main house to care for Remy and Boone as best she could.

Remy cried a lot, and when he wasn't crying, his face was so pained and forlorn, Katy knew he was crying inside. Carl Tyson had no brothers or sisters, nothing but distant cousins that he hadn't seen in decades. A few ladies from the church offered to take Remy for a few days, but he'd refused. He found comfort from Katy's giving presence and gentle touch. She would hold him at night before his bedtime, sometimes for an hour or more, speaking softly to him or praying for him. Then Katy would go downstairs and fall on her knees in a dead man's office and pray for the boys he had left behind and for wisdom from God in dealing with those boys. She would weep, and through her tears she would thank a merciful God that Fritz had made a decision for him in his last days.

Without knowing it, Fritz had given Katy a priceless gift.

Through her sorrow, she was able to rejoice that Fritz was in the arms of God. That comfort allowed her to concentrate more on Remy and Boone and her prayers for them.

Carl was buried beside his wife, mother, and father in a small but growing cemetery on Dos Culebras. At Boone's request, Johann had agreed that it would be appropriate for Fritz to be buried there also. There had been no eyewitnesses to the deaths, because the man who'd been assigned to watch the herd that night had fallen asleep, awoken to the sound of voices, and promptly had been bashed in the head. No one knew how Fritz had come to be with Tyson on his lonely morning trek, but Sam and Moon let it be known what they suspected: that Fritz had died trying to save Tyson. Boone accepted this as the truth and was as upset over Fritz's death as his own father's.

On the short ride back to the ranch in the prince's carriage, Remy fell asleep in Katy's lap, his eyes red and swollen from crying. Sam, sitting beside Katy, watched her run her fingers through his fine brown hair and said quietly, "Kid's really taken to you."

Katy, who'd been absently staring out the window, nodded and smiled dully but said nothing.

Sam looked out the window at Boone and Billy Mantooth riding beside the carriage on their horses. Boone's profile reminded Sam of the day of his beating at Flynn's hands, and Sam could easily recall Carl to mind by the stormy look on Boone's face. "Boone's not taking this too well. I'm afraid he'll try for Flynn."

"What do you mean?"

"Look at him. He's so angry right now he's ready to spit, and you know what's on his mind."

"Sam, you have to stop him."

"What can I do? He's a full half owner of Dos Culebras, and like it or not, he's got a lot of weight to throw around now. Or at least he feels that way."

Johann, Sophia, and Wilhelm sat in front of them, with Johann's head half turned as he listened. He'd been hit particularly hard by Fritz's death, more so than Sam and Katy would have thought. He'd left Katy alone in the house, not even coming by to check on her, and Sam had told her that Johann had barely left his room until the funeral. His face was tired, with dark circles beneath his eyes.

Sam leaned forward. "What do you think we should do about Boone, Johann?"

He didn't answer for a moment as he seemed to be staring at the boy, too. In a low, listless voice he answered, "He is a man now. What *is* there to do?"

"He's a boy suddenly shoved into a man's position. That doesn't make him a man."

Johann faced all the way around, and his face had taken on the life of sudden anger. "You are so smart about everyone, Sam—*you* do something about it."

Feeling Remy stir at the harsh voice, Katy whispered, "Johann, what's the matter with you? Sam's just trying to help."

"Who is he to help? He did not help Fritz!"

Katy looked at Sam in shock.

Sam was watching Johann with slitted eyes. "Now, hold on, partner—"

"Johann, Sam had nothing to do with Fritz's death!"

"You should have been with him!" Johann exclaimed, glaring. "You have said he asked you to go—why did you not?"

Remy stirred and sat up in his seat. Incensed, Katy said, "Sam feels as bad about this as anyone, maybe worse. You have no right to attack him!"

Johann sat forward quickly, the tight set of his shoulders revealing the strain of holding in anger.

Sophia spoke for the first time, so low that only Johann and Wilhelm could hear, "I want to go home."

"What?" Johann said sharply. "That is out of the question!"

"Why?"

"Because we are *here,* Sophia! We made the decision to come here, and here we will stay!"

"We did not make the decision, our father did! Now the war is over and Austria is defeated—why not go home?"

Johann considered his sister closely. "You were more excited than anyone about coming here. What happened?"

Sophia looked down at her hands in her lap. "Fritz is gone—killed by this cruel land that has no laws. Are we next? Will we die here too? I do not want to die here!"

Wilhelm couldn't stand to see her pain and placed his hands over hers. "You are just upset because of the funeral, darling. We are not going to die here."

When the carriage reached the main house, they saw a man sitting on the front porch rocker, whittling a chunk of wood. Boone and Mantooth saw him first and spurred ahead.

"Good afternoon, gentlemen," the man greeted in a Southern drawl, tipping his hat with a smile that revealed perfect white teeth.

"You're on my property, mister," Boone barked. "Uninvited."

"Please, allow me to introduce myself. My name is Jackson Rorke, and you were supposed to have received a letter concerning my arrival."

"Rorke?" Boone wondered out loud as the carriage stopped behind him. Turning to the passengers, he asked, "Anybody know anything about a fella called Rorke?"

"Yes," Johann called as he helped Katy down. "I have been waiting for you, Mr. Rorke."

"Ah, this must be the prince himself!" Rorke crowed as he rushed down the porch steps to shake Johann's hand. "Jackson Rorke, Highness, and it's an *honor* to meet you."

"Mr. Rorke, my sister, Princess Sophia."

"Princess, your beauty is even more than I'd heard or imagined."

"Thank you. You are a . . . reporter?"

"Yes, ma'am. With the *New Orleans Times-Picayune.*"

Johann introduced Rorke to everyone, saving Boone for last. He was still on his horse, glaring down at the stranger. "Sorta made yourself at home, didn't you?"

Rorke shrugged and raised his eyebrows. "I found no one home, so I waited on the porch. I assure you I didn't invade your home, Mr. Tyson." He looked around at their formal clothes. "Did I miss a formal picnic or social function?"

Actually, Carnicero knew exactly where they'd been.

For three days he'd been on Dos Culebras. He heard the commotion of the stampede on his first night; the rumbling roar was headed straight for where he was sleeping when the herd was stopped by the ranch cowboys. He quickly saddled his horse and rode away, staying close to the outskirts of the ranch. He spotted a group of horsemen riding to the north, away from the carnage. Through his spyglass he saw the bodies being brought back to the main house, where mourning began. He sneaked up to a window of the bunkhouse that night and heard cursings and promises of revenge toward a man named Flynn. Spying though windows of Hill House, he got his first glimpse of the prince and princess. And he watched the woman named Katy comfort the boy, then cry out her own grief to the walls of an office, while the stuffed heads of various animals watched in mute sympathy.

Carnicero knew every one of the people on the ranch—he'd observed how each of them had dealt with pain, and all the while he'd done his best to understand why death affected people so much. He himself had never cried over anyone's death, and he was left baffled as to why people did.

Now he looked at the solemn, uncomfortable faces and smiled inwardly.

Sam cleared his throat in the silence. "There's been a funeral. A double funeral as a matter of fact."

Carnicero's face fell as he scanned each face in disbelief. "I'm— I'm so sorry, I didn't . . . who were they?"

Sam told him.

"That's terrible! My timing is awful!"

Johann said, "Nonsense, you had no way of knowing about it."

"If you'd like to postpone our story, Your Highness . . ." Rorke was taking a chance in saying this and inwardly pleaded that he hadn't miscalculated.

Johann shook his head. "No, you have come a long way, I know. We traveled here from New Orleans ourselves and know the difficulty."

"Thank you, Prince Johann," Carnicero said humbly and half bowed to his intended future victim.

Boone told the group, "Me and Billy are goin' over to Briscoe to see the marshal. We'll be back late tonight or tomorrow."

"Wait a minute, Boone," Sam said, stepping forward. "We've already talked about this. There isn't any evidence that Flynn did this."

"Enough, Sam. We're goin'. Remy, you be good for Miss Katy while I'm gone."

Sam shrugged and looked at Johann, who said nothing. After Boone and Billy had ridden off, Sam said to Katy, "I guess it could be worse. He could be heading straight for Flynn's with guns blazing."

Katy's smile was more like a wince. "How do you know he isn't?"

"That's true. You think I should follow them?"

"Who is Flynn?" Rorke asked innocently.

"He is—" Johann started, but Sam cut him off with a curt gesture.

"Johann, Mr. Rorke's a reporter. When you talk to him, or in front of him, it's the same as talking to the *Times-Picayune*. I don't think we want Carl's troubles all over that paper, do you?"

Johann looked at Rorke as if he were a new species of bug. "No, we would not want that."

"I assure you, gentlemen, I'm able to keep confidentialities." *So, Sam's a lot sharper than I'd given him credit for. And he seems to value Katy's advice for some reason. Interesting.*

"At this point, Mr. Rorke, with all due respect," Sam said with a smile, "this is really none of your business if your only reason for being here is to interview the prince and princess. You understand, don't you?"

"Of course, Mr. Bronte." Carnicero was burning to ask what Sam and Katy's business was in this, but that was something he'd been unable to find out through his eavesdropping. He glanced around. "Do you have any idea where I'm to stay? I need to see to my horse."

Grimly, Sam said, "There's an extra bed in the bunkhouse by mine. You could sleep there."

"That would be fine. Please excuse me."

"Let me help you," Sam offered.

"No, thank you, Mr. Bronte—"

"No, I insist. And it's Sam."

Carnicero sensed that the situation was not going as planned, and the fault was Bronte's. He wanted to detach himself from initial contact with these people and examine his next move. He also didn't want Sam to see the assortment of weapons in one of his saddlebags. However, this would be a good time to find out exactly what Sam Bronte was doing on Dos Culebras. With effort, he smiled and said, "Of course. Please call me Jack, all of you."

Katy watched them get Rorke's horse and head to the stable. Sam was acting strangely. She'd never seen him so helpful to a man before—only women. Sighing, she thought about her spooked feelings of the days before and searched for them again. Nothing was inside her but sadness. At least she wouldn't have to wait for the coming fury any longer—what could be worse than losing two good friends in what seemed like a planned murder? Looking down at Remy she said, "Let's go inside and get you something to eat. You haven't eaten since last night."

"I'm not hungry. I wanted to go with Boone, but he left so fast I didn't have time to ask him."

"You don't need to go where your brother's going right now. You need to rest."

"I've *been* resting. I want to find out who killed my father and Fritz!"

"That's enough, Remy," Katy said more forcefully than she'd intended. "That's nothing for an eight-year-old boy to be thinking about."

"Nine."

"What?"

"Today's my birthday."

———※———

"So, you're an actor?" Carnicero asked, as he followed Sam to the bunkhouse.

"If you have to classify me as something, I guess you could say that."

Carnicero, a little behind and to the left of Sam, took in the tall, muscular frame. Sam stood a head taller, and Carnicero knew that the strong physique, coupled with the easy confidence and graceful, coiled way that he carried himself, bespoke more than an actor. Carnicero would have to keep his eye on Sam Bronte.

The bunkhouse wasn't what Carnicero had been hoping for; in the best of worlds, his own bedroom would have been ideal, so that he could slip in and out without detection. That was now going to be impossible. Sam pointed him to his cot, which had a Bible lying on the pillow. "What's this?" he asked, after throwing his saddlebags and valise on the bed and picking up the book.

"That's a Bible."

Carnicero chuckled. "I *know* that. I mean what's it doing here?"

"It was the previous owner's." Sam sat down on his own bunk and watched Rorke. He had the sudden impulse to tear the Bible out of his hands but pushed it away.

"Where is this man now?" Carnicero asked as he flipped through the pages.

"He's one of the ones we buried today." Sam hadn't wanted to tell him that for fear that Rorke wouldn't want to sleep in the same bunk as a dead man, but suddenly he wasn't sure he wanted Rorke sleeping beside him.

"I'm sorry to hear that," Carnicero commented with hardly a pause. "Are you sure you don't want to tell me about all of this?"

"I'm sure."

Carnicero looked at Sam for a moment, put down the Bible, and asked, "Have I done something to offend you, Sam?"

"Tell me about yourself, Jack. Where are you from?"

"I'm from New Orleans, born and raised in Mobile. Why?"

"What did you do before you were a reporter?"

Carnicero sat down on his bunk. The men's knees were almost touching. "I've always been a reporter. Speaking of which, aren't I supposed to be asking the questions here?" Their faces were only a foot apart. The sunlight through the small window nearby reflected in Sam's eyes, turning them the color of slate.

"Where did you go to school?" Sam asked.

"Why are you here, Sam?"

"When did you start working for the *Times-Picayune?*"

"What is your connection with the prince and princess?"

"What did you do during the war?"

"What did *you* do during the war?"

Sam paused. Carnicero kept smiling, but he could tell it looked forced. Sam seemed to be studying him, then he leaned back, a smile lifting his lips. "I guess reporters don't like questions any more than regular citizens, huh?"

"If they're asked politely."

"Touché."

"Why do you distrust me, Sam? You don't even know me."

"Exactly."

Carnicero raised his eyebrows, delighted. "Touché."

Sam smiled.

"Are you—a bodyguard?"

"Not officially. I just watch out for my friends."

"So you consider the prince and princess your friends."

"Of course."

Carnicero reached for his inside coat pocket and found his wrist in Sam's iron grip. He hadn't seen the hand coming and was shocked at Sam's reflexes. Forcing himself to wince in pain, Carnicero whined, "Owww! What's the matter with you?"

Sam opened the coat to find three cigars poking above the pocket and released Carnicero's wrist. "Sorry."

"This isn't amusing anymore. Did you think I had a *gun?"*

Sam shrugged. "Never can tell."

"You're not telling me something, Sam. You're more than you say you are. One second your hand is on your knee, the next it's squeezing mine numb. That's more like the reflexes of a gunman than an actor. Maybe I should be interviewing *you."*

Sam laughed as he stood. "Not a chance, Jack. I've got to go—you'll find the royal party in the house on the hill." He started to turn, then faced Rorke again as if just remembering something. "Say, you wouldn't have a recent copy of the *Times-Picayune,* would you? I haven't seen a paper in weeks."

Carnicero smiled and reached into his valise, producing a wrinkled newspaper. "Of course I do, Sam. Enjoy yourself."

"I will."

Carnicero watched him go. He'd planned on some sort of security around the prince, but in his mind's eye he'd seen an unthinking gorilla or two—not a wild card like Sam that seemed to see right through him. Carnicero's ability to adjust his plans to every unforeseen threat during a task was what had made his talent so demanding the world over.

Carnicero sat on his bunk for thirty minutes, calmly making adjustments.

———— ❧ ————

That night, Katy arranged for Anna, Sophia's servant and cook, to prepare supper in the main house in honor of Remy's birthday. Katy made a cake with Anna's help, but neither the cake nor the singing of "Happy Birthday" could bring a smile to the boy's face. He excused himself early, and Katy took him to his room to say his prayers with him.

When she came back downstairs, Johann, Sophia, Wilhelm, and Rorke were in the parlor, where the first interview was being conducted. Katy searched for Sam and found him in the office, sitting in a leather wingback chair, a newspaper hanging limply over his knee, staring into space.

"Hi, Sam. Can I come in?" she asked at the door.

Sam looked up quickly in surprise and half stood. "Of course."

Sitting in a matching chair opposite him with the bear rug sprawled between them, Katy was glad the bear was facing away from her toward the desk across the room. It was so lifelike, she had the uncomfortable feeling it would suddenly rise at any moment and turn its massive teeth on her. Childish fears, but there it was.

Katy looked at Sam, who was staring at a spot somewhere over her head. When he felt her eyes on him and met her gaze, she asked, "Why are you so quiet tonight? You didn't say a word at dinner, and now I find you staring at walls in deep thought." Katy tried to keep her voice light, but her concern showed through even to her own ears.

Sam kept his eyes on her a moment, then held up the paper. "Our friend Rorke happened to have a copy of the *Times-Picayune*. Do you remember Mark Twain? The fellow that wrote that tall tale about the jumping frog?"

"Of course! That was right after the war, in 1865. 'Jim Smiley and His Jumping Frog' was the name of it. They ran it over and over in the California papers, since that was where it was set. I *loved* that story."

Sam nodded and looked down at the paper but said nothing.

"What is it, Sam? What about Twain?"

"It's not Twain, it's . . ." Dreamily, Sam put his finger on an article and let it rest there.

Katy was getting more concerned by the second. She'd never seen him so confused and disoriented. "Sam, what's wrong?"

Shaking his head as if to clear his mind, Sam said, "Just let me read this to you: 'Mark Twain, fresh on the heels of his new book release, *Innocents Abroad,* was in our town recently to talk about his next project. "It takes place on a riverboat," he told this reporter, "a paddlewheel riverboat on the Mississippi. I wanted to ride the river on one, and this young fellow named James Bronte was kind enough to let me hitch a ride on his boat, the *Dixie Darling.* Smart boy, that Obie—don't tell him I called him that. He hates his first name—Obadiah—but I couldn't resist setting a fire under him every once in a while."'" Sam placed the newspaper across his knee calmly and looked at Katy.

Katy didn't know what to say. She knew about Sam's horrible childhood and that he hadn't seen his little brother since he left home. Now, to have his name appear in a newspaper that Sam had gotten by chance, with Mark Twain himself speaking about him as if they were the oldest of friends was a shock to her—she couldn't imagine how Sam had felt when he'd seen it. She suddenly understood why he'd seemed so distant. "Why, Sam, that's wonderful news! Isn't it?"

Sam continued staring at her.

"Isn't it, Sam? Your little brother has his own *paddleboat!* What a success! Aren't you excited?"

"I really don't know how I feel right now."

"Why? You didn't even know if he was alive or dead, and now you find Mark Twain talking about him in a major newspaper! *Mark Twain,* Sam!"

Folding the paper carefully, Sam said, "I don't want to talk about it."

Katy was dumbfounded. She wanted to scream at him, but she stopped herself. Instead of being excited, Sam was near depression. She watched him set the paper on the small walnut table beside the chair and fold his hands across his stomach. He wouldn't meet her eyes. Though her curiosity was burning inside her, Katy said, "Maybe later, how would that be? You can come to me anytime."

Sam nodded slowly.

Katy leaned back in her chair. "I don't mind waiting. I think we have other concerns right now."

His gaze met hers. "We do?"

"Yes. I've got an odd feeling about our guest, Mr. Rorke. I can't explain it exactly, but there's something about him . . . something that makes me uncomfortable."

Sam nodded again. "I know what you mean. I noticed a few disturbing things about him myself."

She leaned forward eagerly. "Such as?"

As if on cue, the clear laughter of the man in question rang through the hall from the parlor, and Katy felt a sudden resentment against him. Laughter shouldn't be heard in the house of the man they'd just buried that day.

Sam saw Katy's reaction and jerked his thumb in the door's direction. "Like that, for instance. Most men would tend to be more respectful. And when he found out he'd be sleeping in Fritz's bunk, he didn't bat an eye. As a matter of fact, he seemed fascinated by it. He's either got a reporter's morbid curiosity, or death simply doesn't bother him."

"Maybe it *is* just the reporter in him."

"That's not all. His accent's wrong sometimes. I can't explain since it's so subtle, but it's just *wrong*." Sam had kept questioning Rorke in the bunkhouse because he'd wanted to hear him talk. He'd realized early on that Rorke's accent was inconsistent—an inflection here, the disappearance of it on certain words there—*something*. He'd spent many days and nights in New Orleans during his riverboat-gambler days, and he'd had the opportunity to hear and study the native cadence. He didn't think he was hearing that from Rorke.

"Did you notice him at dinner?" Katy asked.

Sam smiled. "He began by eating his steak with his fork in his left hand—"

"—then all of a sudden he switched to his right."

He nodded. "Right. Now think about it, how do *you* eat a steak? Just like everyone else who's right-handed. You take your fork in your left hand, knife in right, cut your meat, switch the fork to your right and spear it."

Katy leaned forward, resting her elbows on her knees. "If I'm American I do that. But the European way is to eat with your left hand, no matter which hand is dominant. Rorke did that two times before he switched."

"Exactly. And we know he's right handed."

She frowned. "How do we know that?"

"Go in there and look." Sam pointed to the door with his chin. "He's got his notepad out, and he's writing with his right hand."

"So, what we have is a man whose accent isn't quite right, who can't seem to decide if he's American or European, and who seems oddly unaffected by the news of someone's untimely death."

Sam nodded slowly. "All of which may mean nothing, or it may mean our Mr. Rorke isn't who he says he is. And if that's the case, then why is he here?"

Katy's gaze met his. "There could be a couple of reasons. He could be working with Flynn. Or he might be after something else."

"The royals," Sam said. With a thoughtful nod, he quoted, "'To have what we would have, we speak not what we mean.'"

Katy rolled her eyes. "I'm supposed to understand that, I guess."

Sam looked at the door, then rose to shut it quietly. Going to Katy, he knelt on one knee beside her and rested his arm on the arm of the chair. "I have a plan."

CHAPTER THIRTEEN

Fury's Challenge

T hat little pipsqueak!" J. B. Flynn raged, as he stalked across his porch. "Sending a federal marshal to question me! A federal marshal!"

Easterling watched the small puff of dust in the distance that was Marshal Floyd Destry. Involuntarily, he shuddered. Destry had had the meanest eyes Easterling had ever seen, and he didn't mind turning them on a man with starburst intensity. Somehow, Easterling had managed to look in those eyes and tell the lies that Flynn expected of him. Somehow.

"Well," Flynn glowered, "I guess that boy's not going to roll over and play dead now that his father's gone. I didn't think he had any fight left in him, but I was wrong."

"So what are we gonna do?"

Flynn stopped pacing and stood inches from Easterling, who took a half step back. "You say there's another boy on that ranch?"

"Yeah."

"How old is he?"

Easterling scratched his cheek while he thought, and this gave him a chance to take another half step back. Flynn's eyes were disturbingly reminiscent of Destry's in their intensity. "I don't know—ten, maybe. Why?"

Flynn spotted a speck of lint on Easterling's shirt and reached

175

for it. Easterling flinched. Surprised, Flynn asked, "What's the matter, B. B.?" Smiling now, Flynn picked off the lint between thumb and forefinger and flicked it away.

"You—uh—ain't gonna hurt that kid, are you, J. B.?"

"Did I say anything about touching a hair on his head?"

The constant wind gusts moaned around the corner of the house as if in sympathy for Easterling's fear. "I don't wanna hurt no kid."

Flynn's calm face grew ugly again. "You'll do what I tell you to do, or I'll have some information for Marshal Destry concerning a buried body on this ranch. Do you understand me? Have you forgotten its previous owner?"

Face burning, tired of being scared and suddenly prodded into a corner, Easterling glared back at his boss. "You said that wouldn't be mentioned ever again. You said that."

"I lied."

"Besides, J. B., I did that for you. You *paid* me for that, remember? If I go down, you go down."

"I don't think so," Flynn chuckled softly.

"What do you mean?" Easterling asked suspiciously, hating Flynn's eerie mood changes when he was angry.

"What *proof* do you have, B. B.? Are you going to look into Destry's eyes and say, 'Flynn told me to!'? Somehow I don't see the stern Marshal Destry taking that as the gospel truth, do you?" Flynn turned and started into the house, ordering over his shoulder, "Come with me."

Easterling followed him into the study and watched as he wrote something on a note.

"This should start the wheels in motion to get Mr. Boone Tyson out of our hair. Have someone take this to him." After handing Easterling the note, Flynn bent over the desk and scribbled another one. "And this one . . . well, this one will put Dos Culebras in my hands."

Easterling had never learned to read, and he held up the note he'd been handed. "What's it say?"

In a good mood again, Flynn smiled and told him what they *both* said.

Katy stood at the sink, washing her and Remy's breakfast dishes. The hot suds felt good on her hands. She took her time and did the job thoroughly while thinking of the future.

She and Johann had barely spoken since his strange outburst on the way back from the funeral. He'd been withdrawn and distant at dinner the night before, not even meeting her eyes. Some sort of change had come over him. Their last intimate conversation, when Sam had snapped at both her and Johann at the picnic, had been calm and polite—more like friends than a romantic couple. Something was bothering Johann; something that was larger and more important than any feelings he had for Katy.

"Katherine?"

Startled, she turned to find Johann standing outside the screen door. "Johann! Come in. I was just washing up."

"I did not mean to scare you," he apologized, as he stepped inside. "I knocked on the front door, but you must not have heard."

"No, I didn't. Sit down." Katy dried her hands quickly on a towel and sat opposite him at the table. He was dressed as casually as she'd seen him, but she spotted grime and hay on his clothes. "Don't tell me you've been mucking out the stables!"

Johann looked down at his clothes and his face flushed. "Yes, actually. I was passing by them, saw Seth inside, and pitched in. He was more surprised than you, I think. I must admit it felt good to do some manual labor after months of doing nothing."

He laced his large, strong hands together in front of him, but Katy saw some angry blisters before he'd closed his hands. "Oh, my, you've got blisters. Better get something on that."

"No, it is all right—"

"There's some salve right here in the cabinet, so keep your seat," she ordered as she retrieved the medicine. Wetting the towel she'd used, she sat back down and gently washed off his hands. "Don't you know about this wonderful invention called gloves?"

"Yes, but I did not think I would need any and . . ."

"And look what happened." Katy removed the cap from the salve jar and began applying the silky smooth ointment.

"Katherine . . . I need to talk with you. About us."

Keeping her eyes on her work, Katy said, "Mmmm?" noncommitally.

"First of all, I am sorry for my behavior yesterday in the carriage. It was rude, but I was just feeling . . . feeling . . . oh, I don't know what I was feeling. Besides being upset about Fritz, maybe I was upset about us, too."

"Why is that, Johann?" Wishing she could keep coating his palms with the ointment so as not to look in his eyes, she reluctantly stopped when he had more than enough on the sores. She replaced the cap and looked up.

"Please try to understand, darling. When we first kissed, I could not stop thinking about you. You are so beautiful to me, and so *alive!*"

Katy blushed. "I'm not beautiful, Johann—"

"Stop saying that!" he said, almost harshly. "I do not want to hear you say that to me again, Katherine." His face softened. "I am sorry—I do not mean to order you around like a servant, but you put yourself down too much. One of these days you will come to love yourself more. I do not know why it is so hard for you."

Katy let this pass, met his blue eyes, and asked what she already knew. "You're going back to Austria, aren't you?"

"How did you know?"

"I didn't. But now I do," she smiled sadly.

Johann started to take her hands in his, remembered the ointment, then grasped one of her hands anyway. They smiled at each other. "You will not come with me, will you?"

"How did *you* know?"

"Because I know you. Whether you know it or not, you are so strong, Katherine. Even when we are together I get the feeling that you are separate from me somehow. That you have your love for God, and that is all the love you need or want to give right now."

Slightly stunned, Katy realized that he had put into words her exact feelings. Throughout their courtship, short as it was, she'd found herself feeling guilty for not loving him, or thinking about him all the time, even though she cared for him deeply.

Johann watched her thinking furiously and said soothingly, "There is nothing wrong with that, Katherine. I thought there was for a while, but there is not. And as for me—" he stopped and shrugged his broad shoulders. "I want a woman to need me as much as I need her. Do you understand?"

"I understand perfectly, Johann," Katy said softly, squeezing his hand and feeling the sticky ointment.

"There is a lucky man out there somewhere, Katherine. He does not know how lucky he is right now. One day you will want to share your life with him, and together the two of you will be happy with each other and with serving God together."

"Thank you. I think it goes without saying that you'll make some woman very happy." Katy's face turned serious. "Do you understand that I'm not the princess type? And that I probably never will be?"

"I have to disagree with that, my dear. You *are* the princess type. You just do not *choose* to be."

Katy kissed him softly on the cheek.

They talked for a few minutes more, then Johann left to clean up. Not feeling clean herself, Katy decided to leave the dishes until she changed clothes. As she left the kitchen and turned toward the stairs, she ran right into Jack Rorke.

"Oh! Mr. Rorke!"

"I'm so sorry, Miss Steele. I knocked, but apparently you didn't hear." He had his hat in hand as if he'd just removed it, and he wore a tan suit with string tie. His hair was slicked down flat on his head, and Katy could smell perfumed hair lotion.

In one swift, clarifying moment, Katy knew he hadn't knocked. She hadn't heard Johann's rapping because she'd been banging dishes in the sink. For that past twenty minutes she'd been quietly talking with Johann, and she was sure Rorke's knocking would have been heard. Also, when she'd rounded the corner of the door jamb, Rorke had just been *standing* there, not walking toward the kitchen. She had the feeling he'd been standing there for more than a few seconds, too. How long? Had he been eavesdropping on her and Johann to add to his story?

Realizing that Rorke was waiting for a response, Katy hid her suspicions and said cheerfully, "What can I do for you, Mr. Rorke?"

"Well, first off you can call me Jack. Secondly, I'm trying to piece together everyone's role at Dos Culebras, and I'd appreciate it if you'd answer a few questions for me."

"Where's Sam?"

"Sam? I don't know."

"I'm having lunch with him. Why don't you join us? That way you can kill two birds with one stone."

Rorke smiled. "Of course. That will be fine."

Katy watched him go, with Sam's cautious warning in her ears. Rorke was neither handsome nor ugly, but extremely pleasant looking, and his charm added to his presence so much that he was almost irresistible. She could detect no mistakes in his accent, but she hadn't been around Southerners nearly as much as Sam had. She looked forward to finding out about the real Jack Rorke at lunch.

Halfway up the stairs to the guest room she'd been using, Boone appeared at the top of the stairs. He'd gotten in late the night before from his visit with the marshal. His suspenders were hanging from his waist and his shirttail was out. Caught by surprise, he quickly spun around the corner of the landing.

"I'm sorry, Boone," she called, turning around to face the other way even though she couldn't see him. She didn't know who was more embarrassed, him or her.

"My fault," he returned. "I'm not used to having a woman around the house." His voice became clearer as he stepped to the top of the landing again. "I was coming down to talk to you, Katy. Do you have a minute?"

"Um—can I turn around now?"

"Oh, yes—sorry."

Katy went up the stairs as she said, "My popularity today is overwhelming."

"Huh?"

"Never mind. What did you want to talk about?"

Not meeting her eyes, Boone shifted his feet. "I—uh—thought . . ." Suddenly he looked down at his hands as they fingered his hat. "I don't know how to say this."

Katy waited patiently.

"I think it would be better—more fittin'—if you were to stay in Hill House now that I'm back. Not that I don't appreciate what you've done for Remy, it's just—uh—"

"I understand, Boone. I was thinking the same thing this morning. Doesn't look too good for propriety's sake, does it?"

"Yeah, and besides that it don't look decent, if you know what I mean. Not to say that anyone would dare think bad thoughts about you, Katy, don't get me wrong."

Katy covered her smile. "Consider it done."

Relieved, Boone put on his hat and nodded. "I'm glad you understand. I'll tell Remy about it later."

Katy noticed that his face was tired and drawn, and she could almost see the bitterness inside him taking its toll.

Boone said, "Well, I'll be goin' to work now."

"Listen—if you ever need to talk . . ."

"Uh—yes, ma'am. Thank you kindly."

He was obviously anxious to get away, and Katy let him go. Sadly, she didn't think he would take advantage of her offer.

———✦———

Katy went ahead and served lunch in the main house, since she'd already made plans for that. Her few things were packed and ready to move back to Hill House afterward. Thankfully, she hadn't seen Remy and needed to explain her departure. That was Boone's job.

Sam and Rorke chatted while she prepared roast beef sandwiches on freshly baked bread. For someone who held a great amount of distrust, Sam was getting along fine with Rorke. They talked of New Orleans: the haughty women, the heat in August, and the French Quarter.

Katy asked, "Jack, would you like pickled okra with your sandwich?"

Rorke wrinkled his nose. "No, thank you."

"A Southern boy who doesn't like pickled okra? I've never heard of that before."

"Just never developed a taste for them."

Katy set three plates on the table and sat down. Rorke immediately picked up his sandwich and started to take a bite.

"Ahem!" came from Sam's throat.

Rorke looked up.

"If you're going to eat with Katy, Jack, you're going to wait for the blessing."

"Oh. I'm sorry, Katy."

"It's all right." They bowed their heads and Katy said a blessing. This time, Rorke waited until both Sam and Katy began eating in case there were more formalities. "So," he began after taking a bite, "what *is* the story on you two?"

Sam opened his mouth to answer, but Katy was quicker. "Why is our story so important, anyway? You're here to interview the prince and princess. Why would your readers be interested in us?"

"Flavor, my dear Katy. Flavor. In my opinion, it makes or breaks a newspaper story."

"Flavor," Sam repeated, rolling it off his tongue. "So we're just background scenery, Katy. Sorry."

"No, no," Rorke protested, "I look at it like this: All are pieces of a puzzle. If one piece is missing, the puzzle is incomplete."

Katy shrugged, then they told their story while they ate. Rorke pulled out his notepad and furiously took notes—right handed—and was still trying to grab a bite every once in a while, long after Sam and Katy were finished eating. He asked few questions since they complemented each other well in the telling.

When they were finished, Rorke sat back and examined his four pages of notes. "Very impressive! I could do a story on the both of you that would probably be more interesting than the royal siblings."

"No, thank you," Sam grunted.

"Publicity shy, are you?"

"I prefer to keep a low profile."

"An actor? That's a first!"

"I'm not in a play here, Jack. These people's lives could be in danger with that idiot Flynn still around."

"What do you plan to do about him?" Rorke finished off his sandwich in one huge bite.

Katy pursed her lips. She wasn't willing to give their plans away to anyone, especially not a man neither she nor Sam trusted. She and Sam had agreed they would try to get to a few of Flynn's men and question them alone. With any luck, one of them would have a grudge against Flynn. Money might be just the thing to loosen lips. If that failed, they would simply wait for Flynn to make a mistake.

"We haven't really decided yet," she answered.

Rorke finished chewing and shook his head. "Imagine the *timing* it took to pull off a murderous stampede! He had to have been watching Carl for days to know where he'd be at exactly what time. Then, to get the herd to go in the direction you wanted it to go . . . amazing."

"Isn't it?" Sam countered, watching Rorke carefully.

Katy asked, "Are you from New Orleans originally, Jack?"

"No, I was born in Mobile, then moved to New Orleans when I was eighteen."

"What year was that?"

"1853."

Katy spoke up, shocked. "Good heavens, that was during the tuberculosis outbreak!"

A slight pause. "Yes. Terrible thing."

"I should say so. Five thousand people died."

"What did you do during the war?" Sam asked, settling back in his chair and stretching his long legs under the table.

"Stayed in New Orleans. I'm *not* a soldier."

"That surprises me. You seem unusually fit for someone that doesn't . . ."

"Doesn't do anything, Sam?" Rorke laughed. "I have a small piece of land where I grow cotton and beans. I like to tend my own crops a few days a week."

"You must have been worried sick about your family when Grant took Mobile Bay."

"I—um—" Rorke paused and looked at the ceiling, as if searching his feelings and memories. Katy thought he was also thinking furiously. "It was a difficult time. Say, I've got a meeting with the princess, so I'd better get up to Hill House. It's been enjoyable, Katy, and thanks so much for the lunch and information."

After he'd gone, Katy and Sam looked at each other without speaking. Then, as if on mutual agreement, smiles slowly spread over their faces.

———◆———

Boone grabbed the handle to the black iron skillet on the stove and yelped, "Owww!"

"That's hot, Boone," Remy informed him.

"I know that! Thank you very much!" Dousing his hand in a pail of water in the sink, Boone grimaced as the coolness closed over his stinging hand.

Remy sat at the table, dressed in his favorite blue pullover shirt and long underwear pants. He hadn't even bothered getting dressed. "I still don't understand why you sent Katy away," he said accusingly.

"And you're not *gonna* understand, either. Just take my word for it, it's the best thing."

"For who? You?"

Boone brought his hand out of the water and examined the angry red welt across his palm. "For everyone."

"Not me. I *liked* having her here."

Boone whirled. "She's not your mother, so don't be actin' like she is!"

"OK, Boone! Sakes 'live, why are you so mean ever since . . ."

Boone saw Remy's eyes lower to the table top. "I ain't been mean to you, Remy—"

"When you've been around, you have." Remy raised his gaze to somewhere behind Boone. "Your taters are burnin'."

Boone whirled back around, remembering too late that he'd left the skillet on the stove after he'd burned his hand. Getting a towel this time, he removed the skillet and quickly scraped out the brown and blackened potatoes. "I don't believe this!" he muttered.

"Who told you you could cook?"

185

"I'm tryin', ain't I?" Boone roared. "Why'd Seth pick today to go on an overnight hunting trip?"

Defiantly, Remy said, "How was he to know you were gonna kick Katy out?"

"It's not like I kicked her out with nowhere to go, Remy."

"You kick her out, you kick out the cook, too."

Boone faced his little brother with a dangerous glint in his eyes. "Would you like to do this?"

"Might do a better job," Remy said under his breath.

"What?"

"Nothin'."

Boone scraped some of the potatoes onto Remy's plate beside thick slices of burned bacon. Setting it down in front of Remy, he paused and dared the boy to say anything else, which he didn't. Going to fix his own plate, though he wasn't the least bit hungry, he said, "I been workin' all day, Remy. I've got a lot on my mind, too, so just have a little patience, will you?"

Remy made no move to begin eating.

Boone sat down across from him and speared a potato with his fork. "Eat, Remy."

"I ain't hungry."

"You haven't eaten hardly at all since . . . since day before yesterday."

"Still ain't hungry."

"What are you poutin' about now?"

"I ain't poutin'!"

"Your lower lip's in your plate—I'd call that poutin'."

Remy looked up at him, and Boone was shocked to see tears in his eyes. "What are we gonna do, Boone?"

"What do you mean?"

"Without Pa. Who's gonna run the ranch and buy and sell cattle and see that things get done?"

"I am, 'course. Who'd you think?"

"Billy."

Boone carefully laid down his fork and laced his fingers together under his chin. "Billy don't own this ranch. I do."

"*We* do!"

The front door slammed, and Billy Mantooth rushed into the kitchen. "Boone, there's something—"

"Hold on, Billy! Me and Remy's talkin'."

"But Boone—"

"I said hold on!" Boone shouted, and he saw Remy give a startled jump out of the corner of his eye. Willing himself to speak calmly, Boone said, "Now. I'm runnin' Dos Culebras, and every-thing's gonna be all right, you understand? We ain't gonna starve, and we ain't gonna lose this here ranch. Not to nobody!"

Remy began to cry. "You can't do it, Boone. You don't know nothin' about runnin' a ranch, 'cause you've always been playin' around! You used to not care about Dos Culebras, and now it's the only thing you care about. More than me, even."

Boone felt his anger rising. "That's not true, Remy—"

Suddenly, Remy rose to his feet and swept his plate off the table; they all watched as it shattered against the wall in a shower of china shards. "You ain't *never* gonna be able to run this ranch like Pa!"

Boone moved with lightning speed. The *crack!* of his palm against Remy's face was more shocking than the splintering crash of the plate. Remy was rocked back a step, and he stared at his brother through tears, pain, and horror.

Mantooth stood frozen in the doorway, stunned at the sudden outbreak of fury.

Still in a half crouch over his chair, Boone blinked at Remy in surprise, as if Remy were the one who had done something un-thinkable.

Remy bolted for the stairs, still holding a hand over his stinging cheek.

"Remy!" Boone called, but Remy's steps didn't hesitate. "Remy,

I'm sorry—!" Both men listened as the small boots pounded all the way up the stairs and to Remy's room. The door slammed like a shot from a rifle.

Boone's legs gave out, and he sat down in his chair heavily. Rubbing his face, he asked Mantooth, "What did you want, Billy?" He looked up to see Mantooth with a dark expression. "Don't look at me like that, Billy! It just . . . happened!"

Mantooth stared at Boone for a moment, then nodded, once. "Thought you should see this." He handed Boone a note. "One of Flynn's boys brought it and rode off without a word."

Boone unfolded the crumpled paper and read: *Meet me at the fork of the Concho and Black Rivers on the edge of our properties at midnight. We'll settle this thing once and for all. Flynn.*

Boone's face flushed and his lips all but disappeared in a flat line. With trembling hands, he wadded up the paper and threw it in the mess that was Remy's dinner. "Get five men saddled up."

"Only five?"

"Yeah. But quietly. I don't want that nosy Sam trying to stop us or followin' along."

"What about Remy?"

Boone's face softened for an instant, then grew hard again. "You stay with him. I'll make things right when I get back."

CHAPTER FOURTEEN

Ominous Messages

Princess Sophia watched as Wilhelm strummed on a banjo in the parlor of Hill House. His face was in half shadow, since he'd doused the oil lamps and lit two large candles on the mantel over the fireplace to his right. Sophia stood at the base of the stairs she'd just come down after hearing the soft but tangy notes from the strings. It was close to midnight, and Johann and Katy had retired to their rooms.

Wilhelm was seated on the edge of the Belter sofa, his tan shirt and pants blending perfectly with the dark green and brown upholstery. In a rare show of ease, his sleeves were rolled up to his elbows and his Hessian boots had been removed and placed neatly to the side. Sophia could count on one hand the times she'd seen Wilhelm so casual. Almost always he was immaculately dressed, and despite his stocky body shape, his clothes invariably fit him well. They were never too snug or loose, and they somehow remained unwrinkled even through the most severe weather, such as the Texas heat.

Frowning with concentration, Wilhelm stared at the mahogany footstool a few feet in front of him. Sophia had never known him to be attracted to a musical instrument. His fingers clumsily but patiently searched the glowing silver strings for the chords that sounded pleasing to him.

Since his last proposal, he'd kept his promise about not asking her again. In fact, he'd gone so far as to avoid touching her. Never was he impolite, because it was not in him, but he'd been distant and aloof. Sophia wished she could blame his actions, or nonactions, on Fritz's death. Wilhelm was definitely disturbed by it, but he'd shown his newfound remoteness in the two days before Fritz had died. He didn't seek Sophia out to spend time with her or talk to her at meals other than polite conversation. Most of the time he'd spent with Johann and Rorke, or in his room, or on sole excursions around the ranch.

Watching him now, Sophia realized just how much she'd missed his presence.

Moving into the parlor she asked in German, "A new hobby, Wilhelm?"

Startled, Wilhelm placed a hand over the strings to stifle the last chord and started to stand.

"Please, Wilhelm," Sophia laughed, still speaking their native language, "do not get up. I am the one intruding here."

Smiling uncertainly, Wilhelm sat down. "Why are we speaking German?"

"I do not know," she shrugged, moving to the mantel. "Do you not miss it sometimes?"

"Yes, I guess I do, now that you mention it."

Sophia ran her fingernail down the side of one of the candles, creating a tiny furrow in the white wax. "Remember when we were young, and I would follow you and Johann around everywhere? You would try to get rid of me, but I would always find you. And the time I stole the candies from *Herr* Schlicter's shop, and you took the blame for me—he took you in the back room. What did he do? You have never said."

Wilhelm stared at her and smiled sadly, but said nothing.

"Even today you will not tell me." She sat down beside him on the sofa. "When we grew older, you were jealous of every beau I had, yet you would listen to me talk about them or hold me when I cried over them. Then you would cheer me up by steering my mind to something else, like chess. You always let me win."

"That's not true—you're a wonderful player."

"And you are a poor liar," Sophia said, smiling. Gently she took the banjo from his hands and placed it on the floor. Taking his hands in both of hers, she moved closer to him and gazed at him. The candlelight behind her reflected as twin sentinels in each of his dark eyes. He watched her in confusion. "I have missed you the last few days. You are the only man that has ever loved me as I am, with all my faults. Ask me again."

"Ask you what?"

"You know."

Wilhelm continued looking at her, his confusion replaced with surprise. "You want me to—?"

Sophia nodded.

"I can't do that, Sophia."

"What? Why not?"

"Because it's not what you want. And I'm not sure it's what I want anymore."

Sophia was thunderstruck. She'd pictured his reaction to be a celebration of fulfilling his lifelong dream. Stunned into silence, she could only stare at him with wide eyes.

"You've already told me the sort of man you wanted. One who is dashing, full of romance, and who will sweep you off your feet. I accepted that on the day you told me—accepted it fully. I meant what I said about not asking you again."

Releasing his hands, practically throwing them back in his lap, Sophia whispered, "You toy with me. I feel like such a fool."

"*I* toy with *you?*" he asked incredulously. In a kind voice, he tried to make her understand. "I have always been there for you when you want comfort, or a friend, or a loving touch. Then when you've had your fill, you push me away like a dog. I'm not putting you down, I would never do that—that's just the way you are, and I find that independence appealing. But please, don't accuse *me* of toying with *you.*"

Sophia acted as if she hadn't heard a word he'd said. Standing, she pointed a finger at him and warned, "You stay away from me, Wilhelm!"

He didn't bother telling her that that had been his intention for days now.

"And—and—" Bursting into tears, Sophia ran from the room.

Wilhelm listened to her quick steps up the stairs, then calmly reached down for the banjo.

A feeling of extreme urgency knotted every nerve in Boone's body. "It's gotta be one o'clock by now—gotta be."

Jasper Lewis stood away from the pacing Boone with the four other cowboys. A three-quarter moon's light glowed on the barrels of the rifles they were holding. They were restless and unsure about being there. Jasper agreed, "You may be right by now. I know it's a far piece after midnight anyways."

Boone forced himself to stop pacing and think calmly—something he hadn't done before riding to the rendevous. *We get out here, and nobody has a watch,* he thought bitterly, shaking his head. His youth and inexperience weighed down on him like an anvil. The adrenaline in his blood had been charging hard as they rode to the river fork, making his hair stand on end and his fingers tingle. Then they'd taken the best defensive position available on the banks of the Concho and kept a sharp watch in every direction.

No one had come. Boone had been ready for the fight of his life, and now he knew nobody *would* show up, either.

Jasper's twangy voice cut through Boone's thoughts: "Why would Flynn fool us like this? Why would he get us away from the ranch and out here for nothin'?"

Boone's head whipped around, and Jasper took a step back, afraid he'd crossed some line. "That's it, Jasper!" Boone nearly shouted. "Away from the ranch. Come on!"

Before Jasper and the other men were mounted, Boone had spurred his horse into a blistering run toward Dos Culebras, an hour away.

Billy Mantooth came awake the instant before the black-gloved hand closed over his mouth. His sleepy, surprised squawk was cut short, and Mantooth saw a dark-clad figure on each side of the bed. The man on his right was the one that clamped his hand over Mantooth's mouth, and before the one on the left moved, Mantooth sent his left fist sideways directly into his stomach. The man's breath left him with a satisfying "Uuuhhh," and he stepped back on wobbly legs.

An instant later, Mantooth heard a dull thud, and his chest exploded with pain. Then another, and another. The one on his right had the fists of a sledgehammer, and he managed to keep his hand over Mantooth's mouth as he pummeled him with his free one. The pain was excruciating, as Mantooth felt his strength and resistance fade away.

The fourth hammerblow hit his stomach directly under his ribcage. Suddenly, his limbs were totally paralyzed, and his thoughts drifted to the helpless boy in the next room. Then his thoughts drifted farther away into a shadowy, still darkness.

Katy wrestled with the covers of her bed, sighed deeply, and turned on her back to stare at the ceiling. Sleep would not come.

She thought she was on the very edge of drifting off when she heard the pounding of footsteps on the stairs. Instantly her feet were over the side and on the floor, but she heard a sob that had to have been Sophia, so she had fallen backward on the bed in frustration. She tried to find the hazy dream state she'd been in, but she couldn't get comfortable, and she couldn't stop her mind from wandering.

The main problem that was bothering her was the same one that she'd battled after the Central Pacific case, but with a different location: What would she do after her work was done at Dos Culebras? She and Sam had been there for almost two months, and already the prince was talking about going back to Austria. Would Wilhelm and Sophia follow? It really didn't matter to Katy, since they were being paid no matter what, but it was the definite ending to another job that left the future as uncertain as before. What would she do?

Every morning and night Katy would read her Bible, pray, and ask for guidance from God concerning this and everything else in her life. So far, there'd been no clear answer.

Lighting the lamp beside her bed, she picked up her Bible through squinted, light-sensitive eyes. Her bookmark was planted close to the center of Isaiah. Throughout the first thirty-nine chapters, the prophet had been full of scathing denunciations of Israel and the surrounding nations, calling on them to repent of their sins. Now, as she looked at chapter forty, she was relieved to find the first sentence gave promise of Isaiah moving on to a different vein: "Comfort ye, comfort ye my people, saith your God." *Just what I needed to hear,* Katy thought, and settled herself back into her pillows to read more.

The last verse in the chapter read: "But they that wait upon the Lord shall renew their strength; they shall mount up with wings as eagles; they shall run, and not be weary; and they shall walk, and not faint." Eagerly now, feeling her spirits lifting by the moment, she read on and came to 41:10: "Fear thou not; for I am with thee: be not dismayed; for I am thy God: I will strengthen thee; yea, I will help thee; yea, I will uphold thee with the right hand of my righteousness."

Katy slowly closed her Bible and stared at the ceiling again. Finally she began to pray a prayer of thankfulness. She didn't ask for anything or request guidance; she merely thanked God for taking care of her and loving her far more than she could understand. He was always there, if she would only look for him.

After a while she heard a door squeak, but this time it was at the other end of the hall from Sophia's room: Johann. He was trying to cushion his steps, but she could hear the pounding of his heavy boots. Jumping out of bed, she put on her cotton shawl and opened her door a few inches. Johann was just passing by, and he stopped in alarm.

"I am sorry, Katherine, did I wake you?"

"I was already awake. Seems nobody's sleeping tonight." Katy noticed he was fully dressed, even with a suit jacket, as if he were going out into the cool night air. "What are you doing, Johann?"

He looked away from her eyes, and Katy saw confusion and worry. "I cannot sleep. I have to go . . ."

"Where? At this time of night?"

Shaking his head, he started for the stairs mumbling, "Never mind. You would not . . . never mind."

"Johann, wait!" Hurriedly, she dressed in what was readily available: a black riding skirt and tan blouse. Barefoot, she stepped back out into the hall, but Johann was gone. *What's wrong with him?* Instantly she ran back in her room, pulled on her boots, and went downstairs. Johann was just coming out of the kitchen, heading for the front door. "Wait a minute! What's going on?"

Johann stopped and turned to her with the same strangely confused look that now held a hint of grimness. Katy wondered if he was sleepwalking. He put a finger to his lips for a moment, then said, "I have something to do. I am all right."

195

"You don't seem all right." She went to him and grasped his elbows. "Please tell me."

He hesitated, then said, "You will not understand, but I am going to Fritz's grave."

Katy did her best not to show alarm and nodded as if it were the most natural thing in the world to go to a dead friend's grave in the middle of the night.

"I have to. I . . . cannot . . ." Johann shook his head as if trying to arrange jumbled thoughts inside. "I have to go."

Katy heard the trembling in his voice and *was* alarmed when she saw his eyes filming over with tears. With iron control, she avoided questioning him further and declared, "I'm going with you."

"Katherine, no—"

"Yes," she said with force. "And I'm waking up Sam. He's going, too."

Johann threw his hands in the air. "What for?"

"Do you remember *why* Fritz is in that grave? He was trying to save Carl. Do you remember why Carl was in danger? There's no proof, but we all know Flynn had something to do with it to get this ranch. That leaves you—you're the only thing left in his way. Flynn's probably *praying* you'll leave here alone, without protection. So, I'm waking Sam."

Katy didn't wait for any more argument but opened the door herself and headed for the bunkhouse. She didn't dare turn around to see if Johann was following, she just hoped he was. The night was cool, and she wished she'd thought to put on a jacket herself, but it was too late now. If she went back in the house, Johann might change his mind, saddle up, and leave without her. A corner of her sensible mind wanted to tell her how ridiculous this was, but she closed the door on the matter-of-fact voice.

Katy reached the bunkhouse, and only then did she balk at entering a roomful of sleeping men. Hesitating, she turned to find Johann passing behind her in his dazed state. "I will start saddling the horses," he muttered. Katy nodded and walked into the house as if she belonged there.

Thunderous snores greeted her. She noted with brief amusement that the cacophony was nearly harmonious. Sufficient moonlight streamed through the windows for her to make her way to Sam's bunk. She was thankful that Sam had taken the time to let her peep inside one day as they were passing by and show her which bunk was his. The matter-of-fact voice piped up again: *What if he's switched cots with someone?* If that's happened, she would wake them *all* up if she had to.

"Sam?" she whispered over the still form. "Sam?" With extreme reluctance she reached down and gently prodded the moonlit shoulder under the thin blanket. "Sam?"

An arm whipped around in a blink, and Katy barely got her own out of the way before it was dealt a crushing blow. Sam's head appeared in the light as he half sat up, his long, dark hair a mess. "What . . . ? *Katy?*"

"Shhhh!"

"What are you doing sneaking around here? It's a good way to get hammered," he warned in a whisper, as he glanced around in confusion.

Katy looked over at Rorke's bunk, but it was in complete darkness, and her eyes hadn't adjusted enough to see if he was awake. No one else had stirred. "Get dressed and come with me. Johann's . . ." She didn't know how to say it.

Sam pushed his hair out of his face and asked in irritation, "Johann's *what?*"

Leaning closer, she brought her voice even lower: "Johann wants to go to Fritz's grave. We're going with him."

Sam shook his head as if to clear it. "What? Fritz's grave! Are you crazy?"

"Shhh! You'll wake up Rorke!"

"Good!" he whispered, but in an almost inaudible voice. "Then I won't be the only one you're inflicting this misery on!"

"I'll explain outside." Katy tiptoed out so he could get dressed.

When Sam emerged, carefully shutting the door, he turned to Katy accusingly. "This better be important."

"It is—come on." She took his arm and started for the stable, then stopped. "Did you . . . ?" She let her question trail off, but nodded back to the bunkhouse with definite intent.

Sam knew what she was talking about immediately. "Yeah. 'What's done cannot be undone.'"

***

Carnicero watched Sam's shadowy figure go out the door. *Did these people think he was deaf? They might as well have been shouting.* He turned over to face the wall and smiled. *Is visiting a grave in the middle of the night some sort of strange American custom that I don't know about?*

Carnicero reflected that his time here was almost done. He'd asked the prince and princess everything imaginable about their lives and had almost run out of questions. There was no reason to stay at Dos Culebras much longer. Besides, a fat money packet awaited him in Prussia. It would be interesting to take a vacation in Austria just to see if *Regimentschef* Dietrich Freissner could pull off his lofty plans.

Carnicero thought Freissner might do it. And if he could, there could be more money in it. Freissner wouldn't want The Butcher to tell what he knew to certain individuals in the Prussian government, would he?

The future looked bright and profitable. Smiling, Carnicero went back to sleep.

***

Coming into sight of the ranch houses, Boone held up a hand to halt the men. "We walk the rest of the way in. I don't wanna ride into any surprises, and I don't wanna wake anyone up. I don't feel like answering questions right now."

They began walking at Boone's pace, but before long he was practically jogging, causing groaning and mutterings among the cowboys. Jasper put a stop to it after a while. "Shut yer yaps and keep yer ears open!" The men didn't dare tell him that they couldn't hear anything but the thud of hooves, jingle of harnesses, and creaking of equipment.

Boone heard the admonishment but kept silent. His mind was relieved after seeing that the ranch wasn't on fire or that a shootout wasn't taking place. However, a dark snake of dread was coiled around his stomach. What *would* he find?

They tied their horses outside the smokehouse to the cooking spit bar and crept around to the front of the house. Inside, Boone waved the men to spread out and search the downstairs and took Jasper with him upstairs. Boone longed to call Remy's name, but held back.

Boone didn't bother waving Jasper to the left; that was Carl's bedroom, and no one would be in there. They walked quietly toward Remy's room, but froze when they drew even with Boone's.

Billy Mantooth was tied to the bed with his mouth gagged. His eyes were large over the gag and filled with pain and discomfort. Jasper rushed to him, but Boone ran for Remy's room, burst through the closed door, and found the bed empty. Beside the bed was one small slipper, stark in its singleness.

Frantically he looked around and in the closet, but no Remy. *I'll kill him!* he thought murderously. *Even if Remy's alive, I'll kill him!* Turning to the door, he was stopped by the sight of a note pinned to Remy's pillow. The paper blended perfectly with the color of the pillowcase, so he'd almost missed it. He strode to the bed and snatched it up.

Bring the deed to Dos Culebras to my office. Make sure you're alone. We'll make a trade.

Mantooth was sitting on the edge of the bed, rubbing his stomach with one hand and his head with the other. Jasper was trying to inspect the side of Mantooth's head, but Mantooth refused. Both men looked up when they sensed Boone standing at the door.

"I'm so sorry, Boone," Mantooth said, his eyes filled with a new pain. "It's all my fault—I fell asleep, and they got the jump on me. Jasper, will you quit playing with my head and help me up? We gotta ride *now!*" Jasper did as he was told, and Mantooth threw another pleading look at Boone. "Can you forgive me, Boone?"

"I can if you can break a speed record riding to Fargo. Marshal Destry's there for tonight before he goes to Abilene in the morning."

"You want me to bring him back here, so we can charge Flynn's place?"

"Nope. I want you to bring him straight to the Box T."

"Well—what are *you* gonna do?" Mantooth didn't like Boone's posture or the look in his eyes. He'd seen the look before. It was one of a man with a mission who didn't care who or what got in his way. "Boone, you ain't gonna do anything crazy, are you? You got all these men that don't want anything but to get that boy back."

Boone didn't answer.

"You hear me? We done lost your pa—we don't wanna lose you and Remy both."

Boone handed him the note and turned for the door. "If I catch anybody followin' me, I'll shoot first. I'm goin' alone—to make me a fair trade."

———◦◦◦———

Carnicero sensed the disturbance before it happened.

One minute he was asleep, and the next he woke to the familiar snoring. Then someone rushed in and began kicking cowboys.

"Get up, boys. Come on—get up!"

Apparently the waker had a tough shell that curses and insults couldn't penetrate, though the sleepy men tried their best.

Carnicero sat up and put his feet on the floor. He had no intention of punching cattle, but he was curious. "What is it?" he asked the kicker.

"Nothing to concern you, Mr. Rorke, just go on back to sleep." He continued rousting cowboys.

Carnicero wondered how often this happened—people wandering around in the middle of the night. He started to insist on an answer from the man, but since he wasn't sure if this nocturnal activity was normal for a ranch, he kept silent. Grabbing his pocket watch, he saw by the dim light that it was three o'clock. He yawned hugely.

The cowboys were remarkably fast at getting dressed and out the door, and soon Carnicero was by himself in the suddenly deafening silence. He shuffled over to the side window and saw a beehive of phantomlike activity in and around the stable. The absence of knowledge about his surroundings irritated Carnicero more than anything. He *had* to know.

At his bunk, he slipped on a dark blue shirt and, since he'd slept in his pants, pulled the suspenders over his shoulders. By touch he searched quickly in his bag for socks, pulled them on, then his boots. He put his hands on his knees to stand, then stopped abruptly.

One of the boots didn't feel right.

Sighing heavily, he removed his left boot and felt around inside, producing a hastily folded and wadded piece of paper. Carnicero unfolded it and leaned toward Sam's bed for light to read by.

Carnicero's heart skipped a beat painfully, then began to pound a churning staccato rhythm. Sweat sprang from every pore at once. He read it again and felt his chest becoming unbelievably tight and heavy, then realized that he'd stopped breathing. Taking a deep, ragged breath, he unconsciously murmured in Spanish, "This can't be!" He had the sensation that a thousand eyes were staring at him and glanced around frantically to see who was watching—but there was nothing but the still room and empty, dark windows.

Breathing hard, staring at the note in his shaking hand but not seeing it, Carnicero felt sick. He sat there for a full minute, blood roaring in his ears and eyes glazed over with a strange, stunned concentration that caused a seemingly catatonic state. When his eyes focused, he read the note yet again, hoping stupidly that he'd been dreaming. But he wasn't.

I KNOW WHO YOU ARE.

It was impossible. Unthinkable. But most of all, shattering.

Who? One of the cowboys? Sam? Johann? Why leave a note? How did they know? What did I do wrong? Who did they think they were, taunting The Butcher!

Anger and bloodlust took him, and he crunched the paper in his hand into a tight ball.

It was time to finish what he'd come here to do.

CHAPTER FIFTEEN

Murderous Ventures

All his life, Boone Tyson had dreamed of the day when he would own and run his own ranch, whether it be Dos Culebras or one that he started from scratch himself. He hadn't considered any other profession; he was born to be a rancher. Now, as he rode across the prairie to his enemy's home, he saw how foolish he was for not taking the experience his father did his best to hand him.

What would the great Carl Tyson do right now? Would he make one last glorious ride into Flynn's house, shooting down men as he went, and kill the man who'd dared to try to take what was rightfully his? Would he negotiate, and calmly sign over his life's work for his son? Would he wait for Marshal Destry to sort it out?

Boone was overcome with the sheer mountain of responsibility forced upon him so suddenly. He slowed his horse to a stop, put his face in his hands, and sighed deeply. "I'm sorry, Pa," he whispered. "I got Remy in trouble, and now I might lose Dos Culebras. And you've only been dead less than a week. How did this happen?"

He raised his strained face to the heavens as if expecting a reply. The smell of sage was strong as he breathed deeply and closed his eyes. The horse stamped his hooves, impatient to continue his run. Boone felt bone weary. "What would you do?"

Deliberately calming himself, Boone started the horse walking.

"I played right into Flynn's hands. That's my fault. Remy got kidnapped because of it. That's my fault, too. And I slapped—" His voice broke on the last word, and he paused to take a deep breath. "I slapped my brother, my only family left in the world. How could I have done that? Will Remy ever forgive me?"

Unbidden, he thought, *I'll do whatever it takes until he does forgive me. So help me God. What's land and grass and cattle compared to the love of my only kin?*

Feeling better, Boone spurred the horse on to a gallop. When he came within sight of the ranch, he stopped again and figured a time frame.

Then he patiently waited for half an hour before moving on.

Wilhelm was sleeping soundly in his room when he woke up at his usual 5:00 A.M. He'd only been in bed for a few hours, but he'd slept soundly despite hearing Johann and Katy go downstairs. Unusual though it was, he didn't try to hear the whispered voices, thinking it something between the prince and his lady. He'd gone right back to sleep.

After getting dressed, he wanted to check on Sophia, but it would be improper to disturb her so early. Nevertheless, as he crept quietly downstairs so as not to awaken her, he cast a glance up to her door, foolishly hoping she would miraculously open it and smile at him.

The door, always closed when she was inside, had a five inch gap between it and the jamb. Then, from that direction, he heard a muted thump.

Carnicero, shedding the foolish sham that was Jackson Simms Rorke, watched as Sophia's fingernails tore at the back of his hands. No sound escaped her because he was firmly holding a pillow over her face. *Such a pretty face, too,* he thought, ignoring the pain and blood from his hands. The princess gave up trying to hurt him and began flailing her hands about, knocking against the bed and frame. Her feet drummed against the mattress in a desperate attempt to avoid her eventual death.

Carnicero pressed down harder.

At last, her motions began to weaken, and he couldn't resist the temptation to speak to her. "Good night, my princess," he whispered, hoping it was loud enough for her to hear over her grunting for air.

Suddenly, Carnicero felt as if a train hit him in the back. Stunned, with his breath knocked completely from his lungs, unseen momentum began to carry him toward the outside wall. Helpless, and in awe of the strangeness of it, he watched the wall speed toward him as if he were a spectator in a nightmare. His body met the wall with astounding force, and he was spun around to face the angry, ferocious countenance of Wilhelm.

Carnicero didn't have time to think about how Wilhelm woke up, or curse himself for not killing the Austrian in the first place, for Wilhelm grabbed his lapels and pulled Carnicero toward him. Crazily, his lungs still burning for air, he thought Wilhelm was taking him back to the princess's side to finish what he'd started. Wilhelm was grunting like an animal, and his eyes were coated with insanity.

But Wilhelm didn't take him back to the bed. Halfway there, Carnicero could see over Wilhelm's shoulder that the princess was sitting up and taking in great gulps of air. Carnicero briefly envied every particle she received, then he was being propelled back toward the wall. *Not again! I can't take another slam like the last one!* On rubbery legs he was danced across the floor, and just as his breath came back, he turned to see that Wilhelm wasn't going to crash him into the wall at all.

He was going to throw him through the window!

Carnicero could do nothing to stop him, since his feet were barely touching the floor. The world exploded in a sharp, shimmering, musical cosmos that scraped and cut and burned, and then he was free from the maniacal Austrian and floating downward. He was vaguely aware of hitting the porch roof, falling again, and impacting unyielding ground. Excruciating pain shot through his back and left arm, and he could only stare at the blurry stars and groan.

He didn't know how long he lay there. Somewhere he heard a deafening explosion and a humming noise. *A bee? In the middle of the night?* he thought dazedly, then he painfully turned his head toward the house and saw the crazy Austrian aiming a rifle at him from the shattered window. Carnicero's natural survival instinct took over, and in agony he managed to roll far enough to put the porch roof between himself and the blazing gun. He recognized that this was only a temporary haven, since Wilhelm could come charging out the front door, so he called on every bit of strength he had left and got to his feet.

His left arm was broken, and his back felt as if a spear were lodged in it, but Carnicero walked in a shambling gait to the darkest shadows on the other side of the house. Keeping an eye on the front door, he knew that he would have to let the princess go—for now.

Carnicero held his broken left arm, blocked out the pain screaming for attention throughout his whole body, and visually plotted a course for the stable.

Prince Johann Kessler was only a short distance away.

Johann spoke little as they rode to Fritz's grave. Sam and Katy tried to draw him out, but he would have none of it. One-syllable answers were all they received.

Sam gave Katy his coat after seeing her shiver, and while they were close and at a relative distance from the prince, he asked, "What do we do?"

"I don't know. He probably doesn't even want us with him, but I couldn't just let him ride off by himself in the middle of the night. He looks so . . . disturbed."

"Well, let's just keep quiet and see what happens."

No one spoke again. Sam and Katy were content to let Johann lead, and he found his way unerringly to the cemetery. The freshly dug graves rose above the ground in two lonely, stark lumps. After they dismounted, Johann walked slowly to the mound on the right—Fritz's. Sam tied the horses to a nearby oak tree. Katy stood behind and to the side of Johann, feeling awkward. The lonely call of a bird sounded far away, ready to greet the dawn.

Johann knelt down by the grave in the red clay.

Katy and Sam waited.

"Warum, Fritz?" Johann muttered. *"Wozu?"*

Katy couldn't understand the words, but the painful look on Johann's face was enough bring tears to her eyes.

"He was around me since my school days," Johann said in a soft voice. "Never did he leave me." He sat back on his heels and rested his hands on his thighs. "Do you know how he lost his tongue? He was working for one of the neighborhood commanders when he was a boy. They were supposed to get the commander's monthly fee from a shopkeeper, and in the process Fritz's partner accidentally killed the shopkeeper's son, who foolishly had pulled a gun. Fritz could not handle the guilt of that death. He went to the police and confessed that he had been part of it. He told them he did not kill the boy. Not once did he mention the commander's name. But that did not matter. A man who worked for the commander cut Fritz's tongue out. The police let the man right into the jail to do the job." Johann shook his head. "It was madness."

Katy said nothing, and Sam shook his head in wonder and disgust.

"Why did he do it, Katherine?"

"He was trying to save another man's life, I guess."

"Not that. That is just Fritz, to give his life for another. Listen to how foolish I sound, I say that is *just* Fritz. That is the wonderful, giving man he was. He only knew how to be loyal to his friends. But that is not what I am asking. Why did he do that in church? Why would a good man like Fritz feel the need to make a peace with God, when he seemed *always* at peace with God?"

"We can't see what is in men's hearts, Johann," Katy said. "Fritz was hurting inside, and only God can heal that deep pain. Fritz figured that out and acted on it."

Johann didn't reply, he only continued staring at his friend's grave.

"Someone's coming," Sam observed, looking behind them.

Boone was met a good distance away from Flynn's house by two grim-looking cowboys, who disarmed him. They led his horse to the house, and just before Boone was taken inside, he glanced to the east and saw that the black sky had turned a deep blue, and the stars on that horizon had disappeared.

Flynn was sitting behind his desk in his office, looking like a cat that had just devoured a mouse. B. B. Easterling stood by the window, managing to look nervous and lazy at the same time. Of Remy there was no sign.

"Boone Tyson, as I live and breathe!" Flynn crowed. "Sit down, my boy, sit down." He gestured expansively to a wingback chair across from his desk. Boone sat, and Flynn waved his cowboy escort away. "I'm glad to see you came alone and didn't try anything chancy. Better for the boy."

"Where is he?"

Flynn gave him a bland look. "He's safe, I assure you."

"I'm supposed to trust your word?"

"If you can't trust ol' J. B. Flynn, who can you trust?"

Boone snorted derisively.

"Now, now," Flynn admonished, raising a finger, "we're about to become business partners, Boone. What kind of attitude is that?"

"Let me see him," Boone demanded. Flynn's gloating was pushing way beyond his patience.

"Not just yet, partner. I believe you have something of interest to me?"

Boone didn't move and kept his hands locked tightly on the arms of the chair. Flynn's eyes flickered anger, and Boone tried not to show his pleasure.

Flynn sighed. "If you don't hand it over, I'll have B. B. take it from you, none too kindly. It's your choice."

"I'm not gonna tell you again. Let me see Remy. Then I'll give you anything you want. I'll be glad to play Easterling's game as long as he wants to, but nothing's happening until I see my brother." He looked over at Easterling, who didn't like what he saw in Boone's eyes.

Flynn placed his elbow on the desk and his forehead in his hand for a moment. "*Why* does this have to be so hard?" he muttered. "All right—go get the boy, B. B."

Boone watched Easterling walk slowly behind him, and tensed for a blow, but none came. Easterling left without looking back.

Flynn clucked his tongue and drummed his fingers on his desk while inspecting Boone. Boone looked right back without blinking. Flynn said, "You Tysons. You've sure got your pride, don't you? Even to the last."

"You'll pay someday, Flynn. For my father and Dos Culebras."

Flynn's expansive mood vanished in a blink. Leaning forward, his chair squeaking in the silent room, he declared, "You just feel lucky, boy, that you didn't end up like your daddy. You've still got your whole life ahead of you—*if* you don't mess up today."

Boone had to call on every ounce of restraint to keep from

leaping across the desk and throttling him. Then he remembered Remy, and loosened his iron grip on the chair.

"Boone!" Remy called from the door and broke out of Easterling's grasp to run to his brother. Boone caught him before he could stand up and crushed the small body to him, relieved beyond words.

"I knew you'd come!" Remy said into Boone's shoulder.

"'Course I did." Boone ran his fingers through the fine brown hair and kissed Remy's head. "'Course I did. I love you, Remy."

"I love you, too." Remy pulled back reluctantly. "Are you all right?"

Boone chuckled, though near tears. "Yeah, I'm fine. Are you? Did they hurt you?"

"Naw, but I got a few good kicks in."

"I bet you did."

Flynn said, "This is all very touching, but aren't you forgetting something?"

Boone moved Remy to the side and reached inside his coat. All joy left his face as he turned to Flynn again. "Here," he said curtly, throwing the paper on to the desk. It teetered on the edge, and Flynn had to move fast to keep it from falling to Boone's feet. He gave Boone a melting glare.

Slowly Flynn opened it, and his face took on a light of satisfaction as he savored what was written.

"What is it, Boone?" Remy asked.

Boone didn't answer.

"It seems to be genuine," Flynn commented. Easterling moved behind him to look over his shoulder. "Now, there's only one more thing to do." He turned the paper toward Boone, dipped a pen in an inkwell, and held it out. "Sign it over."

"Boone," Remy whispered in a horrified voice, "you ain't givin' away Dos Culebras, are you? Tell me you ain't. I know what that word is at the top, it says 'deed.' *D-E-E-D* spells deed."

Boone didn't move.

"Now," Flynn ordered. "Or I'll have B. B. break your arm."

"Boone!" Remy cried. "You can't!"

Boone remained still.

"I've changed my mind," Flynn announced matter-of-factly. "Easterling, shoot the boy in the arm."

Easterling gave Flynn a horrified look.

Remy backed up a step, until he was almost behind Boone's chair.

Boone tensed his muscles.

"Do you remember what we talked about, B. B.? Shoot the boy!" Easterling slowly drew his gun.

Somewhere close by, two shots rang out.

Flynn and Easterling both looked out the gray window, and Boone made his move.

In a blur, Boone reached down and grabbed the bottom of the desk and lifted with all his strength. Both men were completely caught by surprise as more shots exploded outside. The heavy oak desk tilted right on to Flynn's lap and pushed both of them back to the wall behind. Boone continued pushing until they were pinned; then, like the strike of a snake, he reached across and snatched Easterling's gun out of his limp hand. The desk went down hard on Flynn as his chair overturned, and he grunted in pain and loss of breath. Boone smashed the gun against the side of Easterling's head. He collapsed like a felled moose.

The shooting had stopped outside.

Boone jumped up on the desk on his knees, bringing another agonized grunt out of Flynn, and brought the gun around to jam the barrel in to Flynn's flushed cheek. "It's over!" Boone screamed at him.

Flynn's mouth worked, but no sound came out.

"You're gonna hang for what you did to my pa! You hear me?"

In a gutteral whisper, Flynn managed, "Help . . . me! Help!"

Boone got off the desk and motioned to Remy, who ran to his side. Boone looked down at Flynn. "No one can help you now. . . . Except God."

———⬧———

"It looks like . . . Rorke," Katy said, squinting through the blue air of dawn. The sky had grown much lighter while her attention had been fixed on Johann.

"Yeah, it's him. I wonder . . . ?" Sam glanced at Katy, and she shrugged.

Johann stood and watched Rorke ride up. The reporter was sitting in the saddle awkwardly—listing to the side a bit. "Do you think something has happened back at the ranch?"

"I don't know." Katy suddenly felt nervous. Had Rorke been awake when she'd talked to Sam?

Rorke stopped the lathering horse and clumsily dismounted. "Good morning, all!"

Sam noticed the man's left arm dangled limply at his side. He took a step forward. "What happened, Rorke? Is something wrong?"

"Wrong? Why, no, Sam, why do you ask?" He reached behind his back with his right arm, as if to rub a painful muscle.

He's lying. Something is terribly wrong, Sam thought. Rorke's face was pale and sweating in the cool morning air; his clothes were disheveled and dirty. His false smile was a painted leer.

When he brought his arm back around, he held a Colt pistol—and it was pointing at Sam's head.

Sam tensed as Katy gasped and backed up a step.

"Relax, folks," Rorke said, trying to be reassuring, but his voice was ragged and close to a screech. All trace of a New Orleans accent was gone, replaced with a cadence that was foreign. "This will all be over as soon as I get some answers."

"Jack, what are you doing?" Johann asked in horror.

Rorke ignored him and looked at Sam. "It was you, wasn't it?"
Sam stared at him blankly.

"The note? The clever little note?"

Sam inclined his head. "Yes, it was me. So why don't you leave these two out of it?"

Rorke smiled horribly, revealing teeth tinged with blood. "Oh, you are the noble one, aren't you, Sam? No, I believe we'll all take part in this little drama. How much do you know?"

"Not much. Just that you're not from New Orleans or the South. Work on the accent and trivia next time, won't you?"

"Shut *up!*" Rorke shrieked, enraged.

"Jack," Katy said calmly, "put the gun down and let's—"

"You, too!" The gun moved to point at her. "Nobody says a word!" He took two steps toward them, listing to the left side, his face a dreadful mask of pain. "It's all right—everything's all right, I'm just having to rearrange my schedule, that's all. You've disrupted my timetable, Sam. Congratulations. Only one man has ever done that before." He smiled again. "Fortunately, he's dead."

"I'm surprised there haven't been more than the two of us," Sam remarked coolly. "You've made so many mistakes, it hardly seems that difficult."

Rorke's face turned scarlet, and Sam thought he was going to scream at him again—or shoot him. The gun was waving unsteadily in his hand. Then he drew a ragged breath and smiled grimly. "Tell me. What trivia are you talking about?"

"Tuberculosis and General Grant." Two more steps. That's all Rorke needed to take and he'd be able to jump him.

"What?"

"The outbreak in New Orleans in 1853 wasn't tuberculosis, it was yellow fever. If you'd been traveling there at that time, you'd have known that."

"And General Grant?"

"Grant never got near Mobile. It was Farragut."

Rorke's eyebrows tilted, and he nodded slightly. "Ah, yes. So clever." He pursed his lips and took another step forward.

Just one more, Sam thought. *Please.*

Rorke turned to Katy. "And I suppose you had nothing to do with this?"

"Of cour—"

"No, she didn't," Sam interrupted quickly. "It was all my idea from the beginning."

"Excuse me, Sam," Katy said with a smile. "But I believe I can answer for myself, if you don't mind."

He stared at her, dumbfounded.

"I mean, you're a dear, of course, and your chivalry gives me goosebumps, but please, let's give credit where credit is due. You had never heard of the yellow fever outbreak."

"Katy," Sam pleaded, "kindly shut your mouth."

"*Both* of you shut up," Rorke stated through gritted teeth.

"Who *are* you?" Johann asked.

Rorke grimaced and took another step toward them. "Why, my dear Prince Johann. Did you think I'd forgotten about you? Excuse me a moment. Sam, I see you tensing your considerable muscles to try to do me harm. Would you get on your knees and clasp your hands behind your back?"

With a glance at Katy, Sam did as he was told.

"Thank you. Now, Prince. I don't want you to think that I'd forgotten you. You should feel proud. Actually, you're the reason I'm here in the first place." He smiled broadly. "To kill you, that is."

Johann stared at him, lifting one brow imperiously. "Kill me?"

"Yes. I might as well tell you. Certain parties in Prussia want you, your father, and your sister dead. That's where I come in."

Johann's eyes narrowed.

Sam and Katy glanced at each other. They hadn't quite planned on this, and neither one was sure how they were going to get out of it. Or *if* they were going to get out of it.

"My sister?" Johann asked, tilting his chin. "Is she . . . ?"

"At the moment, she's quite alive and well. Thanks to your friend Wilhelm."

"So Wilhelm did this to you." Johann nodded at Rorke's body, not even trying to keep the pleasure from his voice.

Rorke's eyes glittered dangerously. "He will pay, I assure you. Now, if you'll excuse me, I have a lot to do." Without further warning, he raised the pistol, pointed it at Johann's chest, and pulled the trigger.

Nothing happened.

No explosion.

Sam, Katy, and Johann all stared at the gun.

Rorke, too, gazed disbelievingly at the Colt. "A misfire," he muttered. "Imagine the odds." He calmly raised it again.

Sam tensed, ready to throw himself forward, when a hissing sound split the air, followed by a dull thud. Rorke staggered, then looked down in dull disbelief at the bloody head of an arrow protruding from his right shoulder, just below the collarbone.

With a whimper, Rorke turned white, and the gun slipped from his fingers. Katy leapt forward to grab it and toss it to Sam.

Turning in amazement, Katy watched as Seth Moon emerged from a copse of trees fifty yards away, waving his bow.

Sam stood, holding the gun on Rorke, who had sunk to his knees. When Moon reached them, Katy ran into his arms, and Johann shook his hand warmly. Moon then stood over Rorke. "Who is he?"

"An assassin," Sam answered. "We don't know his name."

Rorke, grimacing in pain, spotted Moon through his hazy vision. "Who are you?"

"Seth Moon. Nice to meet you."

"Where did you come from?"

Moon shrugged. "Dos Culebras. I was hunting, and you all

passed right by my favorite hunting ground. I followed to see what was going on."

"You—you live at Dos Culebras? That's not possible! I knew everyone's face before I showed myself! I *never* make mistakes like that!"

"Mister, by the looks of you, I'd say you made one *big* mistake by even coming to Texas." He grinned broadly and drawled, "You're not from around these parts, are you, son?"

———

Carnicero woke from a fever-induced nightmare and looked around. Moving his head caused massive bolts of pain throughout his body, from his hair to the soles of his feet.

Where am I? he thought desperately. The room was familiar, yet unfamiliar. *Spain? France?* A face moved into his line of vision.

"Feeling better?" Sam asked. "Comfy?"

It all came back in a rush. He'd failed. The Butcher had failed. A second face appeared.

"I took the arrow out," Katy told him. "But that's the least of your worries. You've got an arm that's broken in two places that still has to be set, but that's still not the worst news."

"Wha—what is it?" Carnicero was bathed in sweat, but not only from his fever. He'd never been completely in someone else's control like this. Especially not someone he'd been planning on killing in cold blood.

"The prince," Sam said, "you remember him? The one you were going to kill so easily? Well, he's not too happy. He cabled his father in Austria to warn him of a plot against him, and his father's answer should interest you."

Katy said, "He wants Johann to find out the name of the man or men who sent you. But the strange part is, the prince is only supposed to ask you one time. Only once."

Carnicero's tongue felt huge in his mouth, and he tried to lick his dry lips. "Could I have some water, please?"

"Do you hear what we're saying?" Sam asked. "Water is of no concern right now. You could live for a few days without water, but your life will end very shortly if you don't tell us so we can stop the prince. He's in a state of anger like you've never seen before after hearing what you did to his sister."

"I have nothing to say," Carnicero declared.

Katy and Sam looked at each other. Katy shrugged. "It's your funeral."

Sam called, "Prince Johann! He's awake now."

Carnicero turned his head to the direction that Sam was looking. Through the door came the prince. He was dressed in royal splendor, complete with sword. Gold embroidery glistened all over him. Carnicero never had seen such finery, but his eyes were on Johann's face. He also never had imagined that the prince could have a look of such complete detachment. He showed no anger, no lust for vengence, . . . nothing. Somehow, it was more disturbing than looking into the face of a raving lunatic.

Johann stopped by the bed. In his hand, Carnicero saw for the first time, was a finely made Austrian pistol. Slowly, the prince raised it until Carnicero was looking into the black void of the huge barrel. Beyond the barrel were two deadly eyes. New sweat broke out all over Carnicero's body. For a moment, he had the hope that he was caught in another nightmare, but he could feel pain all over, and to prove it further, he squeezed his hand into a fist that caused his fingernails to bite into his palm and bring blood. He was not dreaming.

The prince spoke in a flat voice, totally without inflection, "I will ask you one question. I will ask it only one time. If you do not answer, you will die, which is the punishment in my country for an attempted assassination on the royal family. If you do not answer, we will find out the truth anyway, without your help. If you do answer, you will go back to Austria with me to stand trial, and I will speak on your behalf concerning your aid to us. You will spend the rest of your life in prison, but you will not be executed. Do you understand?"

A thousand questions raced through Carnicero's mind, but he only said in a croaking, dry voice, "I . . . wait, I—"

"The question is, who hired you?"

This can't be the kindly prince that I've come to know—it can't be—this is a trick!

Johann's cheek twitched, once. "Very well. I sentence you to death for—"

"Wait!"

"—the crime of—"

"I can't!"

"—attempted murder against a member of the Austrian royal family."

"Please!" Carnicero began to cry pitifully.

Johann pulled back the hammer of the pistol and moved closer. The barrel was pointed directly between Carnicero's eyes. The blackness inside the barrel became his world, impossibly huge, blotting out everything.

Carnicero, The Butcher, the heartless Spanish assassin, wept and shook and wailed.

And he told them everything he knew.

CHAPTER SIXTEEN

Roses and Verbena

I just can't believe he did this," Boone said incredulously for the fourth time. He was seated behind his father's desk, and Katy couldn't help but think that, at the moment anyway, he seemed like an excited boy that had just gotten word of his first date. Instead, what he held in his hands was worth many thousands of dollars.

"He wanted you to have it," Sam stated simply.

"I'll say! But I was willing to pay him what my father offered. Not at this price! This is almost nothin'!" His eyes couldn't tear themselves away from the deed to the other half of Dos Culebras that Johann had signed over to him at half of what it was worth. Johann had wanted to *give* the land over as a gift, but Boone had stood strong on that point. It was a matter of pride. "He really *is* a prince, isn't he? In every way possible."

"Yes, he is," Katy agreed.

"Let's go look at it today, Boone," Remy piped up from beside Katy on the horsehair sofa.

This brought Boone's attention away from the document. "Look at it? Why? We've seen that land hundreds of times."

"I ain't *never* looked at it when it's been ours. Pa sold it when I was just a little kid. Maybe it looks different today."

"Don't say 'ain't,'" Sam said.

"Sorry."

"You know, you may be right, little brother. Maybe it *does* look different."

Katy watched them smile at each other with absolute love. Since the incident with Flynn two days before, they'd been inseparable. Boone had taken Remy with him while Billy Mantooth had taught him the everyday details of running the huge ranch. Boone had had no conception of the magnitude of the job and felt a bit over-whelmed, but his determination to learn was nearly fanatical.

"What about Flynn's land?" Sam asked. "Will it be sold?"

Boone nodded. "Marshal Destry said it'll be in probate for a while, but Flynn apparently didn't have any relatives that anyone knows of. They'll auction the ranch before long."

"And?" Sam prompted.

"And what?"

Sam smiled and gave him a knowing look. "You've got all this extra money since Johann sold at half price. . . . " He ended the sentence in a suggesting, upward tone.

"Whew!" Boone exclaimed, whistling. "I hadn't even thought of that." He appeared stunned for a moment. "No . . . no, I couldn't do that."

"Why not?" Katy asked.

"Because it's—it's—it'd be too big! I ain't ready to handle that much responsibility."

"Not with an attitude like that, you aren't."

"I'd help you, Boone," Remy assured him in a totally serious voice.

Boone smiled again. "I know you would. Let's think about it, though, OK?"

Remy turned to Sam and Katy and said, "Don't worry—I'll talk him into it."

Katy laughed. "I have no doubt about that."

Sam said, "At least you don't have Flynn to worry about any-more."

"He's gonna hang!" Remy pronounced morbidly.

"Now, we don't know that yet, little buddy," Boone cautioned. "B. B. confessed to settin' up Pa, but Flynn hasn't been tried yet."

"He'll hang," Remy contended stubbornly.

Remy's bloodthirstiness disquieted them all, but Katy knew that he was a confused and hurt little boy who would eventually sort out his feelings. Seth Moon had already begun the process of helping him heal, with the Lord's guidance.

"Are you sure you have to leave today?" Boone asked. "I could sure use your help, Sam. And yours too, Katy."

Sam shook his head firmly. "We've got to move on."

"Still going to St. Louis to look up your brother?"

"Yes."

"And if he's not there?"

Katy answered firmly, "Then we go to New Orleans to look for him, or wherever we have to go. Right, Sam?" Sam had been reluctant to pursue Obadiah, but Katy had pushed and prodded until he'd agreed to go. She knew that deep inside he wanted to find his brother, but his resistance was puzzling.

"Whatever you say, boss," Sam drawled.

Remy suddenly threw his arms around Katy's neck and hugged her fiercely. "I'll miss you."

Katy squeezed back hard. "I'll miss you, too. And I'll pray for you, and I'll think about you every day."

"Me, too."

"You take care of your big brother, Remy," Sam told him as he shook Boone's hand, then looked Boone in the eye. "Think about that property, all right?"

"I will, Sam."

Moon, Johann, Wilhelm, and Sophia were waiting by the wagon when they came out. Without preamble, Johann took Katy's hand

and steered her away from the others to talk privately. Boone and Remy remained on the porch.

Sam went to Moon and shook his hand slowly. They didn't speak for a moment, only stared into each other's eyes solemnly. "You take care of that little boy, Seth. He's depending on you."

"I know. You don't have to worry about either one of them." Sam nodded.

"Go with God, Sam. He's got his eyes on you, you know."

Sam didn't smile. "Believe me, I know."

"Drop us a line every now and then."

"I will." Sam turned to Wilhelm and Sophia. The trauma of Sophia's near murder had affected her deeply. She couldn't sleep unless Wilhelm was outside her door, even though she knew Carnicero was safely in jail in Fargo. The royal party was scheduled to leave the day after Sam and Katy. Now, Sophia held onto Wilhelm's arm as if she'd never let go, and Sam couldn't help but smile at Wilhelm as he shook his hand. "Wilhelm, if anybody's ever trying to kill me, I sure wish you'd appear from nowhere and take care of them."

Wilhelm threw back his head and laughed. He'd never thought he'd hear words like that from *anyone,* much less the indomitable Sam Bronte. "Somehow, Sam, I don't picture you needing assistance at *any* time."

"You'd be surprised, Wilhelm."

Sophia suprised them both by giving Sam a kiss on the cheek. "You know, Sam—you and Katy would make a wonderful couple."

Sam blanched. "Perish the thought!"

The princess watched his reaction and nodded sagely. "That makes you uncomfortable. Good. That gives me more hope than anything you could have done."

"I would hate to see your royal hopes dashed, Highness," Sam said formally. "But I don't see that happening."

"'She's beautiful and therefore may be wooed, she is a woman,

222

therefore to be won.'" Sophia gazed up at Wilhelm. "Believe me, I know what I'm talking about."

"*Henry the Sixth.* But what about that 'tiger's heart wrapped in a woman's hide' of which the duke of York spoke?"

Sophia smiled sweetly. "Tigers can be tamed, Sam."

Across from them, by the rose bushes beside the house, Johann kissed Katy gently on the lips. Their hands were clasped tightly, and Katy felt the first real sadness she'd felt all day. She knew she would never see him again, and in his eyes she saw the same sorrow. When he drew back, he smiled sadly and said, "I will never forget you, Katherine."

"You know, you're the only one that's ever gotten away with calling me that."

"I know. Thank you."

"Thank *you,* Johann. For what you did for Boone and Remy, for your kindness, and compassion, and . . . just for being you. I admire the people of Austria. Their future looks very bright with you to care for them."

Johann sighed, and his eyes were wet. "Oh, *mein Geliebte,* you are making this very hard. I want to kidnap you and make you a queen."

"And I can't believe I'm walking away from those words."

"You are going where your heart leads. That is all that matters." His face turned serious. "I am still thinking about Fritz's decision to follow God."

Katy briefly placed her hand on his smooth-shaven cheek. "I'll pray for you. I know you'll do the right thing and accept Jesus. You're too wise not to."

Johann kissed her again amidst the fragrance of roses.

―――◦◦◦―――

Ironically, the day Sam and Katy left, the weather turned pleasant; no stifling heat or looming thunderstorms on the horizon to cause discomfort. The promise of fall was in the air.

Sam held the reins loosely in his hands as they headed east. He kept glancing at Katy, who didn't seem to notice. "You're awfully quiet. Want to talk about it?"

Katy took off her Stetson and shook her long blonde hair in a spray of sundrenched light. Setting the hat beside her on the wagon bench seat, she brushed her hair back with her fingers and asked, "Do you think Johann would have shot Carnicero? In cold blood like that?"

"Yes," Sam said without hesitation.

Katy looked at him, stunned. "Yes? Just like that?"

"Yes," he said, smiling.

"Kind, sweet Johann?"

"I say again . . . yes. Besides what Carnicero tried to do to his sister, which was bad enough to send any man into an uncontrollable rage, Johann knew that Austria would have *no* future if he didn't stop the Prussians at this game. In my opinion, he came very close to pulling that trigger. Very close."

Katy shuddered. She hadn't thought of Johann in those stark terms, and she didn't know how she would have reacted *had* he pulled that trigger. She pushed the thought from her mind immediately.

"They'll be all right," Sam said quietly, as if to himself.

"Sam," Katy began, wanting to change the subject, but not sure how the new one would be received. "Are you looking forward to seeing Obadiah?"

Sam didn't look at her or acknowledge that he'd even heard her. Katy began to think that he would flatly refuse to talk about it, when he said, "Yes. I was afraid for a while. After all, I practically abandoned him."

"But you weren't the parent—how could you abandon him?"

Sam looked at her. "But I *was* the parent, Katy. I *was* the parent." Suddenly he smiled. "But it'll be good to see him again."

Katy planted a kiss on his cheek. "You're a good man, Sam Bronte."

Sam grinned and put his arm around her, and she put her head on his shoulder. After a while, Katy said, "We have to make one more stop."

"After a compliment like that, you can have anything you want," he said, grinning. "But only for today. Tomorrow, you'll have to come up with a new one."

———————

The sunset over Dos Culebras that evening was filled with brilliant colors that turned the sky a wonderful, fire-tinted orange. Amidst the clouds on the horizon, shining through the blazing hues, were deep purple clouds laced with bright golden light.

They were a perfect complement to the yellow roses and violet verbena that decorated two fresh graves in the middle of the Texas plain.